FORGOTTEN IDENTITY

FORGOTTEN IDENTITY

PENNY ZELLER

Cover Design by EDH Professionals

Print ISBN: 978-1-957847-37-5

Developmental Edits by Mountain Peak Edits & Design
Proofreading by Amy Petrowich

To my oldest. How did I get so blessed to be your mom?

Fear not, for I am with you; be not dismayed, for I am your God; I will strengthen you, I will help you, I will uphold you with my righteous right hand.
- Isaiah 41:10

Chapter 1

Of all the days for the dog to run off.

Mariah Holzman plodded after the family border collie, who continued barking even as he looked back to ensure someone noticed his most recent escape antic. The cold bit her face, and her jacket did little to protect her from the falling temperatures. The weather service had predicted a storm for the area, warning that any travel could be dangerous, but apparently, Nosy refused to heed that advice.

Instead of coming at Mariah's call, Nosy had stopped in a deep thicket of trees with large boulders next to the ravine, his tail wagging. He barked once, then twice, content to ignore the dark clouds forming in the sky.

"Probably another dead rabbit," Mariah muttered. Nosy's shenanigans usually wouldn't be a problem, but the eerie calm that had befallen the forest sent shivers up her spine.

She really needed to stop editing suspense novels right before bedtime. Just because the storm would hit earlier than anticipated and the forest stood too still didn't mean anything was amiss.

"Come back, Nosy!" Seven-year-old Jordan zipped after the dog. His waddle, caused by his bulky snowsuit, would be amusing if not for the lingering sense of unease settling in Mariah's middle.

She shook her head to clear the irrational dread. The events of suspense novels didn't happen in real life, and even if they did, they wouldn't happen in the safe and small town of Mountain Springs.

"Jordan, wait up."

Her son slowed to a deliberate plod. "We can't leave him out here."

"He'll come back in a few minutes."

"What if he doesn't?"

"We can't stay out here long. A storm is blowing in."

Tall lodgepole pines silently swayed in the breeze, their calm movement in direct opposition to what was to come. While she loved the trees, Mariah knew that soon the cabin would no longer be in sight due to the thick mass of pines intermingled with a smattering of aspens.

The wind gusted, causing an aspen's branch to snap.

Mariah took a deep breath. There was nothing wrong. Nothing would happen except the storm hitting sooner than predicted.

Another gust brought a smattering of snowflakes.

If the snowfall increased in intensity, the trees wouldn't be the only things blocking the cabin from view.

Of all the days, you silly dog.

A flock of tiny black-and-white birds zipped past overhead, presumably to get to a safe place before the storm unleashed its fury.

Thankfully, Nosy plopped his hindquarters in the snow and continued to bark.

"No." Mariah grabbed Jordan's shoulder when he prepared to again run to the dog. "It's too slippery that close to the ravine."

"But Nosy's okay."

"Nosy is a dog who sometimes has very little common sense." *Hence his name.*

Mariah bit back a sigh as they neared. While grateful Nosy stopped when he did, couldn't the dog have chosen another place to investigate besides the ravine that could be deadly if someone mis-stepped and fell into it? At least the handful of boulders near its edge warned of the ravine's proximity.

Nosy's barking turned to a whine as he pawed at the snow.

No, not just the snow.

The snow *covering* a shoe protruding from behind a large boulder.

She reached for Jordan and slowed both of their paces even as her pulse quickened. Maybe the object just looked like a gray tennis shoe. Or maybe it was a shoe, but a discarded shoe Nosy found somewhere, brought home, and forgot about until now.

Still...

"Jordan, stay where you are, please."

"Aww, Mom." Despite his protest, Jordan did as she requested.

Mariah advanced. Better be safe than sorry, and on the one percent chance this wasn't a shoe found, forgotten, and rediscovered by Nosy, Jordan did not need to see whatever, or whomever, was attached to the shoe.

"Mom?"

"Just a minute, Jordan."

A few seconds later, she saw an image she'd not soon forget.

Partially obstructed by the boulders and surrounding dormant foliage, a man's body lay face up in the snow, dangerously close to falling over the side of the ravine. Blood dotted the area around him, and not even the slight dusting on his face and body could conceal the blood staining his clothes.

Mariah's breath caught.

"Jordan, stay back for a minute and cover your eyes, please."

She crept forward. Was he alive? No amount of staring could help her determine if his chest rose, and not once did he stir or open his eyes.

So much for it just being a shoe Nosy found.

Mariah held her breath and inched close enough to feel for a pulse.

Weak, but there.

She exhaled out a deep breath of relief. Angry purple bruises marred his face, and a sizable gash covered his right temple. A ripped blue hoodie partially disguised more bruising and wounds on his muscular torso. What had happened, and who had done this?

"Lord, what should I do?" her prayer came out as more of a whispered breath. *Please give me wisdom.*

"Mom, can I look now?"

Could she transport the man herself? There was no way to make it home and ask for Mom's help. Nor could she ask their neighbor. Not with the frigid temps and the worsening weather conditions. The man could easily die before she returned. She didn't have her phone, but even if she did, there would likely be no cell service this deep into the forest. And Jordan would see the man if she assisted him.

But she couldn't leave him there to either die from his wounds or from exposure to the elements.

"Jordan, I need your help." She voiced the words without giving them more thought. She hated for her son to see the man. He was so young, and she wanted to protect his seven-year-old innocence. He shouldn't have to see things like this at his age.

But what other alternative did she have?

"Okay." Jordan neared the man and slowly uncovered his eyes. "What happened to him?"

Mariah pondered her answer so as not to scare her son. "I'm not sure. I think he had an accident."

"Like a car accident?"

"Maybe. Do you think you can help me get him back to the cabin?"

Jordan nodded, his gaze riveted on the man. "His face is hurt. Do you think he crashed his bike? My knee bled a lot when I crashed my bike."

Bike crashes didn't cause such terrible bruising, and the man's wounds didn't resemble road rash.

The wind whistled through the trees, its chill causing Mariah to shiver. Or maybe it was the fact that she'd found a severely injured man knocking perilously on the door of death.

Nosy paced around the man, leaning in every so often to sniff. Mariah looked back at the way they had come. On a clear day, she knew the route back to the cabin by heart. But today...

"Mom, is he gonna die?" Jordan's hazel eyes grew large.

"I hope not. We need to pray for him and help him back to the house."

Jordan bit his lip and fidgeted with his coat's zipper. "I can pray for him, but how are we gonna get him back to the house?"

The snow had picked up, blowing sideways with the increase in wind. Whoever this man was, she and Jordan were his only chance of survival.

Could they find their way back?

Lord, guide me.

She scanned the area for two long and strong sticks. If she

found something with which to create a makeshift stretcher, that could work.

But if there were any long sticks, the accumulating snow obscured them.

She would have to resort to Plan B.

"Jordan, do you remember when we read that book about the man who steered the ship on the ocean?"

"He was a helmsman."

Mariah nodded, grateful that Jordan was dealing well with the stressful situation. "That's right. I need you to be a helmsman. We'll pretend we're in a ship."

"Ooh, like on the Atlantic Ocean?"

"Exactly. You'll hang on to my coat and not let go. Pretend it's the helm. I'll be going backward, so you'll need to be my eyes and get us back safely across the Atlantic and to the house. Are you up for the challenge, sailor?"

Jordan loved challenges, and he loved pretending. "Aye, aye, Captain." He reached a gloved hand toward Mariah's coat.

"Now remember, you must hang on tightly to the edge of my coat and not let go. It's the helm, after all, and you don't want to lose control of the ship."

Jordan giggled. "And the wind is roaring across the waves today, Captain."

Relieved to be able to take Jordan's mind off the task at hand, Mariah leaned over and placed her hands under the man's shoulders. Whispering another prayer for strength, she lifted and began to pull him toward the cabin as the adrenaline surged through her veins.

The man was over six foot in height, with an athletic build and long legs, and Mariah's muscles argued under the weight. She heaved, breaths coming in gasps as she strained. *Lord, please give me the strength I need.*

"Watch out for that tree, I mean, watch out for the whales."

Mariah turned periodically and guided them both from time to time through the endless lodgepoles. The wind pelted her face, stinging as it hit her cheeks. "Come on, Nosy."

"He's the sea dog," giggled Jordan.

"Very clever, son." Mariah gritted her teeth as she struggled to pull the man's weight. She wished Rick, the retired cop who, with his wife, lived in the cottage next to the cabin, was outside to help. But in his wisdom, he would have heeded the storm's warning and tucked himself safely inside.

"I can't see where we're going, Captain," Jordan said.

Mariah craned her neck. The visibility was next to nothing. What if they were unable to find their way back?

No. She wouldn't give that consideration a thought. She must forge ahead.

She squinted, attempting to see beyond the next tree. As she exhaled, her breath emerged in visible misty puffs in the cold air.

The man's head lolled to one side. Was he even still alive? Torn between the desire to take a break and the necessity of getting to the cabin as soon as possible, Mariah begged her muscles to comply with the demands of the stranger's weight. She attempted to ignore the strain on her neck, back, and arms.

Finally, the pines became less plentiful. Good. That meant they were nearing the house. Mariah tried to walk faster, but walking backward in deep snow was no easy feat. Jordan stopped and hid his face in her coat, his feet stumbling. "Just a little farther, Jordan."

"I'm cold, Mom."

"I know, sweetie. Just a little farther."

Jordan faced forward again, and Mariah tugged on the man, his heels creating deep furrows in the snow. White-out conditions would soon be upon them.

She could hear her own heart thumping in her chest. What if they didn't make it?

She lifted her eyes briefly to the sky as the bone-chilling snow stung her face. *Lord, please show us which direction to go. Lead us. Guide us.*

It was difficult to see more than a few feet in front of them. Hazy fog had joined the sideways-blowing snow, and her hands were numb. If they made it to the cabin alive, it would be only by God's grace.

She craned her neck. Jordan lumbered through the snow in front of her, and for a minute, his hand slipped from her coat. She stopped suddenly as Jordan continued forward. "Jordan, hang on to me!" Mariah was about to release the man's body and run after Jordan when he backed up.

Her son turned briefly to face her, snow crusting on his eyelashes. "Sorry, Mommy. My hand slipped. Do captains sometimes get lost when they're steering the boat?"

Mariah's hands shook as she attempted to regain her composure. Did captains get lost at sea? Oh, yes. Did people get disoriented in blizzards and freeze to death? She'd read about one such case just recently. She squeezed her eyes shut and willed the heart palpitations to ease. God would deliver them safely to the cabin.

Wouldn't He?

Lord, protect Jordan, please.

"Mommy? I can't see ahead of me. Which way do I go?"

Mariah swiveled her attention behind her.

"And I'm cold, too. Do you think we can rest for a few minutes? I could build us..." his teeth chattered "I could build us a fort under the trees kind of like the Swiss Family Robinson fort."

If they stopped and sat in the snow, that would be the end. They must proceed. "Sweetie, when a captain sees a storm ahead, he knows he must continue steering the ship to safety. Can you steer us to the safety of the cabin?"

"But I can't—I can't see the cabin."

Mariah's neck and back ached. Had the man gotten heavier? Was he even still breathing? The wind stole her own breath. Maybe Jordan was right. If they could stop for just a few minutes and just close their eyes just for a few seconds. Five minutes, max...

Her thirst-tortured throat begged for water. Was Jordan thirsty too? Was he warm enough? Should she remove her coat and wrap it around him? Was the man still alive? Where was Nosy?

Would God protect them in this perilous weather?

Lord, please...

Mariah's heart hammered in her chest. They couldn't stand here in the weather. They had to keep moving. But her feet refused her order to take a step.

Bible verses jumbled through her mind, including her favorite from Isaiah 41:10. She muttered it aloud, the words sounding incoherent in her own ears. *"Fear not, for I am with you; be not dismayed, for I am your God; I will strengthen you, I will help you, I will uphold you with my righteous right hand."*

Peace settled at the perimeter of her fear. "We're almost there, Jordan. Keep going."

Her son stumbled, then plodded along, and she followed him. She nearly lost her hold on the man twice, and her arms begged for a reprieve.

But no. They would continue to the cabin.

"There's Nosy!" Jordan's chilled voice rang out over the harsh winds, and Mariah ventured a gaze in front of them. She steered herself and Jordan slightly to follow their pet.

Darkness started to fall upon them when suddenly, she heard a voice. "Mariah? Jordan? I was so worried!"

Mom. *Thank You, Jesus!*

Her mother stood just a few inches in front of them and reached a hand to Jordan. A few seconds later, the lights from the house came into view. Then the porch steps.

"Mom, we need help." Mariah took a step up the first stair.

"What on earth? Who is that?"

"We found him near the ravine. We need to get him inside and call for help."

Mom assisted in transporting the man to the front door and inside the house.

"I hope he's still alive," Mariah said.

Jordan's teeth chattered, and she removed his coat, gloves, and hat. Kissing his red-tipped frozen nose, she wrapped him in a hug. "You were a fine helmsman. I'm so proud of you."

"Want some hot chocolate?" Her daughter, four-year-old Presley asked from her perch at the kitchen island.

"Do I ever! But first I need to get warm. It's not easy being a helmsman on the high seas." Jordan trotted toward the fireplace in sock-covered feet.

Mom bent over the man, feeling for a pulse as her nursing skills kicked in. "He is still alive, but just barely. We need to warm him up."

Together, they placed the man next to the fireplace, and Mom covered him with blankets. Nosy placed his head on the man's stomach. The man stirred so slightly that Mariah thought she might have imagined it.

"Whoever he is, he's been through a lot," Mom said.

"Like a car accident or something," Jordan added.

Mariah's gaze met Mom's. This man had been through

more than a car accident. Far more. How could she prevent her young daughter from seeing him? At least until she and Mom cleaned his wounds. Mariah removed her coat and held it up to shield the man's face.

"Presley, honey, can you make sure Nosy has water in his bowl?"

But her daughter peered around the jacket and began to whimper when she saw the man. "He's hurt really bad, Mommy."

Mariah leaned down and folded her daughter into a hug. "That's why we need to help him."

It would take nothing short of a miracle for the man to survive.

Chapter 2

Of all the days for a blizzard to hit.

"Well, the cell service is out completely. No service even at the end of the driveway." Mom pinched the bridge of her nose. "It would have been nice to call 911."

The man needed more help than they could give him. Mariah placed another log on the fire. "Have they said anything more about the storm?"

Mom shook her head. "I know the internet is down, and the snowflakes messing with the signal don't help matters, but that happens occasionally even in good weather. Jordan, would you turn on the TV?"

Jordan found the remote, and the local news appeared.

"And now, in weather, there is a severe blizzard warning for Briggs, Kingsville, and Windfield Counties. Interstate 403 is closed as are the highways and auxiliary roads between Briggs and Mountain Springs and Briggs and Vernon. In elevations above 7,800 feet, such as Mountain Springs, expect lingering snow storms for the next several days. Power outages are being reported, and cell towers are down across the counties. Sustained winds and gusts as high as 35 mph are expected. Freezing temperatures ranging from five above for a high to negative forty with the windchill are expected throughout the next several days. Frostbite can occur quickly so avoid any unnecessary outdoor activity. Travel is advised only in emergency situations due to icy roads and limited visibility. Stay tuned to this channel for further updates."

The lights flickered. "Are we going to lose power?" Jordan asked.

"We'll be fine," Mariah assured her son. "Grandpa made sure we have a generator for times just like these." The thought of her father left a pocket of sorrow in Mariah's heart. Her family had been so close, and her father's death was so unexpected. As hard as it was on Mariah, Jordan, and Presley, it was even harder on Mom. She'd been married to Dad for thirty-five years. They were soulmates. Best friends. For them, there was never any other. High school sweethearts with an affection that grew into a deep abiding love throughout the good times and bad. Mariah longed for the type of marriage her parents shared.

It certainly hadn't happened with Brandon.

With effort, she pushed the thoughts aside.

It took some time to clean the man up and move him to the small guest bedroom just adjacent to the living room. Mom pulled out her medical supplies and went to work. Mariah was relieved that her mother had years of extensive nursing experience. That and a lot of prayer would possibly save the man's life.

"He's hanging in there, but he's badly injured," Mom said in a low voice for only Mariah to hear. "He could really use a suture for that cut in his forehead, and there's just so much bruising everywhere on his body. He has a severe contusion on his left patella, and based on the bruising around his ribcage, I think his ribs are fractured. From the periorbital hematoma around his eye, the blood crusted on his head, and the bruising on his face, I suspect he's suffered a traumatic brain injury. And then there are the stab wounds."

Mariah gasped. "Stab wounds?"

"I saw a few of those in my time in the ER." Mom shook her head. "There's no way to know what type of internal injuries he has. Someone really did a number on him. If he had been out there much longer, he would have died from hypothermia—if he didn't succumb to his injuries first."

"Thank goodness Nosy led us to him. I'm just so thankful we were able to bring him here with how bad the weather was."

"And it's only gotten worse." Mom nodded toward the window, where visibility was now limited to a couple of inches beyond the house. "I sure wish we had some way to get him to the hospital, or at the very least, call 911."

"Even sending an email from the laptop would have been nice," Mariah added. She thought of how far behind on work she'd be when their internet service provider finally fixed the issue. Not to mention, it would have been nice to be able to send an email or search to see if anyone reported a missing man. "I'm sure someone misses him."

"Once we have an internet connection again, that'll be something to look into. Maybe the weather will clear enough to ask Rick his thoughts."

"He would probably enjoy helping us solve this mystery."

"Likely so."

The scenario was similar to the suspense books she edited for a large Christian publisher. While she edited several subgenres beneath the Christian romance umbrella, suspense was her favorite—she just didn't want her life to resemble a suspense novel. Her employer provided a steady stream of manuscripts flowing her way, and she could work from home while homeschooling Jordan and Presley. As a single mom, she was the sole support for her children, and being able to do a job she loved while being able to provide that support proved invaluable.

Mom's shoulders sagged. "I am thankful I haven't gone through your dad's clothes yet. It will be helpful for the man to have a change of clothes. He's about the same size as your dad, although taller. Dad's pants will be capris on him, but I doubt he'll care much."

Mariah placed a hand on Mom's arm. "I know you miss him so much, Mom."

"I do. Every day. I will always miss him."

A half-hour later, they sat at the table eating tacos while the man rested safely in the guest room, dressed in a change of clothes and tucked beneath warm quilts. "What is that man's name?" Presley asked.

"We're not sure," Mariah answered.

"I know that guy's name." Jordan chewed his bite faster, obviously eager to share his information.

Presley clapped her hands. "What is it?"

"George."

Mariah wrinkled her nose. "George? How do you know that?"

Jordan sat taller in his chair. "I just know these things."

Presley shook her head. "But how do you know?"

"All right. So remember when we learned about George Washington in school?"

Presley tilted her head to one side. "He's our president."

"And he was a hero and led the army to victory in the American Revolution. That man reminds me of George Washington. He's brave like him. He stayed out there in the snow after his car accident and even let us drag him to the house without even complaining. And he wears socks just like him," Jordan said, referencing the white compression socks.

Mariah shared a knowing glance with Mom.

"So his name is George," announced Jordan, indicating the matter was settled.

Mariah and Mom took turns staying up with "George" during the night. When Mariah's turn came, she sat in the rocking chair and snuggled into the warmth of the homemade quilt her grandmother made years ago. The man's breathing came in slow soft spurts.

Mariah closed her eyes and again prayed for him. Her body ached from the events of the day. Muscles she didn't realize she had made themselves known through weariness and a deep ache. Sleep remained elusive, so she rocked quietly, thinking about all of the work she would be facing when they again had an internet connection. She had already edited the two manuscripts she'd received last week. Exhaustion overcame her, but yet she was so tired she couldn't sleep.

What was George's story? Had she endangered her family by helping him? How had he found himself beaten up and near death beside the ravine? Had he stumbled there himself? The wind had blown so hard that if he had walked there, footprints would have been easily covered by the blowing snow. Had he been left there to face a deadly fate?

It was still a miracle that he'd both survived and that Mariah had been able to drag him to the house. Perhaps she possessed strength she never knew she had.

She stood to adjust the covers around his body and take his temperature. Even in the dim shadow of the hallway night light, Mariah could see the crusted cut on his head and severe facial bruising. Mom had dressed him in a pair of Dad's sweat-pants—high-water on him—and a red flannel shirt, then covered him with three blankets. But was George warm enough? Mariah shivered in the chilly night air, longing once again to be beneath her warm quilt.

Why did his body hurt so much? And where was he?

He attempted to open his eyes, but only one obeyed. The dim lighting gave him just enough vision to see his surroundings. Near his bed—was he in the hospital?—a woman sat in a chair wrapped in a blanket. Was she a nurse? His wife? Was he married?

What happened to him?

A sharp ache in his ribs jolted him. His head throbbed, and it felt like someone continually stabbed him in the left shoulder. He tried to move his legs, and the pain from one side nearly made him call out. But his mouth wouldn't move.

And his throat was parched.

He had a sense of self, but beyond that, everything remained out of reach.

The woman stirred, clutching the blanket closer to her chin. He was cold too, he realized, and wished he could tuck his own blankets more thoroughly around him.

Why was he here?

He wanted to ask these questions. Wanted to know why his mind was so fuzzy. Why he was so tired?

He took a deep breath—or tried to anyway. Even that hurt.

The woman stirred, her eyes fluttering open. She said something, probably to him, but everything was so hazy. She stood and leaned over him, adjusting his blanket. Maybe he would be warm now. His vision clouded, and he struggled to follow her movements. She reached up and placed her hand on his forehead. Something stung as she did so. She said something to him again, then left the room.

He hoped she was a nurse. Maybe she would do something about this pain that had overtaken every square inch of him.

It was so difficult to stay awake. Maybe he should just close his eyes and rest again.

But before he could, the nurse returned with another woman. The doctor? Voices murmured over him, words that he couldn't quite comprehend. The doctor put something on his arm and some sort of device on his finger.

Would any of this help with the pain?

Seconds later, the drowsiness overtook him.

Chapter 3

Mom set the table, concern lining her tired face. "How did George do last night on the rest of your watch?" she asked.

"He was quiet. I was afraid we lost him a couple of times," said Mariah, using an oversized spoon to scoop the scrambled eggs onto individual plates.

"That was my concern as well. Did you get any sleep?"

Mariah shook her head. "Very little. I had forgotten what it's like to sleep in the rocking chair. Took me back to the days when the kids were babies and I rocked them to sleep. What about you?"

"A fitful night to be sure." Mom reached up and massaged the left side of her neck. "The man was disoriented when he awoke, which is typical of a head injury. I'm sure he has a concussion. If—when—he awakens again, we need to give him some water. We don't need to add dehydration to his list of problems." She sighed. "I wish we could do more for him."

Mom carried the plates to the table. "He's in a bad way. Just the injured ankle and potentially fractured ribs would be enough. Not to mention the concussion, stab wounds, and the deep cut on his head. The bruises all over his body..." Mom's voice trailed as Jordan and Presley, sleepy-eyed and in their pajamas, entered the room.

"Is George still here?" Jordan asked.

It was doubtful the man would be going anywhere for a very long time. "He is," Mariah answered, pouring milk into four glasses.

"Well good. I'm glad he's still here. I want to ask him some questions about being in the military," Jordan scooted his chair from the table and plopped into it, his short brown hair ruffled from a night of sleep.

Presley's eyes grew large. "He was in the mil-tary?"

"We don't know," Mariah answered. Her son had quite the imagination. "What makes you think he was in the military, Jordan?"

Jordan shrugged. "Dunno. It's just that guys named George are always in the military. There's George Washington. And then there was that George guy in that book you read who was a pilot in a war."

"We can ask him," Presley suggested, hugging her doll, Bibby, that she'd brought to the table—and just about everywhere else she went.

George wouldn't be talking much anytime soon, but Mariah was grateful her children had such optimism. "Jordan, would you lead the prayer for the meal?"

Jordan folded his hands and, straightening his posture for what he deemed an important task, began to pray. "Dear Lord, thank You for sending George. Please let him get better and please let him like building blocks and football. Amen."

Mariah's eyes teared at her son's prayer. His sincere heart for George's recovery touched her heart. But the request that the man like blocks and football broke her heart. Her ex-husband rarely stayed in touch with his children, and when he had them for an infrequent visit, Brandon preferred the company of his phone and laptop to spending time with them. Jordan had never known what it was like to have his dad partake in a game of tossing the football around or building a spaceship with his blocks. Grandpa had been the one to fill that male role in both Jordan's and Presley's lives.

She would make sure she set aside time to partner with Jordan in building a new creation later today, even though it wouldn't be the same for him.

They finished breakfast, and Mariah went to check on George. He had awakened again, staring at the ceiling with the only eye he could manage to open. She raced back to the kitchen and grabbed a water bottle. Filling it, she returned to the bedroom, praying he was still lucid. "Mom, George is awake. Should we prop him up so we can see if he'll drink?"

Mom nodded and returned with a wedge pillow and some acetaminophen. "This should elevate him enough," she said of the pillow.

Together, they lifted George's head and shoulders and placed him on the wedge pillow. George moaned in obvious pain, his body stiffening and making it more difficult to re-arrange him.

"I'm sorry, George, we have to elevate you so you can have a drink. It'll do your body good to move a little," Mom said. "As soon as possible, we need to have you do some ankle pump exercises. Those in addition to the compression stockings are necessary for you to avoid getting a blood clot."

George peered up at Mariah, confusion lighting his face. "I'm going to try to give you some water, all right?"

He blinked his eye once. Had he understood what she said?

Mom gently tilted George's head back, as Mariah squirted a meager amount of water into his mouth.

George sputtered, then gulped, the water running down his

chin. Mom reached for a tissue on the nightstand beside the bed and dabbed at the spilled water.

Mariah waited a moment before trying again with the acetaminophen. This time, George appeared to have received some of the water. He swallowed and closed his eye, his head drooping to one side. "I'm going to open the curtains and start the kids with their schooling," she said more to herself than to him.

"I'll finish going through the pantry and seeing what we have. It appears we're going to be snowbound for a while."

Mariah glanced out the window. Snow continued to fall, although now in large, peaceful flakes. The beauty of it never ceased to impress her, as long as they were safe and warm inside the cabin.

Jordan and Presley sat at the kitchen table, paper, crayons, and pencils in hand. Mariah prepared the laptop for Jordan's math program, thankful that she didn't need internet access for it. She placed two coloring sheets in front of Presley. "After you color the shapes, circle the ones that are triangles."

The loud sound of a motor interrupted the otherwise quiet solitude as the children began their lessons. "That sounds like Rick." Jordan bolted from his chair and ran to the window. "It is Rick! He's snow blowing the driveway."

Mariah followed her son to the window. Sure enough, Rick, their retired neighbor, walked behind the snowblower, struggling to clear some of the immense amount of snow that had fallen. Shoulder-high drifts compounded the difficulty of his work.

"Maybe we can make an igloo," Jordan suggested.

Mariah could see the wheels turning in her son's mind. "That sounds like a wonderful idea, but first it has to warm up." She should tell Rick about George and see if he had any suggestions. Opening the front door, Mariah waved at their neighbor, hoping to get his attention.

Rick finally saw her, turned off the snowblower, and headed her way.

Mariah beckoned him inside the house. Rick was bundled from head to toe, with only his eyes peeping above a tightly wound scarf. "How is everyone here with that storm?"

"We're fine. No internet and no phone, but we haven't lost power. How are you and Carol?"

Rick unwound the scarf and removed his hat, revealing his shiny bald head. "Carol, of course, wishes we were in Florida, but she's getting her new quilt done. It's quite something. You know how she is about her sewing projects." He grinned, admiration for his wife and her sewing projects obvious.

"Glad she's keeping busy. It's so peaceful outside right now."

"For now. But it looks like another storm is moving in. I hope to get the driveways cleared, especially a pathway from your house to ours before then. We won't be going anywhere beyond that anytime soon."

Mariah appreciated Rick's dedication. Several years ago when he and Carol moved into the cottage, Dad arranged for Rick to assist with yardwork and snow clearing to reduce his rent. Carol especially agreed, seeing the need for Rick to stay busy during his retirement years. "There's something we need to tell you."

"Oh? Something wrong?"

"Can you stay for a minute?"

"Sure." He removed his boots. "What's up?"

Mariah led Rick away from the earshot of the children and explained what happened. Rick rested a hand on the gun at his hip, likely a habit from his law enforcement days. "There have been recent reports about fugitives trying to hide up here in our little town. I'm glad you and Jordan are all right." A grimace crossed his round face. "Where did the man go?"

"Actually, when we approached him, it was obvious he was badly injured. Jordan and I were able to get him back to the cabin just in time before the blizzard caused zero visibility."

"You hauled him back to the cabin? Why didn't you come get me?"

"The storm hit and there was no time. He's in the guest bedroom. Mom says he's hanging in there, but she's not sure he'll pull through due to all of his injuries."

Rick stroked his beardless chin. "Can I see him?"

"Sure." Mariah led him to the guest bedroom. "He's been asleep most of the time. Mom has been taking his vitals, and she tended to his wounds the best she could. Since we have no cell service or internet, we haven't been able to call for help."

"Not like the EMS would be able to make it up here anyhow. Roads are closed. Wish I could help you with the phone situation, but we never did get a landline again once we moved here. Thought it wasn't necessary." Rick assumed a protective stance and walked toward the bed, his husky frame full of confidence. "So this is our guy?" He leaned over George as if to take full inventory of the man's condition. "Looks to be in terrible shape."

"A concussion, possible fractured ribs, a knee injury, some stab wounds, and a laceration on his forehead to start."

"Man. Someone did a number on him. Attempted murder, it would appear." Rick paused. "Still, this guy could be a criminal or someone on the run. I don't like the idea of him in here with you, Linda, and the kids."

"He can't do anything right now. He can't even stay conscious."

Rick paced the floor in front of the bed. "What I wouldn't give for an internet connection right now. It would put me at ease to check into some things."

"Spoken like a true retired police officer."

"Hey. Once a cop, always a cop." Rick stopped and stared at George for a while longer. "You don't just stop being a cop after thirty-eight years on the force. Remember, I did a stint in homicide for a while. Let me know when he regains full consciousness. I'd like to interrogate him."

"Not sure if George will be up for an interrogation, but yes, Rick, I'll let you know."

"George? You have a name? Did you find some I.D. on his person? Now I really wish I had my internet to look into some databases."

Mariah laughed. "Jordan named him after George Washington. We don't know his real name. The man hasn't been able to speak yet. And no, there was no identification on him."

"That Jordan, he's a character." Rick chuckled. "Well, again, let me know when he regains consciousness. Don't want you to be harboring a fugitive." He paused and gave George one last look over. "I better go finish snow blowing before it snows again or Carol gets worried. Or both."

Mariah led Rick to the door before resuming daily home-schooling activities. She worried, however, that Rick might be right. That they may indeed be harboring a fugitive. Or worse.

Chapter 4

Nosy barked, tail wagging with enthusiasm as Mariah opened the front door. He dashed out into the bleak winter day, not minding that the thermometer registered a freezing 15 below zero.

Mariah wrapped her arms around herself and trotted after him. She stopped briefly at the spot where she usually had cell reception and dialed 911 on the off chance that the tower had been repaired. "Welcome to your wireless service. We're sorry. Your call cannot be completed as dialed."

No surprise. The cell tower must still be down. At some point, they needed to secure more advanced medical care for George.

A chilly wind blew through the trees, and the sound of a saw marred the otherwise quiet ambiance. Rick must be in his garage focusing on one of his many woodworking projects.

Nosy did his business, but instead of wandering back to the house, he ran toward the far side of the yard.

"Nosy!" Mariah called. This was certainly not the day to indulge in the dog's endless curiosity. Last time that happened, she'd found a severely injured man barely clinging to life.

Nosy gave her a dubious glance and began to bury his paws

into the snow. A moment later, he'd retrieved his favorite fetch toy. He pushed through the snow toward Mariah, the toy in his mouth, and dropped it at her feet.

"It's way too cold for fetch today, Nosy," Mariah said, reaching down to pet him.

Nosy's black tail swished in the snow. His eyes begged for some playtime, no matter how brief.

Mariah shook her head. "I never could say no to you," she laughed. "But only a couple of times."

Nosy leaned his head from one side to the other, and he gave her what Presley and Jordan termed his "doggie smile".

Mariah threw the toy and watched as Nosy bounded after it. Her breath clouded the air in front of her, and she tugged her hat more securely over her ears.

The roar of a snowmobile distracted Nosy, and he lifted his head, ears erect and body stiffened to full attention. The machine zipped down the driveway and toward the house with a lone rider who stood while bent over the handlebars as he or she maneuvered it around drifts.

Who would be out in this weather? While it wasn't uncommon for outdoor enthusiasts to pass by on their way to the nearby trails, even the most diehard preferred to embark on their hobby when temps weren't at a dangerous level.

His toy forgotten, Nosy followed the snow machine as it skidded toward Mariah. She stepped out of the way, her own senses on full alert.

The snowmobile stopped and the rider killed the engine.

"Come on, Nosy," Mariah called. If they needed to get inside the house fast, she needed him ready to comply.

Hadn't she just read in one of the suspense novels she was editing about an escaped felon on a snowmobile that resulted in...

Mariah cleared her mind. This was reality. A crazy man with a life sentence escaping from a maximum-security prison wouldn't be riding his snow machine into 430 Deer Lane in Mountain Springs.

Right?

A petite person the size of an older child stepped off the snowmobile and stomped toward her, closing any reasonable gap of personal space between two strangers with the close proximity. Mariah took a step back. The person followed with a step forward.

Should she be concerned?

Or did the person merely need help?

Heavy winter gear and goggles covered their face, concealing their identity. The person's eyes shifted all around Mariah but failed to maintain appropriate eye contact.

Nosy barked, a low throaty growling bark, and planted himself between Mariah and the person. His ears flattened against his head and he tucked his tail. Not a good sign.

For all of his annoying habits, Nosy was protective and had a keen sense when it came to people.

Mariah scanned the neighboring house. The sound of the saw raged over Nosy's barking. A glance at Mom's house told her it was likely no one was looking outside the window. She took another step backward.

"Can I help you?"

The person planted their hands on their hips. It was a woman's voice, smoky and hoarse, that spoke. "Yeah. My brother and I were out riding our snowmobiles yesterday and somehow got separated. He could be hurt real bad."

"Oh, no."

"Yeah." The moment of concern seemed to have passed, and the woman's voice inflection changed. "So I'm lookin' for him and haven't had any luck finding him. Have you seen him?"

Within seconds, the woman's hands fell from her hips, and her hands, covered in heavy winter gloves, balled into fists. "Well?" she demanded.

Mariah weighed her decision and a thought passed through her mind. Could it be George of whom this woman spoke? She wanted to open her mouth and suggest it, but something prompted her to remain silent. Besides, George hadn't been dressed for snowmobiling when she found him, so it couldn't be him.

Could it?

Nosy barked again, and the woman shifted her stance. "What's with the dog? Can't you shut him up?"

"Nosy, come here," Mariah beckoned. But Nosy didn't obey. Instead, he continued to bark at the woman, almost acting aggressively toward her.

"Yo. If your dog bites me..."

"He won't bite you. He's just protective."

"So, have you seen my brother or not? It's cold out here, and he could freeze. I gotta find him."

Nosy growled.

The woman focused a hard stare toward Mariah, her gaze remaining steadfast.

Somewhere inside, a heightened sixth sense kicked in, and a protective fear launched within her. She couldn't explain why.

Something didn't add up.

Mariah knew at this point she'd not share anything with this woman, but she did need to placate her until she left. "What does he look like?"

"About 6'1, 200 pounds, big guy with blond hair. I'm really afraid for him." Her tone again changed. This time to seemingly indicate her concern.

Could this be George's sister? The description sounded accurate.

"I really need to find him. We're close, you know." Her stiffened body posture relaxed slightly. "We were riding and then all of a sudden, I didn't see him. I gotta find him."

"I'm sorry. I haven't seen him, but I'll keep my eyes open."

The woman nodded toward Rick and Carol's house. "What about your neighbors?"

"I would know if they'd seen anyone because we talk daily." *Almost the truth.*

"And who all lives in your house?"

The invasive question struck her as not only presumptuous but also concerning. Mariah refused to answer any question that may jeopardize her children and mother. So, she said nothing.

The blatant stare remained. "Okay, well, I'll be back by to check again."

The woman started the snowmobile, turned an exaggerated circle, and rode down the driveway and out of sight.

Nosy barked and ran after the woman before returning and stopping at Mariah's feet. He nodded toward the toy.

"I'm sorry, Nosy, but we need to go in."

Something about the woman concerned her—call it gut instinct or mother's intuition.

Who was George? And what kind of person had she brought into her home?

Chapter 5

He awoke while it was still dark. He blinked, attempting to focus his eye on the room around him. The rocking chair next to his bed was empty, and the door to what he assumed was a hallway stood open. His right leg had fallen asleep, and he longed to be able to get up and move around. But he knew such a feat was impossible when he shifted slightly.

His stomach growled. When was the last time he had eaten? What foods did he even like? And why could he remember nothing about himself?

That realization unhinged him.

He shivered, igniting pain in numerous spots throughout his body. Reaching with his right arm, he did his best to inch the blanket upward to cover his shoulders, every movement causing excruciating agony.

Was he sick? Was that why his head and body ached?

The clock's ticking counted down the minutes to when someone—maybe the nurse or the doctor—would come to check on him. Would he be able to ask for something to eat when that time came?

He licked his lips, hoping to quench the blistered dryness. He attempted to turn his head toward the nightstand. A bottle of water beckoned him. If he could lean on his right elbow and reach for it with his left hand...

Slowly, he sought to roll over and prop himself up. His right leg still reeling from the pins and needles argued, but his left leg refused. Pain from his knee and ribs surged through him, and he thudded on his back. A loud moan escaped his lips and tears filled his eyes. Pain radiated from his left shoulder to his wrist. His head throbbed.

Was he always this weak?

Exhaustion exceeded his hunger and thirst, and he succumbed to sleep once again.

He had no idea how long it had been, only that the daylight now streamed through the small slits on either side of the window coverings and a delicious aroma filled the air. He opened his eye, the bright light of day causing him to squint. A little girl with blonde braids stood beside his bed staring at him.

"Good morning, George," she said, clutching a stuffed doll in her arms. "How are you?"

He cleared his throat and tried to speak. "Fine," he rasped. Although, he was far from fine.

"Mommy! George is talking!" The little girl fled from the room, only to return a few moments later. "Mommy will be in soon to check on you. We're happy that you're talking. Grandma says that's an answer to prayer."

His mind clouded. Mommy? Grandma? Prayer? *George?*

At least now he knew his name, but just who was he?

"Uh..."

The girl leaned closer. "Do you like pancakes?"

Pancakes? Did he like pancakes? Everything was just so fuzzy. "Uh...sure." He croaked the words. Did he always sound like this?

The girl shook her head. "First we have to ask Mommy. You might need something like soup or something like what I had to have when I was sick."

"Am I—am I sick?" That could explain all the pain.

"Yes. And you have an owie on your face. I once had an owie on my face when I was running after Nosy and fell. Mommy gave it a kiss and fixed it all up."

"Do you know my last name?"

"Your last name?"

George wondered if the little girl even understood what a last name was.

"Oh, yes. You mean like I have three names. Presley Ann Holzman. Your three names are George Ann Washington."

"George Ann Washington?"

The girl bobbed her head. "Yes. We will only use your second name for when you're in trouble."

The name rang a distant bell somewhere in the recesses of his mind, the name. Could that really be his full name?

"I am this many." She held up four fingers. "How many are you?"

How old was he? George had no idea. "Uh...I'm not sure."

"You're probably sixty-seven. That's how old my mommy is."

Could be that he was sixty-seven. He wasn't sure. One thing he did know was that his throat ached for a drink. "Do you know when the nurse will be here?" His voice continued to croak. Yes, he probably was a lot older than sixty-seven.

"The nurse?"

"Or the doctor?"

Presley shrugged. "I'm not sure. But I am going to let you babysit Bibby so you're not scared when Grandma puts the medicine on you. It stings, 'cause I remember that one time when I fell out of the wagon and Jordan was pulling me. I falled on the ground and cut my knee, and Grandma put the medicine on my owie." She tucked her baby doll under the blanket near his right arm. "Bibby will help you be brave."

"Presley, time to eat!" a voice called.

"Well, George, I need to go. We're having pancakes today. Mommy will be in soon." She skipped out of the room, leaving George to wonder...did he know this little girl and her mommy? Were they his family?

The nurse came in a while later. Finally, he could ask her for a drink. He could barely swallow his throat was so dry.

"Hello, George. Presley said you're talking." She came closer and placed a hand on his head. "It doesn't feel like you have a fever, but Mom will be in soon to check all of your vitals."

"Can I..." he cleared his throat. "Can I have a drink?"

"Absolutely." The nurse reached for the water bottle, then assisted him into position on an additional pillow to take a drink. He grimaced at the pain radiating through him. When the water bottle touched his lips, he guzzled thirstily, trying to ignore the fact that in his ineptitude, most of the water drizzled down his chin.

Finally, feeling satiated, George reclined on the pillow. "Thank you." He could feel his throat again and his lips were a little less dry.

"You're welcome." She took a tissue and dabbed at the mess he'd made with the water. "Do you think you could eat something?"

"Yes. I'm—I'm really hungry."

"Good. That means you're healing." She offered what

seemed to be a cautious smile. One he attempted to return, but the movement caused a painful pulling in his forehead.

"Am I sick?"

"You're injured."

His head spun. Injured? "Why? How?"

"We're not sure." The nurse paused. "I see Presley left Bibby here for you to borrow."

"Bibby?"

"Her baby doll."

Remembering the toy nestled beside him, George wished he could chuckle. Whoever he was, he was quite sure he didn't need a baby doll to comfort him.

"Are you cold at all?"

"Not anymore. Just a lot of pain."

The nurse nodded. "Mom will give you something for that after you eat. I have some chicken noodle soup. How does that sound?"

"Do I like chicken noodle soup?"

The woman didn't say anything for a moment as if thinking about her answer. "I think you do."

"Okay. Good. I'm pretty hungry. The little girl said there were pancakes. Do I like those?"

"Probably, but you should start with chicken noodle soup. You've been through a lot."

What had he been through? "Oh, okay." He paused. "What is your name? Do I know you?"

"I'm Mariah. My mom, who will be in here to take your vitals, is Linda."

George would try to remember those names, although he wished he knew whether or not these people taking care of him were related to him. Was Mariah his wife? Was Presley his daughter? Had the little girl told him her last name? He couldn't remember.

But before he could ask, someone called Mariah's name.

"I need to go, but I'll be back in a few minutes with your soup."

George stared at the ceiling. The food and pain relievers couldn't come soon enough.

Mariah busied herself preparing the chicken noodle soup. Last night, she had tossed and turned, wondering how and if George was related to the woman who came in search of him.

She stirred the soup in the pan, her thoughts far from the task of preparing George's meal. Maybe she should have marched right over to Rick's and told him about the peculiar woman on the snowmobile.

On second thought, maybe that wasn't such a good idea. Rick was protective—which was a good thing—but he could also be excessive at times, only because he had seen so much in his former profession. He would worry and fret when, in reality, the woman might never return or cause any more concern. Or maybe the woman—who'd come off as angry—was just worried about her brother.

Mariah hadn't even told Mom. Probably a good idea. The grief over the loss of her husband was enough. She didn't need anything else to worry about.

Lord, I don't know who this man is, but I pray we have not erred in bringing him into our home. Please let him be a law-abiding citizen and keep us safe while caring for him and the wisdom in how to do so. I pray the woman's motives were merely her concern for this man. Please let his memory return and open the roads so we can get him the medical help he needs.

It truly was an answer to prayer that George was awake and somewhat coherent. Mom would likely say he "wasn't out of the woods yet," but this new development was an improvement. Speaking of which, she would have to let Rick know George had awakened and was talking. Rick would likely have some questions, although Mariah doubted George would be able to answer any of them, given how confused he acted. Mom said he likely had a traumatic brain injury, which accounted for that confusion and memory loss.

Turning from the stove while the soup cooked, Mariah set up the day's schooling schedule at the kitchen table.

"George was scared, so I let him borrow Bibby," Presley announced, setting her box of crayons on the table.

"That was very kind of you."

Presley shrugged. "If Grandma puts that medicine on his owie by his eye, it's gonna sting."

"I heard George is awake." Jordan entered wearing the same superhero two-piece pajama set he'd insisted on wearing for three days in a row.

"He is awake and he's talking," said Presley.

"Cool. Mom, can I ask him something?"

Mariah stirred the soup. "How about we let him eat first and let Grandma check on him, then you can ask him some questions."

"Okay."

She finished preparing the soup and poured half of it into a cup. How much would George be able to eat? Opening the utensil drawer, she grabbed a spoon. "I'm going to take this to George. I'll be right back to help you get started with school."

Mariah entered the guest room with the cup of soup and sat in the chair beside his bed.

The black and blue that marred his face was so profound

that Mariah wondered what George looked like without the facial injuries. His matted, stringy blond hair gave him an unkempt appearance. Would Rick recognize him from some photo in an article he'd perused online?

Mariah spooned some soup and held it toward his mouth. "I'm really hungry," he rasped, after taking the first bite.

"I know. It'll be hard not to eat it fast, but we don't want to overdo it. There's plenty if you need more."

They sat in silence while George finished his soup. "I think I do like soup," he said.

Mariah smiled. "Do you remember anything—anything at all?"

"No."

"You probably have amnesia. You were hit pretty hard on the head."

"What? How? Who did this?"

Mariah wished she had answers. "We don't know."

Mom entered then, her doctor bag in hand. "I'm here to check some vitals. How is our patient doing this morning?"

Mariah stood to the side and watched as Mom first took George's blood pressure. "Doctor?" George asked.

Mom and Mariah exchanged a glance. Did George think Mom was a doctor? "Doctor?" he repeated.

"I'm not a doctor, but I am a nurse. My name is Linda."

Mariah sensed George was somewhat disappointed by this news.

Mom unsnapped the front of his flannel shirt, revealing severe bruising on his torso. "It hurts to breathe," George said.

"I suspect you have some fractured ribs, although I can't know for sure without an x-ray." Mom gently pushed the flannel a bit farther off the side of George's left shoulder. Two angry red wounds marred his flesh.

Bile rose in Mariah's throat at the sight of the stab wounds, and she swayed slightly, clutching to the nightstand for support.

"Mariah, honey, I think I've got this," Mom said.

Mariah nodded. "I'll refill the water bottle."

How had George survived a possible attack on his life?

One thing was for certain: those wounds weren't from a snowmobile accident.

Chapter 6

George winced as Linda checked his injuries. With every breath, his ribs hurt, and with every movement, his head throbbed. He wanted to mention it to her, but just the thought of speaking hurt.

"I sure am concerned about those stab wounds on your shoulder."

Stab wounds?

How had he gotten stab wounds?

It didn't make sense.

And why did—what had Linda called her?—Mariah?—appear squeamish about his injuries? He couldn't crane his neck and see the wounds himself, but for some reason, he had a feeling the sight of them wouldn't bother him.

Had he experienced such wounds before?

Frustration filled his thoughts. How could he know anything about anything when he couldn't even remember who he was?

"I'm concerned these are getting infected," Linda said, dabbing medicine onto his shoulder with gloved hands. "It's hot around the wounds and they look irritated. It'll be good to be able to get you to a doctor." She then put medicine on his forehead.

George groaned. Presley was correct—the medicine did sting. "When can I see a doctor?"

"We're snowed in for the time being. Still no internet or phone service. Apparently, this has happened one other year in recent times. We'll keep praying for you and doing the best we can."

Praying? Somewhere in the recesses of his mind, the word evoked some sort of recollection. Was prayer a part of his life?

Linda assisted him with a sip of water. "Can I get you anything else?"

"No thanks."

She smiled warmly, then left the room.

His next visitor was a young boy with a colorful toy in his hands. "Hey, George," he said, standing next to the side of the bed. "I'm Jordan, and this is my spaceship I built out of my blocks."

So many names to remember. George stared at the spaceship. Obviously, the boy had put a lot of work into it. "Looks great."

"Thanks. Do you think maybe tomorrow when you're all better you could help me build some new things? After I'm done with school, of course."

George could only wish he would be all the way better tomorrow. Jordan's eyes lit with expectation. He wasn't sure who this child was and if he knew him, but one thing George did know, he didn't want to let him down. And from the excitement in the child's eyes, creating things sounded like a worthwhile endeavor. "Maybe tomorrow when I feel better." He paused to catch his breath and adjust to the pain in his ribs at this lengthy conversation. "Think of something to make, okay?"

"Oh, I already have lots of ideas. Mom says I'm an idea factory when it comes to building block creations. I can't wait until you help me. Mom sometimes builds things with me, but..." Jordan leaned closer and whispered, "She's a girl, so you know...she doesn't really know much about building spaceships and stuff."

"What about Presley?"

"Presley?" Jordan wrinkled his nose. "No way. She's a girl too and just a little older than a baby and not much fun at all."

George wanted to laugh. Tried to laugh. But his head and ribs ached.

"Do you have any sisters or brothers?" Jordan asked.

Did he? "I'm not sure."

Jordan scratched his head. "How can you not know if you don't have any sisters or brothers? Presley never lets me forget she's here."

"Something—something happened to my memory."

"You mean like it got erased?"

"Something like that."

"Jordan, time for history," a woman's voice called. Mariah's?

Jordan shrugged. "That's my mom. I better go do some history. I'm pretty excited because today we're learning about Benjamin Franklin. I'll leave my spaceship here to keep you company." Jordan placed the toy on the nightstand near George. "See ya later!" He waved and left the room.

This family all seemed to care a lot about him. Was he related to them?

If only he could remember.

Mariah found George awake in bed and staring out the window. "George? Are you all right?"

"Yeah. Just wishing I felt better and knew who I was."

"That has to be frustrating." She sat in the chair she had placed next to his bed and proceeded to help him with his breakfast. "You're talking more. That's good." She paused. "Pancakes are on the menu today."

"I think I like those," he said.

Who was this man? Would they ever find out why he had been left for dead near a ravine in their small mountain town? And what if he was the one that the woman *had* been looking for? She must be worried sick about him. "At least the snow has stopped for a while."

"Linda said we're snowed in. Does your family have enough supplies?"

"Yes. Dad built Mom several storage areas she has put to good use. We'll be fine."

George took a bite of the pancake and chewed slowly. "Your dad?"

"He passed away last year."

"I'm sorry."

Mariah swallowed hard. "Thank you. We all miss him."

"I don't know if—if I have parents and siblings. Jordan—he—asked me."

At times, George seemed to be having a difficult time articulating his words. "I see he was in here and left his toy to keep you company." She was proud that her children were considerate of others.

"He wants me to build something—with these blocks. I'm

43

not familiar with those."

"They fit together to make things." She paused. "Jordan is clever and smart. I love his eagerness to learn. It makes teaching him super easy."

"If I feel better, I can help him build something."

Mariah stared at the man in the bed. He didn't know Jordan and Jordan didn't know him, yet George was willing to take the time to do something that meant so much to her son. "Thank you, George. Thank you for offering to do that."

"Don't know how much I can do."

"Just the time spent will mean the world to him."

Mariah set the plate on the nightstand. "We're praying that the Lord will restore your memory. I can't imagine not recalling anything, especially things that are so important."

"Sometimes." He closed his eyes. "Sometimes I wonder if there are—there are some things I don't want to remember." George's voice lowered, and he averted his gaze to the ceiling. "Just hope not."

The sound of the doorbell interrupted them. A moment later, she heard Rick's voice. "That's our neighbor coming for a visit. Can I get you anything else?"

"I'm good. And, Mariah?"

"Yes?"

"Thanks."

"For?"

"For taking care of me. All of you."

George's gratitude stirred something within her. "You're welcome."

She turned and left the room, nearly causing a head-on collision with Rick in the hallway.

"Hey there, Mariah. Linda said George was awake, so I thought I'd come do some interrogating."

44

"Be nice, Rick," she warned.

"I always am. Ask Carol."

Mariah laughed. "Carol's biased."

"Maybe." His eyes crinkled at the corners. "Don't worry. But I do aim to get to the bottom of this investigation."

Whatever Rick uncovered, Mariah hoped it was good.

George strained to hear the conversation in the hallway. Something about an interrogation? A man entered his room a moment later. Husky, sturdy, and bald, he carried a gun on his hip. He strode toward George, and lifting the chair, flipped it around and straddled it. "Wow, someone did a number on you," he said. "So, they tell me your name is George."

"Yes."

"I'm Rick. I live next door with my wife. We rent the cottage from Linda." He paused, resting his hand on the gun at his side. "I'm extremely—did I mention extremely?—protective of this family. Just thought you should know that upfront."

"They seem nice."

"They are. So, tell me, George, what's your last name?"

"Washington."

Rick narrowed his eyes. "Oh, a wise guy, are we?"

George had no idea what Rick was talking about, so he remained silent.

"So, tell me, Mr. Washington, who did this to you?"

"I—I don't know."

Rick nodded but didn't appear convinced. "Someone beats you up, attacks you with a knife, and leaves you near a ravine, and you don't know who did this?"

"That's right, sir. I have—I have no idea. Linda says I have memory loss." The lengthy sentence took the air out of him.

"Apparently so."

George held his gaze. "It's tough not knowing any details about your life."

"I can sympathize with that." He stroked his chin. "I'll put it straight to you. I'm retired law enforcement, but as I always say, once a cop, always a cop. I worked homicide for years. I worked in fraud during some less-exciting tenure on the force. No matter what I did, I worked for justice. I'm direct and to the point and always get the answers I seek. I *will* find out who you are."

Something rattled in George's mind as Rick carried on about his former profession. He gazed at Rick's gun in the holster on his hip. George closed his eyes. There was something there—some recollection just out of his reach. He squeezed his eyes tighter, trying to ignore the pain it caused in his swollen eyelid. What was it? Why was this triggering some type of memory?

Everything was so elusive.

Finally, he gave up. Nothing would come, and it obviously didn't help to force it. "Well, nice to meet you," he finally said.

"Yeah. You too. I'll be back to visit again." Rick stood, and with his right hand, pointed two fingers toward his eyes, then toward George. "In the meantime, I'll be watching you."

George only hoped Rick didn't have reason to be concerned.

Chapter 7

Mariah finished the dishes and glanced at the clock. Eleven-fifteen. Weariness overtook her. It had been a long, but good day. The wind whipped through the trees outside, and standing close enough to the kitchen window enabled her to feel the drafty air that made its way beyond the sealed window.

Tossing the dishrag into the sink, she padded across the floor and down the hall to check on George one last time before heading to bed. He snored lightly, a good sign that he was sleeping hard. He needed quality rest to heal properly.

Nosy had taken to sleeping in George's room, and tonight, the dog curled up on the floor next to George's bed. In the glow of the light from the hall, she could see Nosy twitching as he barked small yipping noises. She smiled. No doubt Nosy dreamed of a plethora of doggie toys at his disposal. Or maybe playing nonstop fetch with Jordan. Or Presley feeding him all-he-could-eat treats from a doggie buffet. Whatever the case, the dog appeared as peaceful as George.

Next stop: Jordan's and Presley's rooms. Then off to bed.

Her weary legs ached as she headed up the stairs. She was a night owl, always doing her best work in the late evenings and preferring to sleep from midnight to 8:00 a.m. Mom was the opposite. Their opposing schedules complimented each other well.

A clicking noise caught her attention when she reached the third stair. Her mind groggy, Mariah figured it was just her ears playing tricks on her. Either that or the wind batting against something outside.

Realization dawned when she heard it again.

Someone was trying the lock on the front door.

The potential threat caused an adrenaline rush. Why would someone be trying the door? Who would even be out in this type of weather? And at this time?

Could it have been my imagination?

The clicking sound happened again, putting to rest her thoughts of an overactive imagination.

Her mind wandered back to the incident with the creepy woman on the snowmobile. Was it her again searching for her brother?

But if so, why would she try the door rather than knock on it or ring the doorbell? And why at night?

Finally, all she heard was the roaring wind and the ticking of the clock on the mantle.

She released a deep breath. Best get to bed and get some sleep.

But if she was asleep and someone broke into the cabin...

A screeching pitch caused her to jump. Gripping the railing, Mariah attempted to formulate where the sound had come from and what it was.

She didn't have to wait long. The origin of the sound soon became clear. Someone had opened the sliding screen door off the back deck. The glass door still separated her from whoever desired to enter the home, but just the thought of someone attempting to enter caused a chill to ripple through her.

Would they succeed in entering the house?

Should she go upstairs and retrieve her gun?

Awaken Mom?

Offering a prayer for guidance, she rushed up the stairs and into her room. Opening the biometric safe in her drawer, she pulled out her 9mm pistol, already loaded and ready to protect.

Passing by Jordan's and Presley's rooms, she peeked in quickly, just to reassure herself they were both in their beds.

Why did she feel like someone had stuck her plumb in the middle of a suspense novel?

When Mariah mentioned she'd like to write one someday, she didn't anticipate having the real-life experience of a nerve-wracking and suspenseful life to do so.

Mom's door was closed. Should she wake Mom and tell her what she heard?

No, she would investigate for herself. Rarely had Mom been able to get a good night's sleep after Dad's death. No need to disturb her on what could be a night where rest finally came.

Mariah inched down the stairs, her back to the railing. *Always be aware of your surroundings.* Rick's words from the situational awareness class he offered last fall rang through her mind. She tiptoed to the front window and peeked out into the darkness.

Nothing but swaying trees.

A breath she didn't realize she'd been holding escaped her lips. Turning, she edged her way toward the back glass door. Dad had cut a thin board to place in the track to avoid someone opening the door and entering the home.

But nothing would stop someone from breaking the glass and entering were that their intent.

Mariah pushed the drapes aside. She squinted across the deck and into the unlit backyard. The gate swung open and closed in the wind.

A gate that had previously been shut and locked.

No one was on the deck, but was that someone in the backyard? Mariah pressed her face against the glass, straining her eyes to compete with the darkness and blowing snow.

Yes.

It was a person.

Escaping through the open gate.

What had they been doing in the yard? Why had they been trying to break in?

George.

He had to be the reason. Whoever it was—the woman maybe?—it was a smaller figure that escaped through the gate—they were obviously still looking for George.

She'd never get any sleep now.

Chapter 8

He was actually having a somewhat of a lucid day. He'd slept *a lot* and didn't remember much of yesterday, but at least he'd slept.

That morning, Presley rushed into his room with the force of a windstorm. She held her hands behind her back. "I have a surprise for you."

Jordan stepped beside her. "I'll go first because I am the oldest."

"I was here first," Presley shoved her way closer to George's bedside.

George had no idea how to react to their squabbling.

Presley thrust a piece of paper at him nanoseconds before her brother did the same. He reached a shaky hand toward the gifts.

"We made them in art class." Presley beamed and peered from the paper to George, then to the paper again. "Do you like it?"

"Yes, I do."

Presley pointed a bright-pink-painted fingernail at her drawing. "Do you know who that is?"

"Is it me?"

She clapped her hands. "Good job, George! Yes, it is you. And these..." she pointed to several scribbles on the drawing. "Those are bandages covering your owies. You have a lot of them, you know."

George was about to say something when Presley continued. "And that's your hair. Kinda messy. And next to you is a picture of Nosy because he found you. He's glad you're here."

"My turn now," insisted Jordan.

Presley held up a hand. "Not so fast. And Bibby helped me drawed it."

"Bibby can't draw. She's a doll."

"A special doll."

Jordan rolled his eyes. "I only let you go first because Mom would tell me it's the gentlemanly thing to do. But now it's my turn." He edged his way to George's bedside and pointed at his drawing. "This is the fastest race car in the world. And you're driving it, George."

"Thank you."

The thought of driving a race car was preferable to languishing in a bed with bandage-covered owies.

"You're welcome," Jordan stood tall. "You should put it up for all to see."

"I know where to get some tape," Presley said.

A glint lit Jordan's eyes. "Good idea. Go get it."

The exchange amused George. Did he have children of his own? Did he have siblings?

Doll in hand, Presley dashed from the room only to return a few minutes later with the tape. "Do you want to tape them up, Jordan?"

"Since Mom would want me to be a gentleman, why don't you?"

"Okay." Taking both drawings, she taped them with numerous pieces of tape each to the wall beside George's bed.

George wanted to ask if she had permission to decorate the walls, but he didn't want to ruin her enthusiasm.

"There. This room could use some decorations. And George needs something to look at. Besides, Mom and Grandma have hung up pictures in other rooms," Jordan said as if reading George's mind.

"Do you think it's enough tape?" Presley asked.

"No, not if a strong wind comes in the window. Better use more." Jordan unrolled some tape and cut it on the dispenser. Presley proceeded to tape every side of each picture—more than once.

"There," she said. "Whenever you are sad, just look at this picture of you."

"And the race car," added Jordan. "Wow, look. We used that whole roll of tape."

One thing was certain. Neither picture was coming off the wall anytime soon.

The first thing Mariah saw when she entered George's room was the drawings taped haphazardly to the wall beside George's bed. She was confident she knew the artists.

Her eyes teared at the kindness of her children. Already at such tender ages, they were compassionate and thoughtful. No easy feat in today's world.

But she would have to sweetly, but firmly, let them know that taping pictures to the wall with an entire roll of clear tape was not acceptable. Mom had recently painted the room, and the tape would remove all of her hard work, albeit in two odd-shaped rectangles. Not wishing to deter her children from their thoughtfulness, Mariah instead would remove the bulletin board from above her computer and prop it up on George's nightstand. Then she would encourage Jordan and Presley to draw more pictures. Such a kind gesture on their part would no doubt assist in speeding George's fragile recovery.

Mariah turned her gaze from the drawings to George. "Looks like the welcoming committee delivered some get-well cards."

His attempt at a smile pained his expression, and he winced as the gash on his forehead puckered beneath his scraggly hair.

At least he was able to open his left eye a little more than the previous few days. "How are you feeling today?"

"In pain," he muttered, lines of melancholy emerging on his bruised face.

Mariah gave George some acetaminophen and a sip of water. "I'm sorry. It's the strongest we have." If he was in the hospital where he should be if the roads weren't closed, George would be given much stronger pain pills. He needed them with the abuse his body had endured.

She made sure that the window coverings were completely closed today. Yes, having the curtains open would likely cheer up George, but Mariah couldn't take the chance of the bizarre stalking woman seeing him if she was again in the vicinity.

The thought caused Mariah to shiver.

She took a seat beside George's bed in the chair and attempted to remove the woman from her mind. What could she say to cheer him? "Not sure if you remember this, but you're a snorer."

"I am?"

The expression on his face was priceless. "Yes, but I haven't heard any complaints from the neighbors yet."

Was that a slight grin? Mariah smiled in an attempt to encourage it. Her plan worked and George's smile grew slightly, his hand reaching up toward his forehead.

"Don't worry. They haven't called the police on a noise disturbance yet."

He placed his hand by his side again and his expression changed to that of confusion. "Noise disturbance?"

"As long as it's not loud enough to be heard in Briggs, we should be fine," she laughed.

"Briggs?"

"Yes. We're in Mountain Springs, but Briggs is about twenty miles away."

"Briggs. Do I know that name?"

Mariah inclined toward him. "Are you from there, maybe?" If he was, that would certainly narrow down their search in determining his identity.

"I don't know. I can't remember."

"That has to be frustrating, but Mom says it's good news that you are pretty coherent overall. You're actually doing quite well, considering what you went through. We weren't sure you'd make it at first. And now you're talking, eating, and your eye looks a lot better." All the truth. God was healing George.

"That's good, I guess." He still rasped when he spoke, but even his voice was getting stronger.

There was much to be thankful for when it came to the miracle of this man's survival.

Still, George sounded down. An idea came to Mariah then. One that just might give George the boost he needed.

If she could accomplish it.

But it wouldn't be today. Not when the snow continued to

fall and the temps registered well below zero. And not when that woman could return. No, she'd wait before acting on her idea.

George drifted in and out of sleep that night, failing to find a comfortable position. Nights had become more difficult as his mind would not allow him to rest.

Things popped into his brain unannounced.

Things better left far from his failed memory.

If he hadn't been in such pain, George would have shifted from one side to the other. But because his left side was pretty much doomed and his injured ribs spanned both his right and his left, he'd have to settle for staying on his back.

Sleep finally came when something in the night suddenly startled him. Fists slamming into his body—face, ribs, back.

He couldn't move. Couldn't extract himself from the all-encompassing pain.

The nightmare shook him awake, sweat beading down his face and his breath coming in gasps causing even more pain in his ribs.

He adjusted himself on the wedge pillow, crying out against his better judgment at the ache in his knee that throbbed worse than before.

No sleep came for the remainder of the night. Dawn whispered through the curtains, and George allowed the relief to spread over him. When morning came, he could cope because there were other things—other people—to take his mind off the nightmare.

The dog was the first to greet him. Nosy stood up on his back legs and placed his front paws on George's arm. His tail wagged.

"Good morning, boy," George whispered. "Anyone else awake?"

Nosy let out a yip. If the dog needed to go outside, George wouldn't be able to accommodate him. He reached a weak arm toward the dog and patted him.

Instantly, some of his stress left him. Nosy buried his face against George's arm. "Good boy," George murmured. Did he have a dog?

"Good morning, George," Mariah stepped inside the room with a bowl. "I have oatmeal for you today."

Did he like oatmeal? It was like trying new food all over again.

She sat on the chair beside him as she always did. Nosy put his paws down and sat and watched, likely hoping someone would drop a morsel for him.

Mariah scooped some oatmeal on the spoon. George reached for it with his right hand and carefully put it toward his mouth. He needed to try to feed himself.

So he wouldn't be dependent on the kindness of strangers forever.

The oatmeal warmed his stomach. Add it to the list of things he did like.

"Nosy is particular. It's good to see that he likes you."

That was good news. Who knew what kind of guy he was? He certainly had no idea.

Mariah continued. "It's no longer snowing, which is nice. And it's warmed up to a tropical minus one degree."

Her smile made him want to smile.

"It was a hard night," he whispered.

"The pain?"

"Yeah. And a bad dream."

"I'm sorry."

He swallowed the oatmeal. "Have you ever had something like this?"

"Like the trauma you've experienced? No. But I was really sick with the flu one year. The sickest I've ever been about four years ago." Something akin to sadness crossed her face.

"Was I there for you like you've been here for me?"

Mariah's brows knitted on her forehead. "We didn't know each other before you came here."

"We didn't?"

"No."

"Oh. So, no relation to each other?"

"No relation."

Why did disappointment wiggle its way into his mind? With her assistance, he took another bite.

Guess it made sense now why the former cop wanted to interrogate him. Rick wouldn't have done that if George and Mariah had known each other.

Why then did he feel a connection to her if he'd never known her before?

"I don't know any of you?"

"No. I'm sorry. We found you and brought you here."

George allowed the thought to sink deep into his mind. "Thank you," he whispered.

"You're welcome."

Silence followed while he took a few more bites. Everything jumbled around in his mind. The present, the unknown past, the uncertain future.

"You've been through a lot, George, but we're going to help you get through this, and once the roads open or the cell tower is restored, we'll get you the assistance you need."

"How can I repay you?" If only he wasn't so banged up and

worthless lying in bed all day.

"Just get better."

Her smile was all he needed.

It was the main thing that kept him going.

Chapter 9

It was a bizarre thing, caring for someone you knew nothing about. Especially in light of the woman on the snowmobile and the intruder in the backyard. Mariah couldn't help but wonder if she could have handled things differently. Been upfront with the woman. Told her about the man.

Could it be that George was of the same caliber as the woman? Coarse and disrespectful? Hardened?

If so, did that make him a bad person?

A criminal?

Or maybe just someone with a difficult past?

Questions whizzed through her mind at a nonstop pace. If she had told the woman and George wasn't truly related to her, what then? What if George was an innocent person and the woman and intruder, who were likely one and the same, meant to do him harm?

Just how big was the risk of having him here?

She needed to pray.

"Deep in thought?" Mom asked, placing a load of clean dish towels in the kitchen drawer.

And then there was Mom. How much should Mariah tell her?

"Just thinking about things."

Mom laughed. "You have always made this certain face, even when you were a little girl, when you were engrossed in contemplation."

"Engrossed in contemplation? I like that. I'll have to use it someday if I ever write that suspense novel that's been rolling around in my brain."

"You have my explicit permission. No credit required."

Mariah smiled, then sobered. "Mom, I think maybe we need some sort of code word."

"Code word? Like the ones you tell Jordan and Presley in case of emergencies?"

"Exactly." She thought of the "who can be the quietest contest" she'd invented for when they were in places and situations that needed indoor voices.

Mom's brows knitted. "Is there something you're not telling me?"

"Actually, yes. There's been a strange person, or maybe two people, lurking around lately, and I'm not sure why. Well, not exactly sure. I think it has something to do with George."

"George? And what do you mean 'lurking around'?"

"As in a woman stopped by on a snowmobile the other day and—"

"What woman?"

"Mom, I'm not sure who she was. She said she was looking for George. That he was her brother. I told her I hadn't seen him. Something about her just gave me the creeps."

Mom nodded. "Well, as your dad and Rick would say, 'Always listen to your gut instinct.'"

"Right. So then last night, someone was in our yard." Mariah omitted the part about someone trying the doors. Mom would panic for sure.

"Who?"

"Not sure. It was hard to see, but I'm betting it was the woman again."

"Hm. And you were going to tell me this when?"

"Sorry, Mom. I didn't want to worry you."

Mom shook her head. "Please always tell me, especially things like this." She paused. "Do you think we need a code word in case we're in danger?"

Mariah blew out a breath. "Exactly. Mom, we have no idea who George is. He could be some nice guy just in a bad situation or..."

"It's the 'or...' that bothers me," said Mom. "We should tell Rick."

"I thought about that, but he's a little over-the-top sometimes."

"He'd want to know about this," Mom insisted.

"True." Mariah would tell him. At some point. "So, what should the code word be?"

"How about your Dad's name?"

"So if I say, 'Walton,' then you'll know it's an emergency."

Mom nodded. "Yes. That will be the clue."

"All right."

Mariah wasn't sure if the idea of a code word comforted her or enhanced the awareness that someone was out there perhaps intending to cause harm to her family.

Mariah curled up on the couch and continued editing the most recent manuscript. It would be her last assignment until they again had internet capabilities. She adjusted her laptop and focused on the story, one that had a lot of potential.

The house was quiet, and everyone else was in bed asleep.

Except for Nosy, who had dashed to the front window and had begun to bark.

"Nosy, you're going to wake everyone up," she said, placing the laptop on the couch and walking toward the dog. A glance at the clock told her it was 10:30 p.m.

A knock at the door sounded, causing Mariah to jump.

The only ones who would stop by at such a late hour would be Rick or Carol. She offered a prayer that nothing was wrong with either of them.

Mariah turned on the porch light and peeked through the curtain. A large figure stood outside the door. Was it Rick, his girth accentuated by heavy layers of clothing?

She squinted. Regardless, no one should be at her door at this hour unless it was an emergency. Was Carol all right? Rick mentioned she hadn't been feeling well. Perhaps Mom should check on her.

Mariah backed away from the window. Her heart raced, and she wished she could call 911. *Lord, please just let it be Rick.*

The knock came again, so forceful this time it made the glass rattle. She again peeked out the window at just the wrong time. A large man's face covered in a ski mask stared at her. Or at least, she thought it was a man.

Mariah jumped, her pulse pounding in her ears.

It was definitely not Rick.

This man could do her family harm, and she would have no way to stop him.

"Can you open the door?" the man shouted.

Mariah shook her head.

Absolutely not!

"I'm an EMT. I'm looking for an injured man."

Nosy growled again as he propped his paws on the low

window sill.

Someone else looking for George? Who were all these people, and why were they looking for him? An EMT wouldn't be out in the dark at this time of night by himself in bitter cold temperatures.

Especially since no one was getting in or out of Mountain Springs until the road opened.

Something wasn't right. And even though the porch light wasn't the best, nowhere did Mariah see the EMT letters on his coat.

The man pulled up his ski mask, revealing corroded teeth. He spit into the snow. "Open the door!"

Nosy bared his teeth at the man.

"Shut the dog up and open the door." He pounded hard on the window, causing the glass to shake. His breath clouded the window.

"There's no injured man here!" Mariah shouted, her voice shaking.

"Mariah, is everything all right?" Mom's voice sounded behind her.

The man narrowed his beady eyes at her. "Are you sure?"

Mariah nodded again.

"I need to find him," the man continued. "He may have wandered this way." With a slight hand movement, the man exposed a gun tucked into his waistband. Did all EMTs make it a habit of silently threatening with their weapons?

Did they even carry weapons?

"Mariah, who are you talking to?"

Mariah held up a finger to Mom. She'd explain it all as soon as the man left.

He glared at her again and fingered the gun. "If you're sure."

"I'm sure."

She watched as he trudged away through the snow. Closing her eyes, Mariah willed her heart rate to return to normal.

"Mariah, what is going on?" Mom padded toward her in her flannel pajamas. "Who were you talking to?"

"Some guy looking for an injured man. I'm presuming he's looking for George."

"At this late hour?"

"Says he's an EMT. I'm sorry it woke you up, Mom."

Mom shook her head. "I'm more concerned about strange people stalking our house at late hours than being awakened. I'm far from a paranoid person, but something about an EMT at this hour going from door to door is bizarre."

Mariah placed a hand to her chest and contemplated the wisdom in voicing her concerns to Mom. "Do you think George is on the wrong side of the law? That man didn't look like an upstanding citizen."

"Didn't sound like one either." Mom put her arm around Mariah. "There's no way of knowing who George is until his memory returns. One thing is for certain—Rick needs to know about this."

———

The following day, Mariah slogged through the fresh layer of snow to Rick and Carol's house with her 9mm tucked in the holster on her waist. Her attention was on high alert for anyone who might be in the area. Thankfully, all was quiet. She quickly stopped at the end of the driveway to see if there was cell service.

None.

She continued on her way to Rick and Carol's, her mind reeling with frightening possibilities. Had the supposed EMT visited them last night after paying a visit to Mariah?

Mariah knocked on the door. Rick answered. "Hey there, Mariah. I'd invite you in, but Carol's coming down with something. With Presley's asthma, I wouldn't want her to catch it."

"Is she all right? I could send Mom over—"

"If she gets worse, I might take you up on that offer. She's got a terrible cough, body aches, headaches, a fever, and awful fatigue."

Poor Carol. "I'm so sorry, Rick."

"Was there something I can do for you?" Her neighbor slipped on his shoes, grabbed his coat, and stepped onto his porch.

Mariah peered behind her "Did you have a visitor last night—a man stalking around outside? He probably knocked loudly on your door?"

"What time?"

"It would have been about 10:30."

Rick's jaw stiffened. "Someone was knocking on the door last night at 10:30? Was there some type of emergency?"

"He claimed to be looking for an injured man."

"George."

"Yes, that's what I believe, but—"

"But?"

Mariah took a deep breath and shivered at the thought of the man's dark eyes and the gun on his hip. "And this was the second time someone was looking for an injured man."

"The second time?"

"Yes. The other day, a woman stopped by on a snowmobile and said that she was looking for her brother who had been snowmobiling with her and they became separated. Then there was someone in the backyard."

"And you failed to tell me this because..."

"I should have told you, but I thought maybe she was legitimately looking for her brother. And then this guy stopped by last night, pounding on our door and demanding to come in. He said he was an EMT."

"Well, for one thing, EMTs don't come out in the middle of the night in this weather and they don't come alone. For another, no EMT is going to be showing up out of the blue because the roads are closed."

"He definitely wasn't an EMT, Rick. No emblem on his jacket and not professional at all. He looked and acted more like a thug. He didn't stop by here?"

"Not that we're aware of. Of course, by 10:30, we're both asleep. My CPAP does drown some noises out, although Carol was sleeping in the recliner due to coughing. But she didn't mention she heard anything." Rick steepled his fingers. "Something is going on here, and it has to do with George. We need to find out who he is, how he's connected to these people, and why they are looking for him. In the meantime, do you still have the gun your dad bought you?"

"I'm carrying it right now."

"Good. I'll keep a closer eye out for anything suspicious and you and your mom do the same. If Carol wasn't sick, I'd invite ourselves to stay at your house until we get this matter settled."

"I understand, and I appreciate all of your help. Please tell Carol we'll be praying she feels better soon."

Chapter 10

Thankfully, there had been no further sign of the man at the window nor the woman on the snowmobile. Perhaps they'd given up.

She certainly hoped so.

Mariah had an idea now that George was becoming more cognizant and he seemed to be doing better at managing his pain. "Mom, what do you think about that old wheelchair of Dad's for George?"

"That's a great idea, although no one has used it since Dad had his surgery. It's in the shed, but it might be buried."

"I'm willing to look for it if you think it would help him."

Mom nodded. "I do think it would help. We need to get him up and with his swollen knee, he won't be walking for a while. And it's always better for his ribs for him to sit upright."

"I'm going to see if I can find it." Mariah walked toward the entryway closet to retrieve her coat.

"It's minus five with the windchill. I'll come looking for you if you're not back within twenty minutes."

Mariah zipped up her coat and pulled on her gloves. "I'll go out the back door and be back as soon as I can. Do you have any idea at all where it could be?"

"My guess would be in the back by the canoe, but I truly have no idea."

She opened the door and a rush of cold air stung her face. She pulled the hood of her coat over her hat and wound her scarf to cover her mouth and nose. There was some sunshine, but it did little to warm the air. Aware of the possibility that the supposed EMT and the snowmobile rider could still be lurking about, she did an efficient perusal of the backyard.

All was quiet.

Unlocking the shed door, she slipped inside. Memories flooded her at the sight of so many of Dad's possessions. Come summer, she and Mom would have to go through the items and determine what to keep and what to sell or donate.

The lawnmower and weed trimmer were the first things she saw, followed by shelves housing lawn care supplies and garden tools. She made her way down the narrow shed toward the back where the canoe rested on a nifty contraption Dad had made. The oars and life jackets rested beside it. His treasured fishing poles stood unused against the wall. Nearby, several boxes full of items littered the floor. Items that had been packed and forgotten years ago. Some boxes were labeled, others remained a mystery.

Mariah fought the sadness that permeated through her. Dad had loved to go canoeing and fishing, especially with his family. Her ex-husband never could understand her close-knit family. But that was a thought for another time.

Swallowing hard, Mariah tried to focus on her reason for being in the shed, rather than the pain of losing her dad. Lifting a couple of the lighter boxes, she searched around for the wheelchair. It would be folded to conserve space. Not seeing it, she rummaged further toward the back of the shed. "Where is it?" she muttered aloud.

The wind whistled beyond the thin walls. How long had she been inside? A gust caught the door she'd left ajar and sent it banging against the front of the shed.

Mariah jumped.

Willing the hammering of her heart to slow, she again searched behind more boxes, carefully lifting the ones she could and attempting to push the other ones aside. "If I were Dad, where would I pack the wheelchair?"

Dad hated being confined to the wheelchair while he recovered from his double knee replacement surgery. He detested anything that kept him from being able to do the things he enjoyed, which included always being on the move. There was always another project to complete, another fish to catch, or another elk to hunt.

If Mom hadn't insisted he keep the wheelchair in case someone else needed it later, Dad would have dropped it off at the dump. He hated that thing.

Mariah perused the entire area. Just as she was about to give up on her search, she looked up, and there, on the rafters, Dad had carefully constructed to implement even more space in the shed, was the wheelchair folded and attached. Out of sight, out of mind.

That sounded like Dad.

Standing on a nearby step stool, Mariah reached overhead and released the wheelchair from its bindings. Taking care so it wouldn't come down on her head, she awkwardly teetered with it in her arms before resting it on some nearby boxes.

Now to surprise George with her new find.

———

She adjusted the wheelchair in her arms and plotted her steps back to the house.

"What're ya doin'?" A voice she didn't recognize echoed in the shed, and she whipped around, searching for its source.

"I saw you come in here."

Who saw her come in here? *Always be aware of your surroundings.*

But this time she hadn't been. Hadn't even seen the tall thin frame leaning against the door.

Could she get past him and make a dash for the house? Leave the wheelchair behind? She set the wheelchair on the floor in case she had to dodge past him.

Then felt the side of her pants for her holster.

The holster and her 9mm she'd failed to attach to her waistband in her rush to go to the shed.

Since when did she need to carry a gun into the backyard?

Her heart constricted in her chest.

The man was waiting for her answer.

And Mariah was planning her escape.

"Just getting something from the shed." Her voice in her ears sounded exactly as she felt—scared, shaky, and fearful. *Lord, please keep me safe.*

The man maintained his stance. "Like what?"

"Just my dad's old wheelchair."

Should Mariah approach him and convince him to allow her out of the shed and toward the house? What if he followed her? What then?

"Can I help you with something?" she asked a moment later, hoping her voice sounded more confident, although suspecting it didn't.

The man advanced toward her and she gasped as the air deserted her lungs. Had she seen him before? Was he the one in the backyard? He definitely wasn't the one at the window

71

the other night.

How many crazed people were there?

"Just lookin' for someone."

"Oh?" *Let me guess—George?*

"Yeah. Someone who might have come this way. Got lost in the blizzard and all." The man stopped in front of her. He wore a thick brown coat with a fake-fur fringe around the hood. His face was thin and droopy with several sores that had been picked at and scabbed over. His bloodshot green eyes and an ungroomed mustache and goatee completed his unsettling appearance.

Good, Mariah. Get a good physical description of him. You might need it.

"So have you seen a guy come this way? One who got himself lost?"

"I have not."

Something passed across his face. Did he not believe her? "You sure?"

"I'm sure."

"'Cause, you know, I'm lookin' for him and I been all around this neighborhood asking folks, and ain't no one seen him. I think he's in your house."

What was so important about George that everyone wanted to find him? While this guy caused alarm bells to go off in her mind, he wasn't nearly as scary as his two predecessors. Still, he could trap her in the shed and no one would hear her. Not Mom and not Rick.

And if Mom did make good on her promise to come look for her, the kids would be left alone in the house vulnerable.

"Is this man related to you?"

"Related? Ain't related. Just a friend is all."

"An important friend?"

"Yeah. Something like that. He and us, we got some business to tend to."

What kind of business? Obviously from his appearance and slurred speech, this guy was on drugs, or at the very least inebriated.

"Well, I better get inside the house." Mariah attempted to walk around the man.

He placed an arm across the doorway. "Not so fast. 'Cause if he ain't at those other houses, then he's here or he's died somewhere out there." The man nodded toward the outdoors.

"Yes, it's cold out there. I hope you find him soon."

"Me too. Don't want the rest of them to get mad."

The rest of them? "It's awfully cold to be out looking for someone."

The man scratched at his covered arms. "Kinda. But we got ourselves a nice place to stay in the meanwhile. 'Sides, I got me a snow machine to ride back to the place."

"Well, glad you have a place to stay." Mariah forced a smile.

"Okay then, if you haven't seen my friend, you can go." The man lowered his arm.

"Thank you."

Lugging the wheelchair, Mariah squeezed past him and out the shed door. Glancing behind her, she noticed the man leave the shed, light up a cigarette, and disappear into the trees. Was that where he'd hidden a snow machine?

She just wanted to get inside the house, lock the door, and check on her family.

Mariah heaved the cumbersome wheelchair into the house and slammed the front door. Setting it haphazardly against the wall, she locked the front door, and peeked outside just to be sure no one had followed her.

The house was eerily quiet.

Where was everyone?

"Mom?"

Mom came around the corner. "Mariah, is everything all right?"

"Where are Presley and Jordan?"

"In George's room."

"And Nosy?"

"He's in there too. Mariah, what is going on?"

Mariah took a deep breath. "Mom, there was a man in the shed."

"What? This has got to stop."

"Yes, it does. He was looking for George. Why are all of these people looking for him?"

Mom shook her head, clearly rattled.

Mariah relayed the entire conversation to Mom. "We need to tell Rick."

"I can go over right now and tell him."

"No, Mom. That guy could still be out there."

"Did you hear him leave on the snow machine?"

"No, but that doesn't mean anything. I was panicked and rushing toward the house." Mariah's heart rate still pulsed in her chest. "We'll tell Rick next time we see him outside."

"All right. And then once the roads open and we have cell service, we're making some calls to the police."

If it wasn't too late by then.

Chapter 11

Mariah assisted George to a sitting position and handed him some apple slices and a cheese stick. Each day, Mom cut up a piece of fruit, and along with a cheese stick, gave it to the children as their morning snack. Something so seemingly minor had become an anticipated tradition.

"Thank you," said George, biting into the first apple slice.

For peace of mind and to quell the unsettled mass of emotions tangled in her stomach from the recent events, she needed to ask him the questions that had pervaded her mind since the day that first stranger arrived looking for their patient. "George, can you recall at all if you have a sister?"

He stopped chewing and looked at her intently. Was he remembering something? "I don't know about siblings, but I guess it's possible."

"Do you like to snowmobile?"

"Snowmobile?"

"The little snow machines that people drive around on the snow."

George frowned, confusion lighting his face. "No idea."

"Someone stopped by and mentioned she was your sister and that you were in a snowmobile accident."

"I was?"

Mariah shrugged. "I'm not a nurse, but your injuries appear to be from more than a snowmobile wreck." *Like maybe an assault with a deadly weapon.* "And you weren't wearing snowmobile gear." To the contrary, George's attire was hardly sufficient for winter outdoor activities.

Should she describe the woman's appearance? Tell him about the supposed EMT or the drugged-up man in the shed? From the blank expression on George's face, it was doubtful he would remember anything about people of those descriptions.

George compared his mind to a web of wires that had become unhooked from their power source. Or something like that, anyway. But he did know enough to know that Mariah appeared troubled by the fact he couldn't remember if he had a sister, liked snowmobiles, or was in a snowmobile wreck.

A wreck could explain the intense bruises and pain that wracked through his body and from which he struggled to find relief.

All George could do was live in the present and do his best to recall any pieces of the past that might make sense to both him and to those who'd opened their home to him.

He averted his attention to the bulletin board that Mariah had propped up against the wall. It gave him a perfect view of the ever-increasing pictures drawn by two young artists. Better than the former location where a temporary square of stripped paint gave evidence to their good intentions.

"George! George!" Presley's voice interrupted his thoughts, as she burst through the room.

He wished he had half of her energy.

"I made you another picture in art class." She stood beside his bed and presented him with a drawing on a sheet of blue paper. "This is you when you were a little boy. Do you remember when you were a little boy?"

George shook his head. He could only hope to remember his life as an adult, let alone as a child.

"I made you a picture too," said Jordan, handing him a sheet of yellow paper. "This is a t-rex."

"Wow. I'm impressed by your drawings."

"Do you want us to pin them on the bulletin board?" asked Presley.

"That would be great."

Presley took both drawings and pinned them on the board with the other pictures. "There. Now you can enjoy them for always. I better go. It's time for Grandma to read me a story." She skipped out of the room, her doll securely in her arms.

Jordan sat down in the chair beside George's bed. He chewed on his lip and bounced his foot.

"How are you today, Jordan?" George asked. It was clear there was something on the boy's mind.

He shrugged. "Okay. Hey, George, can I ask you a question?"

"Sure."

"You're from Briggs, right?"

George wished he could remember where he lived, what his occupation was, if he was married, had kids, or even what type of car he drove. But everything was so hazy. However, looking into Jordan's eyes, he knew the boy needed an answer besides George's typical "I don't know." What should he say? "I think so. The name sounds familiar."

Jordan's eyes lit with his answer. "Then do you know my dad? He lives in Briggs, and his name is Brandon Holzman."

His expression showed eagerness and expectation.

An expectation that George could not fulfill. "Where does your dad work?"

"He works in an office with numbers. He's real important."

Did George know him? Maybe. Maybe not.

Before he could answer, Jordan continued, sadness filling his eyes. "But..." He hung his head. "I haven't seen him in a long time. Mom has a picture of him with me and Presley and sometimes I look at it, but..." Jordan shrugged.

"Maybe you'll see him soon."

Jordan shook his head. "No. He sometimes says he'll come over to see us, but he doesn't. I would really like to play football and build something with building blocks if he does. Do you think my dad would like to do those things?"

"I think he'd really enjoy building something with you. Probably have to wait on the football because of the snow." He smiled at Jordan, hoping to solicit a return smile.

"Yeah. You're right. It's too snowy for that. Well, when you go back to Briggs, if you see my dad, can you tell him 'hi' for me?"

"I sure will."

Jordan stood. "Okay, thanks. I better go do some math."

"Hey, Jordan?"

"Yes?"

"Be thinking of something we could build, okay?"

"Really?"

"Just waiting until I feel a little better, and then we'll be able to build." George hoped he could make good on his promise.

"I have all kinds of ideas. We might have to build lots of things. Bye, George!" Jordan waved and bolted from the room.

George sighed. The poor kid really needed his dad. There was a story there somewhere, one he wasn't sure he wanted to hear. He hoped that if he himself was a dad, that he wasn't a father like Jordan's.

Chapter 12

It was odd how the brain worked, but Linda told him with traumatic brain injuries that he would be confused and disoriented. She reassured him he was doing remarkably well considering all he'd been through.

George was just grateful he could carry on conversations and knew what most things were. His memory could use some help, but Linda reassured him that would come in time.

Had he always been this impatient?

Mariah brought in a wheelchair that afternoon. Had he ever been excited about a wheelchair? Probably not. But he was now. Just to get out of bed would improve his mindset.

Mariah and Linda eased him into the chair. Pain struck him in nearly every part of his body.

But it was good to be in a different position.

And good to move from the bed.

Linda propped his feet on the footrests. If only his knee wasn't swollen and painful. Maybe then he could hobble around. Of course, he struggled with dizziness and headaches, so he likely wouldn't be walking anytime soon anyway.

Mariah pushed him out of the room and into a hallway.

"George! You're out of your room!" Presley rushed beside

him. "Can I push him, Mommy?"

"Thank you for offering, but I think I'll push him right now. We have to take it really slow."

"Are you scared, George?" Presley asked.

Should he be? "No."

"'Cause if you are, then I can give you Bibby while you go for your ride. Do you want to hold Bibby?" she asked, stretching a doll toward him.

"George doesn't want to hold a doll. He's a boy." Jordan rolled his eyes.

Presley's expression turned hurt. "Bibby always helps me when I'm scared."

"Mom's not *that* bad of a driver."

"Thank you, Jordan, for your confidence. I'm going to push George to the table so he can join us for dinner."

The blinds were closed, but George could see through the window high above the front door that it was snowing. He wished he could shovel snow, bring in wood, cut up vegetables...something.

He felt so helpless.

With his good arm, he reached for the cup of water Mariah had placed in front of him on the table. "I wish I could do more than just sit here." Perhaps he was the type of man who appreciated being busy. If only he could remember.

Mariah flashed a pretty smile at him that brightened her already pretty face.

When did he begin noticing she had a pretty face?

His brain was addled. Literally.

"Your job is to get better."

"That's a tall order."

"It is, but you're already doing a lot better than you were."

George appreciated her upbeat attitude. "It's the pictures Presley and Jordan keep drawing for me."

Mariah laughed. He decided he liked the pleasant sound. "They are quite the artists, aren't they? I homeschool both of them, well technically, I'm only really homeschooling Jordan. Presley is only four, so she's still a preschooler, but she wanted to be like her big brother and be homeschooled too."

"They seem like really smart kids."

"Not to brag because I am a bit biased, but they are. Jordan has such a love for history, and he recalls things I don't even remember teaching him. Presley has a gift for art, and she already wants to sound out letters and read. They have a co-op we attend in the spring and fall, but during the winter months, we're pretty much hunkered down here in Mountain Springs because of the weather, besides church and an occasional trip to Briggs for groceries or play dates. Wow, listen to me, just rambling on."

———

Mariah shook her head. What had gotten into her? Why would George care about her children's schooling or how they got along with each other? Or their homeschool co-op? The poor guy was overwhelmed with just remembering his own name. Yet, here she was, yammering on like she hadn't spoken to a soul for months.

At least George was a good listener.

She turned and busied herself finishing putting together a salad for dinner. The last salad until they could get to the store again.

"I have a beard?" George's voice interrupted her thoughts. She spun to face him. His right hand was stroking his scruffy dark-blond beard, and his eyes lit with a bit of disgust.

Mariah found it difficult not to laugh at his incredulous tone. "Yes."

"I don't think I had a beard in my former life."

Would they ever know much about the man who had nearly lost his life in a ravine not far from the house?

The wind howled that night. Mariah snuggled beneath the quilt and tugged it to her chin. Was anyone outside in the yard? Snooping at the windows? Arriving by snowmobile? In the shed hunkering down?

Time to switch gears before she kept herself awake all night.

Mariah turned her attention to receiving more assignments from the Christian publishing company to edit. With the internet down with the storm, there was no way for her to work. She needed the money to support Jordan and Presley. Yes, they lived with Mom now, and she was so grateful for that, but she still owed so much on the credit cards on which Brandon had charged an exorbitant amount for purchases. The court order deemed them jointly liable for the charges.

Brandon. She hoped for her children's sake, he would be more present in their lives. Even before the divorce, there hadn't been room in his life for his children. His laptop, his golf, and his job absorbed the majority of his time. When he was home, he was impatient and brushed aside any attempts from Jordan and Presley to spend time with him. The looks on their young faces would forever haunt her when Brandon made it clear that they were the least important thing in his life. He was unwilling to help Mariah with any of the children's care or the expensive home he had insisted they purchase.

They later defaulted on the mortgage and lost the house.

It wasn't an issue for Brandon, however. He now resided with the new woman who had taken Mariah's place—while they were still married.

A year after the divorce was final, Mariah still reeled from the pain of betrayal. One thing was for certain, she'd think twice before ever falling in love again.

Mariah rolled to her left side. She worried about Mom after Dad's death. She worried about supporting the kids. She worried about the threat to her family. She worried about George and the people who kept looking for him. Now she worried about his true identity. Crimes rarely occurred in their tiny town of Mountain Springs, with the exception of a few cases of trespassing each year. But the much larger town of Briggs, twenty miles away, had its share of crime with a recent uptick of drug-related offenses. Especially with the population continuing to increase.

For now, he couldn't do much with his injury limitations. But at some point, George would be able to independently move about. If, for whatever reason, he remained in Mom's house, would they discover he was dangerous? Was he part of a gang or a drug deal gone wrong?

Rick had reason to be concerned. A strange man now lived in the house, one whom they had no knowledge of his past or his present. He didn't even know anything about himself.

Was such a prospect of having him here even safe?

Not that they had a choice. Mariah would never leave him to die in the cold and Rick and Carol had no room in their one-bedroom cottage for a guest. Besides, having him here with Mom's extensive nursing skills was George's best bet.

Still...

While his scruffy appearance could be indicative of someone in trouble with the law, George *did* have kind eyes. And he didn't *seem* dangerous. Didn't *seem* related to or friends with those who were on the hunt for him. He had a sense of humor, and he *was* patient with the children with all of their pestering.

Mariah flopped again to her right side and angled the old digital clock that had been Dad's toward her. The big red numbers read 3:41 a.m.

Sleep failed to come.

So much on her mind and no real answers.

Staring at the ceiling, she prayed for a good night's sleep, what was left of it anyway.

And for the peace not to worry about the many things that plagued her mind.

Chapter 13

Mariah headed out to the garage to retrieve a hammer to hang a new picture for Mom. The draft from the attached garage blew in a colder-than-usual breeze as Mariah opened the door and stepped into it. Hers and Mom's SUVs lined up side-by-side, leaving room on the perimeter for Dad's numerous toolboxes. "You can't live in Mountain Springs and drive a van," Dad had said. Dad, in his wheeling-dealing way, had sold Mariah's van and found a used older model mid-size SUV in excellent condition. It set Mariah back a meager amount after the van was sold, but she hadn't regretted her choice.

She wedged herself behind the vehicles and over to the more spacious side of the garage where Dad housed the hammers in a tall red tool chest.

A strong breeze blew the edges of an old tractor calendar Dad had hung on the wall.

And that's when Mariah realized.

The side door from the outside into the garage was open. How did that happen? Rushing toward it, she slammed it shut against the fierce winds outside.

"I was enjoying that breeze," a deep male voice said, causing her to jump.

Mariah spun around to face an oddly familiar thickset man. The same one from the other night who'd peered into the window? Same build, but no ski mask this time.

She gasped.

He laughed, and she shivered at his harsh chortle. He stalked toward her and pinned her against the tool chest. "Have you seen an injured man?"

"No."

Leaning his face closer to hers, Mariah could see the enlarged pupils of his hazel eyes. His breath wreaked of a combination of alcohol and cigarette smoke and she nearly gagged. A brownish-red beard covered his chin and his left ear housed numerous piercings.

"I don't think you're telling me the truth."

She wasn't, but how could she keep him from coming inside to prove he was correct?

Mariah's mind kicked into high gear with all of the self-defense tactics Rick had taught her. The man was mammoth in a wide and burly way, although not exceptionally tall.

"Today is your lucky day. Today I'm going to go inside your house and look for myself. Should have done that sooner." He spat the words at her, and she noticed his top teeth corroded into black stubs.

How could Mariah prevent him from going inside?

Of course, if the man did find George, she would relinquish him to save her family. She would do anything to protect those she loved. But George could no more travel in this weather than stand on his own two feet. Surely the man wouldn't haul him off on a snow machine and expect him to survive.

The connecting door from the house to the garage opened "Mommy?"

Go back inside, she silently willed her daughter.

"Mommy is just looking for a hammer. I'll be back inside in a minute, sweetie." Her voice shook. Would Presley notice? Would her daughter see her and the man through the car windows?

Presley shut the door, and Mariah breathed a breath of relief.

"Well, now, ain't she cute?"

The powerful desire to do anything to protect her daughter permeated through her. "Stay away from her."

The man leaned in toward her, his face inches from hers. "Or what?"

"You just stay away from her." Mariah's heart pounded. She could not, would not, let this horrid man near her family. But how could she prevent it? Mariah offered a desperate prayer for the Lord's protection.

The door opened again and Mariah heard Nosy bark. "Mom?"

"Jordan, I'll be right in. Take Nosy and go back inside."

The door shut, but Nosy apparently hadn't listened, as he ran toward Mariah, his bark shrill and deafening as it echoed in the garage. Nosy stood at the man's feet and growled, his teeth threatening to make good on his bark.

The man pulled his gun from the back of his waistband and pointed it at Nosy. "Tell the dog to shut up or I'll shoot it."

Keeping an eye on the man, Mariah leaned over, her arms trembling, and took hold of Nosy's collar. "It's okay, Nosy."

If only she could calm herself. Sweat had begun to trickle down her back, even in the sub-zero temperature of the garage.

Nosy finally calmed until he emitted only a low growl.

The man's posture relaxed slightly, and he placed the gun inside his waistband. "So you're going to take me inside and tell everyone that I'm here for a short visit. I'll wander around your house, check every room, and see what I find. Or should I say, *who* I find."

Mariah shivered. What would he do when he found George? Would he punish Mariah and her family for Mariah's lie?

The man laughed, evil emanating from his voice. Mariah's knees wobbled, and she grasped the nearby tool bench to steady herself. If only she could get away from him, run inside the house, and lock the doors. And when he tried to break through the door, she and Mom would be ready for him.

"Please, just leave. The man isn't here." She lamented the quivering in her voice.

"What, a little scared, are we?"

Nosy barked again, and immediately the man again pulled his gun. "Shut up, dog!"

Mariah comforted Nosy the best she could. Her racing heartbeat caused her chest to hurt, and with the tenacity she had only with the Lord's help, she looked the man square in the eyes. "What is so important about this guy you're looking for?" Her voice wavered.

"Important?" The man leaned in, the gun still in his hand. Mariah held her breath as the gun dug into her side. "I'll tell you why the guy is important. He's a friend of ours. We have been going from house to house looking for him. Not an easy thing to do when it's freezing cold outside." He released a stream of profanities that caused Mariah's ears to burn. "Everyone has let us into their houses without a struggle—well, of course, some weren't home—but the ones that were, they let us in. You are the only one who has pitched a fit about it. That's why I think our friend is hiding in there. Got it?"

"Yes."

"Good. Now lead the way and don't do anything foolish. If you do, those kids of yours won't make it to see their teenage years."

Worry snaked through her, and her stomach knotted. She'd protect her children at all costs. But would she even have a chance against the man, especially with a gun in his hand?

As if reading her mind, her nemesis reached for her arm, squeezed it hard, and then forced it behind her back. She let out a sob as the pain traveled from her arm up to her neck. He released it from behind her back and slammed it into the tool chest, the pain of the metal zapping the tender part of the front of her hand.

"Now go!"

He followed her into the house. Presley and Jordan sat at the table and looked up as she stumbled in. "Mommy, who's..."

"Do you remember that game we played called 'Who Can be the Quietist?'" she asked them, heading their questions off before they could ask them.

"Oooh, I like that game," said Jordan.

The man shoved her. "Hurry up."

"We're going to play that game," Mariah said, forcing herself to smile to calm her children.

Presley made a motion of zipping her mouth. Jordan nodded and shuffled through a stack of papers, presumably to keep score with tally marks on who was the quietist.

The aroma of chocolate chip cookies baking in the oven filled the room. Quite the contrast between that and the man's body odor mixing with the stench of alcohol and cigarettes wafting from his clothes.

Mom came down the stairs, an alarmed look on her face. Mariah shook her head ever so slightly. If Mom thought there was any threat to her family, Mama Bear would emerge. Mariah sensed the man's volatile nature and knew they likely couldn't win. She tilted her head toward the man. "Walton."

Mom gave her a knowing look and focused on the oven.

Mariah led the man down the hall to first the pantry, then the laundry room. Was George in his room sleeping? Would he awaken at the commotion? From what she knew of him so far, he slept soundly and wasn't disturbed by the everyday bustle of life at Mom's house.

"Here's the pantry and the laundry room. And here we have a craft room and further down, a bathroom."

The man muttered a string of foul words. "This ain't no tour," he hissed.

Lord, please protect us.

It was likely George was who this man wanted, and if that were true, it meant George was a criminal of similar caliber. Mariah grimaced. What would this man do if he discovered she had lied about George?

Pressure built in her chest, and she released a shaky breath. If protecting George meant protecting her family, then so be it.

The guest room where George stayed was the next. "We have an upstairs too," Mariah said, praying the man wouldn't be wise enough to notice she'd skipped the door on the right.

She whipped around and headed up the stairs. At just over 2,000 square feet of living space, the cabin wasn't rustic by a long shot. Rather, it was well laid out and full of amenities, all on a budget Mom and Dad planned long before building the home. Since Dad had been able to complete so much of the work on his own, an incredible amount of money had been saved. The cottage had been the only home on the property in the beginning, and Mom and Dad had resided there while their dream home was being built.

If only Dad had had the chance to enjoy it longer.

The man shoved her and she toppled forward, barely catching herself before falling. "I don't have until next year."

Mariah opened the door to Mom's room, then her room, the bathroom, and finally each of the kids' rooms.

"I know he's here, and I will find him."

"He's not here," she said, trying to keep her voice calm.

"What about there?" he pointed to a room on the left.

She opened the door to reveal a tiny storage room where Mom kept the Christmas tree and decorations. The man glowered at her before turning and stomping back down the stairs. Would he go back through each room and this time discover George?

Mariah followed the man downstairs, while in her mind plotting how she could eliminate the threat. But he glared at her as if reading her thoughts, and raised his gun and pointed it in her direction, his finger hovering dangerously near the trigger.

Thankfully Presley and Jordan weren't in the vicinity. But where were they? And would they accidentally say something about George?

Mariah's heart pounded in her ears. When the buzzer on the oven sounded, she jumped.

The man holstered his gun and barreled his way to the kitchen where Mom was removing a cookie sheet from the oven.

He reached for a cookie off the cookie sheet and stuffed it into his mouth, inhumanly impervious to the heat. "Load the rest of them up in a bag," he growled while chewing.

Mom's hands trembled as she reached for a plastic bag, and using the spatula, placed the hot cookies inside.

Before Mom could even zip the bag, the man yanked it from her grasp. He marched back toward Mariah and jerked her hard by the arm. She bit back a scream just as she noticed Jordan and Presley at the top of the stairs.

She stumbled as he pulled her after him.

Where was he taking her?

He called her a crass name then hissed in her ear, "Got something to tell you outside. Now move!"

Mariah dug her feet into the flooring, making it more difficult to drag her. Somewhere in the recesses of her mind, she heard Mom tell the children to go inside their room.

No way would she go with the man. She knew if he was able to hoist her away from the house, her chances of survival declined.

Dramatically.

He reached around her waist and lifted her off the floor. She bit, pounded, and pulled on his hair and ears.

The man slammed the door to the house shut and flung her against it. Throwing the bag of cookies on the ground, he reached into his waistband and produced a knife. Its glittering blade glimmered. Mariah searched for a weapon. Anything that she could use to defend herself.

Where was Mom?

The shiny blade came closer to her face, causing her eyes to blur. She flinched. "Please just leave me alone."

"If I find that guy inside your house after you told me he wasn't there, I will kill you. Then I will kill your family."

He twirled the knife in a fluid motion toward her coat. It caught the material and ripped it.

Blurriness smudged Mariah's vision as weightlessness invaded her limbs. *Please, Lord, let me stay conscious.*

"I'm gonna go. For now. But I'll be back to get the man.

You understand?" The man shoved her hard against the door again, her head hitting it.

The world spun around her. The man leaned toward her, the knife still in his hand. He could kill her right there in front of Mom's house. Her children would never be able to forget the horrific memory of finding their mother dead at the hands of a heinous stranger.

Lord, please give me wisdom...and strength.

In an act concocted purely on adrenaline, she eyed the bag of cookies and kicked it hard against the snow.

"Why did you do that?" he yelled, leaning to retrieve the bag.

In an instant, she reached for the small decorative rock by the front door. The one Mom had purchased for Dad during his brief stint of interest in geology. She slammed the rock hard on the back of his head, causing him to fall face-forward in the snow.

Blood poured from the gash.

Panic assailed her, and for a moment she couldn't move.

Finally, she stumbled into the house, slammed the door, and locked it. Mom stood there, two guns in her hands. "I sent the kids and Nosy upstairs to their rooms for a few minutes," Mom whispered, handing Mariah her pistol. "We may need these."

More like maybe needing to carry a gun at all times.

The man stood and lumbered toward the front door. How had he survived the blow to the back of the head without losing consciousness?

He rapped on the door, blood seeping into the collar of his coat.

A snowmobile sounded, and within seconds pulled up to the front porch. The man climbed onto the back of it and the driver zipped through the snow and into the trees.

A prayer of gratitude escaped from Mariah's lips thanking God for protecting her family.

And then a desperate plea. *Lord, protect us when that man visits again.*

Because if history proved her theory correct, it wouldn't be *if* the man returned, but *when.*

Chapter 14

Mariah clung to Mom. Things could have turned out so differently. The prayers of gratitude would never be enough to express their thankfulness for the Lord's protection.

"Mommy?"

Mariah and Mom both turned to see Presley and Jordan standing a few feet from them. Oh, but to think of how close she had come to...

"Why was the mailman here?"

Presley's innocent inquiry caught Mariah off guard, and she caught Mom's eye. Only God, in His mercy, could have orchestrated something like this—that Presley would believe it was the mailman in the house and not a deadly criminal.

Jordan folded his arms across his chest. "I saw him eating cookies, but I guess it's nice of us to share, right, Mom?"

Mariah finally found her voice. "Yes, it is nice of us to share, and he was hungry."

That seemed to satisfy both children, and Mariah closed her eyes and exhaled a breath that blew away the strain and stress of the last hour.

God was good. And they would get through this.

A few hours later, Mom headed upstairs to read to the

children, and Mariah placed another log on the fire. George sat on the couch, his feet propped up on a footstool and an ice pack on his knee. He'd just finished doing another round of ankle pumps to prevent blood clots. She eyed the wheelchair. At some point, George would be able to walk. At some point he would be feeling much better. The questions lingered in her own mind about his identity and whether or not he associated with the likes of the woman and two men who'd wreaked havoc on Mariah's family.

"I thought I heard some commotion earlier, but I wasn't sure if it was real or just another nightmare."

Mariah sank into the comfortable leather seat cushion as weariness beckoned her. The heat from the fire warmed her, and she fought closing her eyes. The fire had always relaxed her.

"Yes. It was a man looking for you. He was in the garage and then..."

"What? In the garage?" He strained to turn his head. Concern lit his eyes.

How could this man possibly be a part of the group that sought to find him?

"I went to the garage to get something, and he followed me back inside." Her hands in her lap trembled as she recalled all that had transpired. The threats. The knife. The tossing her against the house. The headache she still had. The fear and the uncertainty.

"Was he looking for—me?"

"He was." Her voice wavered.

Something flickered in his eyes. "Mariah, you need to tell him I am here. I can't keep putting your family in danger."

She shook her head. "No, I can't tell them now. He threatened that if he found out you were here after I said you weren't—"

Clearly, there was no easy answer to the dilemma they faced. The flames glowed a bright orange and crackled, drowning out the howling wind outside, and they sat in silence for the next several minutes.

Finally, George spoke again. "If you don't mind me asking, what happened to your dad?"

Mariah hadn't expected that question, but it took her mind off the events from earlier today. "He died a few months ago of a heart attack. It was all so unexpected."

"I'm sorry to hear that. It must be hard on your family."

"It is. He was just always there, always the rock for all of us, and had the best personality. Always full of gratitude, never complaining, just thankful for all God had given him."

"Sounds like a great man."

"He was. Mom is having such a hard time, which is to be expected, but I do worry about her." Mariah bit her lip. Why was she sharing so much with a stranger? "Sorry. Too much information."

"Not at all."

"Do you remember anything, anything at all about your parents? Your family?"

George shook his head, quietly wincing as he did so. "No, nothing. Mariah, I'm really grateful for all you and your mom have done."

"You're welcome. I'm glad we can help."

"Do you have enough food until the roads open?"

Mariah laughed, the memory lightening the burdens weighing her down. "With Mom we always have enough food. She's one of those people that if she sees that beans or rice or some other staple is on sale, she'll buy out the store. My dad used to give her such a hard time about it. She would leave with a list with about ten things on it, and return with enough food to feed an entire army."

George laughed too and wrapped his right arm around his ribcage. "Shouldn't laugh like that. It's not good for the old ribs." He paused. "Still, the thought of your mom with all these grocery bags and the look on your dad's face must have been something to see."

"Oh, it was. And she would always bring Dad home some little treat. She would hide it in one of the grocery bags—almost like a treasure hunt for Dad. Sometimes it would be his favorite candy bar or other times an iced tea. One time she forgot to buy him something and Dad did his best not to be disappointed, but Mom knew he was. She tells the story much better than I do, but I can imagine my dad trying his best to act as though it didn't matter that she forgot a special treat she'd picked out just for him. His face always gave him away."

"With the treats she brought home, he probably quickly forgot that he had one hundred bags of rice and beans to carry in from the car, huh?"

"Pretty much. But he loved Mom more than anything. I don't think he really cared about the groceries. He just liked to tease her about it." Mariah shook her head. "I don't think Dad could truly be mad at Mom for anything. He was so easygoing, and she was his world."

There was silence then, and their eyes met. There was something about him. Something that made it so easy to hold a conversation with him. Something comfortable. She couldn't explain it, but it was as though she had known him for longer than the days he'd resided at the cabin.

His gaze drifted to her hand. "Did you hurt yourself?"

The front of Mariah's hand still ached from the episode with the vicious man who slammed it against Dad's toolboxes.

A purple bruise marred her otherwise pale skin. Her upper arm also boasted a bruise, which was covered by her sweater. "Yes, courtesy of the man looking for you today."

George leaned toward her with effort. "He did this to you?" He lightly touched her hand with his fingertips, causing a hint of electricity to travel up her arm.

Strange.

"Yes. He slammed my hand against Dad's toolbox in the garage."

"I am so sorry, Mariah." George removed his fingertips from her hand, removing the warmth his hand had provided.

His touch had been comforting. Reassuring. Caring. That was all. So why did she miss it?

"Mariah," George said, his voice low and husky. "I wish I could have protected you and your family from this, especially this guy bashing your hand into the toolbox. If he's a friend of mine, he'll answer for treating you this way."

She smiled at him, relieved George would take that stance. Whoever he was before his accident, he possessed a seemingly genuine, considerate nature in the here and now. Would that stay when his identity was revealed?

Mariah had never really thought about it, but now looking into his sympathetic expression, she realized the depth and soulfulness of George's brown eyes. They weren't harsh and piercing like some brown eyes, but soft and tender.

What on earth had gotten into her?

Delirious came to mind.

Why else would she be contemplating a potential criminal's eyes?

Mariah broke the contact and glanced at the clock on the mantle. "Wow. It's almost 11:30. Can I help you into your wheelchair?"

"Thanks."

Mariah stood and assisted George to the wheelchair. She released the brake and pushed him quietly down the hall and to the guestroom before giving him another dose of acetaminophen, hoping it would at least take the edge off of his pain.

"Good night, George."

"Good night, Mariah."

Chapter 15

He hadn't been able to fall asleep easily that night after his meeting by the fireplace with Mariah. The thought of someone hurting her because of him tore him up in ways he had no clue how to process.

Someone, or several someones, had attempted to locate him. At first, George had been thrilled at the possibility that whoever it was could offer some answers to his mile-long perplexing list relating to his identity.

But when Mariah had mentioned the man had injured her, anger and protectiveness had risen within him. He wished he could take away the pain the bruise obviously caused. What else had the man done to her that she hadn't told him?

This family had taken him in. Saved his life. Cared for him. And this was the thanks they received?

Not on his watch.

While staring into Mariah's pretty face last night, something else had occurred to George. Was he worthy of this family's help?

When he finally did fall asleep, restlessness overwhelmed him. He couldn't turn over and reposition himself in any other position, which made for a long night. He awoke tired and sleepy.

The aroma of toast and eggs wafted into his room. Still unable to propel himself into the wheelchair on his own, he was grateful when Linda arrived to assist him. She wheeled him to the table where Jordan and Presley sat. Mariah was in the kitchen frying the eggs, and Linda retrieved milk from the refrigerator.

Presley climbed from her chair and stood beside him. Leaning her small round face toward him, she asked, "Do you like jelly, George?"

"I think so."

"We have grape jelly. It's so good. It's my favorite." She rubbed her stomach. "When I was little, it's all I wanted to eat."

Jordan shook his head. "You're so 'zageratted, Presley. How can you remember when you were little?"

"I can. Just ask Mommy." She paused and leaned over George again. "Do you think I'm 'zagerrated, George?"

George chuckled lightly, just enough to avoid excruciating pain in his ribs. He looked forward to the day when he could actually laugh as much as he wanted. "Maybe just a little bit." He held up his finger and thumb on his good arm, indicating a miniscule amount.

"Yes, just a little bit," agreed Presley.

Minutes later, they were ready to eat. He bowed his head as Mariah led the prayer.

Was he a praying man?

He had no clue.

When they were finished, he reached with his good arm toward the plate that held several pieces of toast slathered in purple jelly to add to his plate of eggs. "I think my appetite is coming back."

Linda nodded. "That's good news. You need your strength

for the road to healing that's ahead of you."

He wished he were healed right now. Perhaps patience hadn't been one of his strong suits.

Presley and Jordan both scraped the grape jelly from their toast onto their plates and ate it plain, then proceeded to eat the toast. From the looks on their faces, it was obvious that grape jelly was an important staple for this family.

George salt and peppered his eggs and took a bite. His stomach growled for more. He finished his eggs and took a bite of the grape jelly toast.

That's when he nearly gagged.

Placing the toast back on his plate, George held back the urge to vomit. Had he ever tasted anything so vile? Not in recent memory.

At the thought of recent memory, he would have chuckled again were it not for the gag reflex that overtook him. And the painful ribs every time he laughed or coughed or even took a deep breath.

It took a while to swallow the bite of toast, but once he did, George finished his milk in one gulp, hoping to wash down any remnants of the awful toast. When he glanced up from his ordeal, the family was staring at him. "Are you all right?" Mariah asked, a look of concern lighting her expressive blue eyes.

"No. Not really."

Linda rose from her chair. "What can we do to help?"

He raised his hand and shook his head. "What I meant was that I don't think I like grape jelly."

Everyone began to laugh then, probably relieved he wasn't in some grave danger with his injuries. Or maybe truly grateful he didn't vomit the grape jelly toast. "Guess I know something about myself now."

"It's a start," Mariah said, taking a bite of her own grape jelly toast.

Presley helped herself to a second piece of toast. "Grandma, do we have more grape jelly in the pantry? I could eat it all day."

"We have several jars. It was on sale at the grocery store last week, so I stocked up."

George met Mariah's eye. She smiled a knowing smile, and he nodded. Hadn't they just spoken last night about Linda's "ability" to take advantage of sale items in stocking the pantry?

"I think I'm going to rest for a little while," George mentioned, as Mariah retrieved his dishes from the table a short time later.

"Here, I'll help you." Mariah assisted him from the table into his wheelchair. "Has Mom taken your vitals yet this morning?"

"She did, and she gave me some ibuprofen."

Jordan ran toward him, two of his books in hand. "When I'm done with school, will you help me build something super cool out of blocks?" he asked.

"I did promise we would do that, didn't I?"

Jordan scratched his head. "Yes, and I have a great idea. How about you and me build a police car?"

The words triggered something deep inside George's brain—blurred colors, the slap of shoes against the pavement, the wail of sirens. But George couldn't articulate where he ran to—or whom he ran from.

"George, are you all right?" Mariah's words interrupted his unsettling thoughts.

"Yeah, it's just that something..."

"Did you have another memory?"

Jordan's brow furrowed. "Is it okay to build a police car? We can build something else if you want."

"No, Jordan, a police car is fine. You get your schoolwork done, and after I've rested for a while, we'll build that car, all right?"

Mariah pushed his wheelchair to his room. "Did your memory have something to do with Jordan mentioning a police car?" she asked, helping him from the wheelchair and onto the bed.

"It did. I don't know what, just me running somewhere or from someone. I don't know. It's so irritating not to be able to complete the train of thought I have when something triggers a memory."

Her compassion drew him to her.

"It'll come back, George. It will just take time. From what Mom said, traumatic brain injuries can be complicated."

"I just..."

She looked at him expectantly, but he couldn't say it.

Wouldn't say it.

Wouldn't tell her he feared he might be on the run from the law.

Chapter 16

George awoke sometime later. When he opened his eyes, he noticed Presley standing near his bed. "You're awake!" she exclaimed.

Still foggy from his nap, George turned to face her, only to notice that Bibby the doll had been planted right next to him. Again.

"When you said your owies were hurting, I thought Bibby would make you feel better. So, do you feel better now?"

"A little bit. Thanks, Presley."

"You're welcome. I have to go get Jordan and tell him you're awake. He put me in charge of lookout."

"Lookout?"

"Yeah, you know. I have to be on the lookout and let him know right when you wake up so you can build a creation."

George wished he could laugh a full laugh at the look of seriousness on the little girl's face. "Okay. You better let Jordan know then."

"I will. I'll take Bibby too." Presley gently pulled the doll from the bed, clasped it tightly in her arms, and ran from the room calling Jordan's name.

Both Jordan and Linda appeared in the doorway seconds

later. "I'm all done with my schoolwork. I'm ready for us to build a police car."

"Did you ask George if he felt up to building a police car?" Linda asked.

"Oh. George, do you wanna build a police car?"

"That sounds fine, Jordan."

Wished he knew why it had triggered a memory. Even now in his mind, he saw the lights swirling, heard the sounds of sirens, and saw vehicles driving at a high rate of speed.

And saw himself running with another man away from the police car.

Crazy stuff.

Just how bad of a person was he? And what had he done to be running from the police?

Linda pulled her stethoscope and thermometer from her bag. "Before you build anything, I want to check on a few things, including that infection in your shoulder."

Jordan's looming face peered down at George. "I already have everything all ready at the table. I've been ready for about eight hours. Mom said we can even have some hot chocolate while we build. Hot chocolate always gives me 'spiration."

Linda laughed while taking George's temperature. "Eight hours is a long time. Hot chocolate is a good inspiration for just about anything, especially with marshmallows."

"See you in a couple minutes, George." Jordan waved and disappeared.

Mariah stood in the doorway in a pink sweater and jeans. Not that he was noticing what she wore.

All right. Yeah, he was noticing.

"How is he doing?" Mariah asked.

"I just finished checking on his infection. It's not worse, so that's a huge answer to prayer. But it's still red and a little hot to the touch. His fever is low. I put some more medicine on it, and we'll keep monitoring it." She sighed. "It'll be nice when we can get in touch with the doctor."

George shifted so Linda could take his blood pressure. "Why do I have an infection in my shoulder?"

"The cuts are quite deep. They probably would have stitched you up both there and the laceration on your forehead had we been able to get you to the ER."

"Knife wounds? That's what the cuts are?" Why had he not realized that before?

"Yes."

He watched as something passed in the glance between Linda and Mariah. "How did I get the wounds?"

"We don't know," Linda said. "Do you remember being in a fight or something?"

George closed his eyes. Had he been in a fight? Nothing but blackness filled his mind. When would he remember something? Anything? "I don't know. The only things that have triggered anything have been your neighbor's gun and the police car that Jordan said we were going to build."

"We'll keep praying you get some of your memory back. In the meantime, we'll do what we can to manage the infection and the pain." Linda handed him two acetaminophen tablets. "I wish I had something stronger for the pain, but all we can do is alternate the acetaminophen and ibuprofen to manage the pain, inflammation, and fever."

"I feel better than I did this morning, at least."

"That's good," said Mariah. "Have you recovered from your grape jelly incident?"

Her auburn hair, which she normally had pulled up in a ponytail, was down today, hanging just past her shoulders. She was attractive, but more than that, she was kind. He was drawn to her not just because of her beauty, but because of that kindness, because she was a good mom, and because she seemed to truly care about people.

People she didn't even know.

Like him.

Mariah averted her eyes, and George realized he had been staring. "Yeah. I'm recovered from that. I don't want to be picky about the food choices when you all are taking such good care of me, but I will be passing on grape jelly from here on out."

She laughed, a sweet laugh that had grown on him in a short amount of time. "Good. We'll remove that from your diet."

Linda packed up the items into her bag. "Do you need help with your wheelchair?"

"I can help him, Mom. I know you want to get your photo album finished today."

"Sounds good. Let me know if you need anything else." Linda patted him gently on the arm. "We'll start some physical therapy exercises later today to begin building your strength, and please remember to do the ankle pumps several times a day."

"Thank you, Linda. For everything."

"You're more than welcome. If you need me, I'll be in the craft room putting together photo albums from decades past."

Mariah assisted him into a sitting position, then into the wheelchair. As she did so, he caught a whiff of her shampoo and inhaled.

The realization hit him, likely harder than whatever had caused his brain injury had.

He was starting to fall for Mariah.

Mariah watched from afar as Jordan and George went to work on the police car. Even in his injured state, George was happy to oblige Jordan's request. It warmed her heart.

If he struggled with the police car memory, George didn't show it but instead did his best with one arm to snap together the pieces.

After partaking in some physical therapy exercises, George rested on the couch. The children were putting a puzzle together, and Mom was organizing the pantry. Mariah finished clearing the table of homeschool items, then took a glass of water to George.

"How are you feeling?"

"Better today."

Mariah sat on the edge of the couch beside him. "Thank you for helping Jordan with the police car. That really meant a lot to him."

"It was fun. You have great kids."

"Thank you. I'm pretty partial. They do have their moments, as all kids do, but I'm blessed. They get along well and are really learning to have hearts of compassion." *Unlike her self-absorbed ex-husband.*

"They have excellent role models in you and your mom."

She turned to smile at him, noting he was closer than she realized. "Thank you. We try. I don't have any siblings, so I love to watch the interaction between them. Jordan can be bossy, and Presley can do her best to annoy him, but overall, they get along so well. I always wanted to have a sister or brother."

"I hope I find out someday if I do. I don't even know who my parents are."

"Hopefully pieces of your memory will start to come back soon." She wouldn't elaborate that Mom said sometimes symptoms like what George experienced could last a lifetime if severe enough.

"It will be nice to know what side of the law I'm on."

Mariah's pulse thumped. Another reminder that just because she felt comfortable with him and he was good to her kids, didn't mean he was a safe person. What if he had an extensive criminal past? What if she was being too trusting? At some point, he would be well enough to cause harm if that was his intent.

"So, how long have you guys lived here with your mom?" George asked, changing the awkward subject.

How much should she share? "About a year now. We used to live in Briggs, but after my—after my divorce Mom and Dad offered for us to live with them. We'd lost the house anyway, so it was a welcome offer. At first, I didn't want to impose, but I really needed my parents. We've almost always been close, and while Briggs is only twenty miles away, I figured a change of scenery would do us all some good."

"Briggs?" George closed his eyes. "There's something about that town."

"Maybe you live there?"

"Maybe. Not sure." He sighed. "Why did you lose your house?"

"The divorce. Brandon always handled all the money during our marriage. When everything happened, he promised to continue paying the bills, including the mortgage. Our house was huge, and we owed a lot on it. He stopped paying the mortgage and it foreclosed. By then, he was long gone. I thought about getting an apartment or trying to save up to buy another house, but it'll take some time to restore my credit between that and the credit card bills Brandon racked up over the years."

"I'm sorry, Mariah. Sounds like you've had a rough time of it with the divorce and your dad's passing."

"It's been tough. But I've always had a strong support system and an even stronger faith. That's what has gotten me through it."

"I wonder sometimes if I have a strong faith or even a faith at all. I don't know much about myself. Although..." he stroked the bushy growth on his chin then reached a hand to his head. "I feel confident I was not a bearded man in my former life. This thing is driving me crazy. And did I always have long hair?"

"Maybe we can solicit Rick's help with that."

"As in Rick, your neighbor? I don't know. He doesn't seem to like me too much. Might be dangerous for him to be that close to me with scissors and a razor."

Mariah shook her head. "It's not that he doesn't like you, it's just that he's protective of us."

"I appreciate that. I wouldn't want anything to happen to you either, especially with those people asking about me." George paused and once again turned to face her. "Mariah, you have to know that whoever I am—whatever I've done—I will never hurt you or your kids or your mom. Please believe that."

Did she believe that? Did she believe that once he regained his memory he would still be above the law? Did she believe that, if he was a wanted man, that they could continue to have any type of friendship?

George's eyes held a look of expectation. How could she respond?

"Mariah?"

"It's just that you don't really know us and we don't know

you." She could hear the uncertainty in her voice. Fear that something could happen. Fear that she was getting too comfortable. She couldn't promise she believed him. For how could she when she knew so little about him?

Chapter 17

George sat in the backseat of the van, staring at the back of Tiny's misshapen head—narrow at the top and wide at the bottom near his neck. Two folds of thick skin rested on Tiny's collar and were accentuated in size each time Tiny turned his large head. He sported a short spikey reddish-brown buzz cut and three piercings in his left ear, and his enormous stomach snuggled the steering wheel. Keeping his gaze off the road more than on, he used one beefy arm to steer the van while the other arm hung out the window.

George shivered at the frigid air flowing in through the window. Who had their window down in below-zero temps?

Psycho Eyes sat beside Tiny in the other front seat, smoking his crystal meth, a powerful odor wafting from his pipe. Greasy wisps of blond hair hung in strings just above the collar of his stained sweatshirt that appeared to have at one time sported a hood.

Tiny and Psycho Eyes chatted back and forth as Tiny whipped around the corners on the thin two-lane icy road, causing bile to form in George's throat from motion sickness. His head throbbed from what, he didn't know, just that the pounding of his headache was in perfect sync with his heartbeat. George closed his eyes, hoping to ease both the pain and the nausea. He needed to rest, just for a minute.

A blow to his right shoulder woke him from his nanosecond of rest, and his eyes flung open to see Deb up close and in his face. "Wake up!" she snapped, her breath foul from a mixture of cigarette smoke and alcohol. "We got stuff to do."

Stuff to do?

George forced his eyes to stay open as Deb remained inches from his face, likely ensuring he obeyed. Finally, she settled back into her own seat.

In the third-row seat, Dawson chuckled. "Yo, Deb, you woke even me up with that one."

She scowled. "Shut up, loser."

Dawson leaned forward and exhaled a vape mist right into George's face. "I love this flavor. It's like apple pie or somethin'," he said. He gripped the seat, his dark eyes scanning the van. "Are we almost there?"

"What are you, some kid?" asked Tiny from the front seat. "Just shut up and be patient."

Dawson laughed again and hit the ceiling of the van with his fist. "I can already smell the money. This is gonna be a good day and ain't no one gonna find the goodies this time. Not when they're hidden in the ceiling. Ain't no police doggy gonna find it there." He slapped George on the back of the head. "This is gonna be a good day, huh?"

George bit his lip to keep from crying out in pain.

"We're just gonna be chill and it's gonna be good, right, Deb?" Dawson took another puff on his vape pen.

"Yeah, whatever. Just shut up, already." Deb spun around to face Dawson, and George could see from her profile and flared nostrils that she offered him a hateful glare.

"All right, all right," Dawson muttered. He kicked the back

of the seat, his apparent nervous energy not allowing him to sit still.

In a split second, Deb leaped from her place next to George and climbed over the seat. George turned slowly to watch as she met up with Dawson in the third row. She backhanded his face in conjunction with a swift string of Spanish. George didn't know a ton of the language, but he caught something about shutting up and kicking the seat.

"Ow! You hurt my nose," Dawson whined. He dropped the vape pen on the seat beside him and covered his nose.

Deb wielded her petite frame back over the seat next to George. He avoided looking at her or saying a word. Two punches to his face wouldn't bode well with the excruciating headache and nausea.

"Good job, Deb. Keep him in line," Psycho Eyes said, admiration in his icy blue eyes. He allowed his gaze to travel from the top of Deb's short black pixie haircut to her feet and lingered everywhere in between. "You something else, Girl." He smiled, a barrage of missing teeth lining his meth mouth.

Why was he with such repulsive people?

George's eyes fluttered open in the darkness. He jerked to a sitting position, causing a rapid ache in just about every part of his body. Where was he? Was he still in the van? He shivered. Who were these people?

His breathing came in rapid gasps, and he tried his best to keep his breathing shallow to avoid more pain. Darkness surrounded him. Why could he not see?

Had he just imagined all that he had dreamt? Or was it real?

Had he been on his way to deliver drugs hidden in the ceiling of the van? Were the people with him his friends?

Who was he?

The dream about the van and its occupants haunted George throughout the next day. If he was involved in some type of drug trade, or worse, he could put Mariah and her family in danger.

And that was something he did not want to do.

George sat in the wheelchair in front of the round portable mirror in the bathroom. Today was the day he would attempt to shave his beard. Mariah had suggested asking the neighbor to help.

Something didn't sit right about that Rick guy. But George couldn't do this on his own. Not shaving his beard and not cutting his scraggly hair.

Rick took the scissors to his hair first before the clippers. Did the man even have any experience with this type of thing?

As if to read his mind, Rick offered an answer to George's unspoken question. "My dad was a barber. Taught me a thing or two. Not that I've used it on my own head recently." He chuckled.

"No, I don't suppose so," muttered George.

The beard was next, and instantly the relief from the itch made George feel better.

After clipping his hair and shaving his beard, Rick handed George a handheld mirror.

The appearance of the man staring back rattled him. This was the first time he had seen himself. Purple and black, although fading, marred his cheeks. A crusty horizontal scab puckered the left side of his forehead above a black eye. Bandages on his shoulder protruded beneath his t-shirt.

What happened to him?

And why?

The need to know pulsed through him. Frustration at the unknown pummeled his mind.

He rubbed his right hand across his clean-shaven chin and ran his fingers through his short-cropped hair.

"Not too bad for a rookie barber, eh?"

Rick's words jolted him from his thoughts. "No, not bad at all. Thanks, Rick."

"Any recollection?"

"Not yet."

"At least now you look somewhat normal."

That was a compliment, George supposed.

"Look, so some creep friend of yours stopped by and threatened Mariah and her family. If Carol wasn't still so sick, we'd move in here. I *will* find out who you are."

George had no doubt the man would. But when he did, would George be disturbed by the answer?

Rick wheeled him to the kitchen. From the expressions on everyone's faces, they were just as shocked at George's new appearance as he was.

"Still no idea who I am, but it's much better without that beard."

Mariah offered him a reassuring smile, and an unexpected thought sucker-punched him in the gut. Did he have someone like her waiting for him back home, wherever that was?

If so, he couldn't allow himself to be attracted to her.

Rick left with a bowl of soup for Carol, and the family sat around the table for lunch. Mariah led the prayer today and prayed for George's healing and for him to remember who he was. He'd begun praying himself—prayers similar to the ones the family prayed for him. Had he prayed before his injuries? He couldn't be sure, but George had some recollection of a modern church with rows of chairs. *Lord, please don't let me be the man I believe myself to be.*

For whom he believed himself to be would not be the kind of man who should be staying with a nice family.

Chapter 18

The change in George's appearance was astounding. His battered face notwithstanding, he was a handsome man.

And not one who looked to be one who spent time with the three searching for him. But as Mariah reminded herself on numerous occasions, looks could be deceiving.

George took a nap the following day in the early afternoon. Mariah schooled the kids, threw a load in the laundry, and prepared lunch. She wandered down to the laundry room to transfer the load from the washer, and Jordan and Presley, finished with their schoolwork, headed upstairs, and played with their toys. Mom powered the vacuum and cleaned the rooms.

Mariah grabbed the laundry basket and carried it toward the living room. Later, she would gather some more dirty clothes from the rooms.

Nosy began to bark. She cautiously opened the door and let him outside for a bathroom break. A cool gust of air greeted her, as she scanned the area. Thankfully, she saw no one and heard no snow machines. Only the wind whipping through the pines.

She perused the area next to the house. How were Rick and

Carol? Was Carol feeling better?

Even from outside, she could hear the vacuum roaring upstairs, blocking out all of the other household noises except Nosy's persistent bark. She called to him, and when he didn't come, she trampled after him as he bounded around the corner.

"Nosy!"

The dog growled, and his ears stood at attention. "Come on, Nosy. We need to get back inside." She reached down, grabbed his collar, and pulled him toward the door, even as he resisted.

Finally, she opened the door and slipped inside. Nosy continued to bark as he left wet pawprints on the floor.

And then she saw him.

A burly man, one whom she recognized, sat at the table eating Jordan's lunch.

Mariah jumped. Gooseflesh covered her arms, although not from the cold. How had he gotten into the house? Could it have been when she chased Nosy around the corner? She sucked in a shaky breath.

"Ah, we meet again. Are you surprised to see me?" The man had removed his hat and placed it on the table. A heavy winter coat had been tossed on the floor. He bit into a carrot and chewed with his mouth open, exposing orange pieces of food meshed between decaying teeth.

She noticed the grip of a pistol tucked in the front of his waistband beneath his abundant abdomen. "I didn't appreciate what you did last time," he growled in between bites. The man turned his head, revealing a red wound. "Seems to me I owe you one for the headache you gave me."

Mariah's knees shook and she struggled to maintain an appearance of calmness, although she was anything but calm.

"What, you a little shy today?" The man pulled a vape pen

from his pocket, prepared it, and held it to his mouth. He inhaled the vapor and removed the vape pen from his mouth and exhaled a puff of foul-smelling odor. "It's blue cheese flavor. My favorite."

Blue cheese-flavored vape? Nausea swirled in her stomach both from his choice of flavors and from the threat he posed. Mariah commanded her legs to move, but she stood frozen not far from the trespasser. Nosy continued to bark, this time edging closer to the man and baring his teeth.

"Better shut him up."

The vacuum stopped for a moment, likely indicating Mom was picking up things off the floor before she resumed.

"Mommy, why is the mailman here again and why can we see his breath even though he's in the warm house?"

Lord, please no!

It was a blessing their mailman was thickset with reddish-brown hair like this man, but that was where the similarities ended.

Jordan emerged at the top of the stairs.

"Kids, please go back to your room for a few minutes and read some books or play with toys."

"Do we have to?" Jordan asked.

"Yes, you do." Mariah's voice shook and instead of looking at her children, she maintained eye contact with the man.

Thankfully, Presley and Jordan did as they were told.

The man's back was to the stairs and he didn't bother turning to see the children, but instead took another puff on his pen. Nosy growled again and the man reached for his pistol and pointed at the dog.

Mom proceeded to turn on the vacuum again.

"No!" shouted Mariah.

"Then shut him up!"

Mariah reached for Nosy and attempted to calm him.

Presley ran down the stairs and stood next to Mariah. "Mommy why is the mailman yelling and what is that pewey smell?"

Mariah raised her voice over the noise of the vacuum and commanded Presley to go to her room again.

"Oh, all right. But I'm still just so curious." Any other time, Mariah would be proud that Presley remembered the new word she'd learned.

But this wasn't the time for even a smile, let alone a laugh. She watched as her daughter skipped up the stairs to her room.

The vacuum clicked off and she heard Mom's voice. "Mariah, is everything all right?"

Nosy barked.

"Walton!"

There was no response. Would Mom remember their code word?

"Walton!"

The man narrowed his eyes. "Who's Walton?"

"Walton's the dog. Come on, Walton. Let's go to the other room." Nosy looked at her as if she'd lost her mind. And maybe she had with all this frightening stress provoked by the man at the table. "Come on, Walton." Mariah tapped her leg with her hand.

Nosy tilted his head to one side then to the other. He turned briefly and growled once again at the man. "Come on, Walton."

The man rested his gun on the table and proceeded to alternate between vaping and eating a leftover piece of a half-eaten chicken nugget.

Nosy finally followed her down the hall. She passed by George's room. Carefully peering around the corner to see if the man was watching, she opened his door. He was snoring.

She locked the door and closed it.

Then she put Nosy in the downstairs bathroom.

When she returned to the kitchen and living room area, the man was removing himself from the chair. "Where is he?"

"Who? Walton?" Mariah turned her head and peered up the stairs. *Where was Mom?*

Were the kids safely tucked in their rooms?

Would George wake up and give his location away?

While her head was turned, the man bent forward and grabbed Mariah's ponytail. He yanked, hard, causing her head to jerk back. She winced, tears streaming from her eyes. Calling her a string of vile words, he put his face within a few inches of hers. "You know I'm not talking about the dog. I'm talking about the man you're keeping here somewhere."

"He's not here."

The man glowered at her. His breath, a combination of the blue cheese vape and chicken nuggets from Jordan's plate, caused bile to rise in her throat.

Mariah's neck ached. She found it difficult to breathe with the angle at which he held her neck.

Lord, please...

He muttered under his breath. "There are four of us and I get the pleasure of being the one to keep coming to this house. Why is that?"

Four of them? She knew of three. The woman or the other thin man from the shed would have been preferred over this bully.

"Maybe I should have sent P.E. He's good at getting people to tell him stuff."

Cold chills ran up Mariah's spine. They were protecting a man they didn't know. A man who could be a friend to the monster who now held her hostage.

Yet she knew from some peculiar gut instinct she couldn't explain that she could not, *would not*, let this man know that George resided in the house.

"There are several houses in the area. We've checked them all over and over including that old pathetic guy who lives next door. He's going to be hurting for a while, by the way. If he recovers." The man emitted a thunderous and evil laugh.

Tears stung her eyes. What had they done to Rick? To Carol?

Mariah's neck felt as though it was stuck in the bent position the man held it in. He grasped her ponytail tighter and gave it another yank. "But you, you seem to be hiding something from me, and I don't appreciate that."

"I'm not hiding anything. Please just leave us alone."

"You haven't seen the last of me. I won't stop until I get the answer I want." The man roughly let go of her hair and her head popped back into normal position.

Despite her best attempts not to do so, Mariah cried out at the pain. She didn't want this bully to see her pain. Her weakness. Her fear.

From the corner of her eye, Mariah spied the man's gun on the table. Dare she make a race for it? Her heart beat wildly in her chest. Her head pounded from the pain of her neck. And her mouth internally whispered words of prayer begging God to go before her.

The man remained glaring at her with those hateful eyes. She had to be able to get around his girth to get to the table. The man might be strong, but he was slow.

High school track becoming a more recent memory, Mariah pivoted to one side, then dashed toward the table. She grabbed the gun, its grip feeling too large for her small hand. She seized it tightly and pointed it toward the man.

"Get out of my house."

The man laughed and produced the knife from his baggy pants. "So you wanna fight?"

She could shoot him if a round was chambered, and Mariah felt confident it was. She would do anything to protect her family.

"The bad thing is that I can't kill you...yet. P.E will want that privilege. He hates liars more than I do."

Mariah took a firm stance, legs enough apart to hopefully help her from toppling over should the bulky man lunge toward her.

Lord, please...

Out of nowhere, she heard a voice. Mom had flitted down the stairs, unbeknownst to either Mariah or the man. "Get out of my house and away from my daughter or I will shoot."

"Two of you. That's funny. Still no match for me," the man roared.

"I'll shoot," warned Mom.

The man lifted his hands.

Would he give up this easily?

He leaned over to retrieve his coat, acting as though it was a pleasant social call and he was preparing to take his leave. That's when he threw his coat at Mariah. She struggled to untangle herself from the thick garment, and just as she was able to free her face, something grabbed her shoulders and shoved her. She teetered and she would have maintained her balance were it not for a kitchen chair in her path. The gun flew from her hands as she went down.

Mariah's head hit the floor with a thud.

Dazed, she stuttered a moment before attempting to reach for the gun before he did. The race placed him once again in close proximity.

"Get away from her or I'll shoot," Mom shouted.

Mariah grappled for the gun. The man lunged toward the weapon. Her fingers brushed the grip a second before the side of his palm karate-chopped the top of her bruised hand. She cried out in pain. Adrenaline overtook her and instinctively she drove her kneecap into his elbow, causing his arm to buckle, give out, and tip him off balance.

Seeing an opportunity, Mariah snatched the pistol and scrambled away. Dizziness caused her to stagger as she rose to her feet. She backed into the island in the kitchen, trapped as the man regained his bearings. He rose and advanced toward her, a guttural growl rumbling from his portly frame.

Mariah raised the gun. At the same time, Mom barreled toward the man. Gun in one hand and a can of bear spray with the orange safety clip removed in the other, she lifted the canister. Mariah turned away, guarding herself. The man howled as the spray doused him square in the face. He coughed and wheezed, bending over as far as his girth would allow.

Mariah pointed him toward the door and shoved him outside. He stumbled, eyes closed and one hand pawing at his face while the other grasped into the air for direction as he groaned. She locked the door behind him, and she and Mom watched from the window as the man floundered through the deep snow drifts and into the woods.

Mariah set the man's gun on the table, planning to lock it in Dad's gun safe.

Her own breath coming in gasps, Mariah turned toward Mom and they embraced. They both sobbed, tension mixed with relief and gratitude that they had survived what could have been a deadly attack. How many times would the man keep coming back?

And would they survive the next time?

Chapter 19

Mariah's legs wobbled and her head throbbed as she made her way up the stairs to check on the children.

"Mommy, what was all that noise?" Presley asked.

"When I saw the mailman being mean, I went into Presley's room and we shut the door," said Jordan, his arm around his sister.

"That was very wise and very brave. You did the right thing."

Mariah always knew she had the best mom in the world, but she'd never seen Mom react in such a courageous manner as she had today.

She hugged her children as tightly as she could. Life was precious. She'd not let a day go by without making sure they knew how much she loved them. Tears formed in Mariah's eyes again and she kissed the tops of their heads. "I love you."

"We love you too, Mom," said Jordan. "Say, is George awake?"

Thankfully the children didn't have any apparent distress from hearing the commotion, Mariah told them they could come downstairs and have a snack and she'd check to see if George was awake.

"Did a her-cane come through here?" Presley asked.

Mariah perused the kitchen. Chairs knocked over, food spilled on the table—a mess rivaling a natural disaster awaited her and Mom.

But at least they were safe.

And alive.

She needed to check on George, and then she or Mom would need to check on Rick and Carol. When they did, what would they find? She shivered. *Lord, please let Rick and Carol be all right.* Rick was a brave man who could defend himself and his wife, but someone high or bent on being evil and vicious, as the man had been, would likely offer intense competition.

Mariah situated the children on barstools at the counter and gave them some fruit snacks. She and Mom would tackle the kitchen after they checked on George and the neighbors.

Wandering down the hall, Mariah let Nosy out of the bathroom, then came to George's room. She unlocked the door. "George?"

"Come in," a groggy voice answered.

Mariah opened the door. George blinked. Had he just woke up? She rushed to the blinds and made sure they were completely closed. She and Mom had talked about how they needed to remember that, both in George's room and in the other parts of the house whenever he was present.

"How are you doing?" she asked.

"How long was I asleep?"

Time had passed at a crazy rate of speed given all that had happened. The clock on the wall indicated it was 3:30 p.m.

"A couple of hours. But sleeping is good for you. It helps the healing process."

Looking at the man in the bed, his face bleary with sleep and his hair ruffled, she wondered once again how he could be a part of the gang that had terrorized her family. How could someone so "normal" looking, even handsome, be a cohort with someone like the man she'd found in the kitchen a couple of hours ago?

And George was handsome. Especially now that he had shaved off his scraggly beard and had a haircut. Signs of the assault still shown on his face, but Mariah saw beneath that. Of course, criminals could be handsome. It was a fallacy that all of them were greasy and creepy looking like the one Mom had bear-sprayed.

She assisted him into the wheelchair and took a seat beside him in the vacant chair. If she could just sit. Just for a minute and get her bearings about her again.

"Are you all right?" George asked, his voice interrupting her thoughts.

"Yes. It's just been a wild afternoon."

To say the least.

"Mariah?"

His voice, tender with concern, drew her attention to him.

"I thought I heard some noise, but I wasn't sure if it was one of those nightmares I've been having or if it was real. Did I hear some noise?"

"You did."

"Is everything okay?"

His compassion was all it took for the emotions to rage within her again. Mariah swallowed hard. She would not lose it in front of George.

But her unsettled emotions won. She began to sob, her face in her hands. God had kept them safe, but what about next time?

An arm reached around her shoulders. She leaned into him, finding a comfortable spot against his strong chest, but hoping it didn't hurt his injuries.

When he didn't give any indication that it did, she leaned in further, thankful for the strength he radiated.

George said nothing for several minutes. Instead, he allowed her to rest in his arm. It was an awkward position, but pleasant all the same.

When was the last time she'd had a man care enough to hold her in her time of need?

Brandon had never been the type to offer comfort. Even in the good times. But why was she comparing George to Brandon?

"Want to tell me what happened?"

She did, yet didn't. How could George possibly understand? How much should she tell him?

"One of them stopped by again. He got inside the house. I need to tell Rick and check to see if we have cell service yet and if the roads are open."

"Did he hurt you?"

"Yes."

As she looked up at him, she felt him tense against her.

"What did he do?"

"Yanked on my hair and shoved me."

A muscle in his jaw bunched before the anger was replaced with compassion in his eyes. He reached around her shoulder and placed a gentle finger on her face, wiping away the tears that fell freely.

She closed her eyes at the softness of his touch.

"I'm so sorry, Mariah. I would do anything to protect you and your family. Please, just tell them I'm here."

"I can't. Not after I've told them you're not. Besides, I think they're—this man anyway—won't do something worse as long as he thinks I know where you are."

George balled his fist. "These aren't my friends. They can't be."

"They claim to be."

"Friends or not, I'm not going to allow them to hurt people I care about."

He cared about them? Mariah supposed she knew that, but hearing him say it warmed her. "They want to find you and will do anything to achieve that goal. But it's not like a family member or close friend who's concerned. It's...I can't explain it." Mariah had shared some close friendships in her lifetime. Those friends would never threaten someone innocent if they were looking for her. But then, those friends weren't in a gang, which Mariah was convinced this man and the two other visitors were.

"I know with the dizziness and unsteadiness I'm still experiencing it wouldn't be a good idea, but I do wish I had a gun."

He was right. In his condition, a gun wouldn't be helpful.

"I can't exactly protect you by leaping out of my wheelchair and taking him down. Why would I have friends like this?"

Mariah shrugged. Why would anyone have friends like that, unless they were of the same caliber?

He pulled her close again and she inhaled the scent of the woodsy deodorant he used, likely one of the new deodorants Dad never had the chance to try. If she could just rest peacefully here in his embrace for a few moments longer and forget all that had happened, everything would be right with the world.

Chapter 20

Mariah glanced over her shoulder, noting how Mom stood at the window where she could see Mariah's journey from the cabin to Rick and Carol's. Mariah followed the clear path from one house to the other, afraid of what she would find. She'd brought her gun, but hopefully she wouldn't need it.

Her heart pounded. Would any of the unwanted visitors arrive again while she navigated her way the short distance to her friends' home?

She felt a sensation of the hairs on her neck standing on end, and she quickly assessed the area. Snow fell at a medium rate. A few brave birds chirped, and the air smelled of a wood-burning stove.

But no one was around that she could see.

What would she find once she reached Rick and Carol's home? Would they be injured? In need of dire medical assistance?

A thought pummeled her then. Had the man taken the lives of her friends?

No, Lord, I won't even go there with that thought. Please let them be all right.

The wind stung her cheeks. How had the criminals continued to visit in this weather? They must not be far away. Where were they hiding? Were they watching her, even at this very moment?

When she reached the cottage, Mariah rapped on the door with three hard knocks.

No answer.

Walking to the front window, she peered inside and saw their vacant living room. Were Rick and Carol gone? But if so, where would they go? With the roads closed, their only option was to drive down the street if it was cleared. Otherwise, they'd get no further than the driveway.

Mariah turned and gazed beyond the driveway. It was doubtful any of the roads had been cleared. When blizzards hit Mountain Springs, the town shut down.

But for this long?

She could see Mom's face in the cabin window. Mariah returned to the door and knocked again. The cottage was about 800 square feet. No matter what room they were in, they should be able to hear her knock.

Mariah held her breath. *Lord, please let them be all right.*

Trying the door handle, she found it to be locked. Had the man broken through a side window? Mariah shuffled through a few deep drifts to the side of the house. Through another window, she could see the kitchen. Deserted.

Dare she go around to the back of the house? What if someone was watching from the woods? Surely, if the man was still in the vicinity, he would be unable to see much given the injury to his eyes from the bear spray.

But if he sent reinforcements...

Mariah shivered, both from the cold breeze and from the frightening possibilities. Yes, she was armed this time and Mom was watching for her, but these were ruthless people.

She returned to the front of the house so as not to worry Mom. Mariah flicked a quick gaze toward the cabin, the driveway, the woods, and the backyard.

Eerily desolate.

Maybe she should have taken Nosy as Mom suggested. But all she needed was for the dog to take off again.

One final time, she rapped on the front door, louder this time.

Finally, after what seemed an eternity, the door flung open and Rick stood in the doorway. "Mariah, is everything all right?"

She now knew why people fainted from relief. Mariah clutched the molding on the doorway. "Yes," she whispered.

Rick appeared fine, and Mariah breathed a prayer of gratitude. She pivoted and gave Mom a "thumbs up" signal. "I was worried when you didn't answer."

"I'm sorry. I was in the garage and Carol has been sleeping. Are you okay?"

She hoped she hadn't awakened Carol with her incessant knocking. "We had a break-in."

Rick balled his fists. "What is it gonna take to get these people to leave us alone?"

"They're serious about finding George."

"Wish it was as simple as them leaving us alone if we turn him over, but I'm not that naïve."

"I've already been told they'll express their displeasure at being lied to if they find out George is in the house."

Mariah shared the story of the man's entry and his attack on her. Rick's face and his bald head turned red. A vein in his jaw twitched. "He made it sound as though he had harmed you and Carol. When you didn't answer the door..."

"They haven't been by."

136

"The only good thing is that we were able to attack him with bear spray."

Rick's normally small eyes enlarged. "Bear spray? In the face?"

"Yes. Let's just say he was temporarily put out of commission."

"Probably a little longer than temporarily, what with the respiratory issues and blisters that stuff causes.

Mariah nodded. "He wandered off into the woods. I think they're riding snowmobiles in from somewhere. Somewhere close."

"That very well could be. Were it not for Carol being sick with what your mom thinks is pneumonia and the concern of Presley catching it with her asthma, we would have moved in long ago. All right. Here's what we're going to do. I will be doing perimeter checks three or four times a day and once at night. Once the weather clears, I'm also going to wander down the road a bit. I won't go too far with leaving Carol alone." He rubbed the back of his neck. "If anyone shows up and give you any trouble again, place a flashlight in the upstairs window—I think it's Jordan's room that faces us—and that will be our code. Until we have the ability to call law enforcement, we'll have to take matters into our own hands." Rick's idea held a lot of merit, but Mariah still worried about her older friends. "They're callous people, Rick. Please be careful."

"Don't you worry about us. I dealt with worse people than this when I was in law enforcement. Besides, I'm a tough old coot."

Arrogant and cocky too, but that could be a good thing in times like these.

What would Mariah do without these dear friends that God had placed in her life?

"Good. Then I'll walk you back home and we'll be more aware of our surroundings in these coming days than we've ever been. Oh, and speaking of being aware, I'll be by to have a chat with George tomorrow. I don't particularly like the friends he chooses to keep. You know what they say, 'birds of a feather' and all that."

That particular worry had continued to needle Mariah. Was George only nice to her and her family because he didn't remember who he was?

George heard Rick's voice before he saw him. Frustration at not yet being able to do much consumed him. His body failed to hold up for long at any given time. Weakness overcame him easily and without much effort.

Sure enough, the older man entered George's room with Mariah moments later. "George, are you awake? Rick wants to ask you a few questions."

Her gentle voice lingered in his ears. "Yes," he answered, dreading what type of questioning Rick would deem necessary today. He opened his eyes, and his gaze fell upon her. She had pulled her hair into a ponytail, her bright eyes drawing his attention to her face.

He found himself staring.

"Thanks, Mariah. I got it from here," Rick said.

"Be nice to him, Rick," Mariah warned, her voice sounding like she was half-teasing him. George watched as she left the room.

"Don't worry. I'll only be here a minute." Rick placed a chair backward and straddled it next to George's wheelchair. The same gun was holstered at his hip. A Sig, not that George knew why he knew that.

Rick stroked his nonexistent beard. "Any more memories?"

Not that George wanted to lie or be evasive, but telling Rick about the drug van would likely not gain an ally in the man.

"You look a whole lot better."

"Thanks."

"Look, George, these people we're dealing with are ruthless." Rick paused and inclined forward. He articulated his words. Making sure George understood, perhaps? "I'm a retired cop. It's my job to protect this family. I am a justice seeker, always have been. I don't know who you are, and I don't know if you're telling me the truth that you don't know who you are. I aim to get to the bottom of this mess. Were it not for my wife being sick in bed, we would have moved in here. Your friends wouldn't appreciate seeing me face to face."

"I'm sorry your wife is sick." George had known Rick was law enforcement. And he'd known Rick aimed to protect Mariah and her family. He only wished he knew if he, himself, was a threat.

"Thanks." Rick steepled his fingers, and as the sleeve of Rick's t-shirt rose up his arm, George noticed a tattoo for the first time.

The words "Psalm 91" and the picture of a bird partially covered his bicep.

George closed his eyes, the tattoo provoking a memory in his blurred memory. It was cold and snowy, ice covering the road. He was walking closely behind Psycho Eyes, one of the men from the van. Psycho Eyes walked fast, while George seemed slow, almost lethargic, stumbling behind him. Ahead on the road, George saw the large beefy guy, but no sign of the other two or the van.

Psycho Eyes turned to say something to George, but George

couldn't comprehend nor hear the words. When Psycho Eyes faced forward again, he leaned his head down to look at something in front of him. George saw the tattoo on the man's neck. The letters "d-a-n-j-r-u-s-s" were tattooed on the back of his neck, likely an incorrect spelling for "dangerous."

Where were they going?

"Hey, man, you okay?"

Rick's voice removed George's thoughts from the scene that played in his mind. He opened his eyes. "Yeah. I'm good." Well, as good as he could be in his current predicament with an odd feeling washing over him from the recently-triggered memory. His eyes veered toward Rick's tattoo again, now more hidden by Rick's new arm position.

"Did you remember something?"

"Just..."

"Just what?"

How much, if at all, could George trust Rick? Yes, he wanted Mariah and her family to be safe, but if he truly was a wanted criminal...

The thought suffocated him.

"I don't know. Just something about your tattoo."

"My tattoo?" Rick flipped up the shirt over his bicep. The man was fit for a guy his age. Definitely not one to mess with. "This here is my favorite chapter in the Bible. Psalm 91. Heard of it?"

"I'm not sure."

"It's about God's protection. *Whoever dwells in the shelter of the Most High will rest in the shadow of the Almighty. I will say of the Lord, "He is my refuge and my fortress, my God, in whom I trust.'* There's much more to it than that; that's only the beginning. Sound familiar?"

"Can't say it does."

Rick tapped his chin with his finger. "So, what kind of memory did the tattoo evoke?"

"I just remembered a tattoo I saw."

"On yourself? Do you have any tattoos?"

George didn't think so but honestly, he really didn't know for sure. "Not that I've seen."

"So, a tattoo on someone else?"

"Yes."

Rick nodded. "What did the tattoo say?"

"Some word. Letters. Something spelled wrong, but I can't remember." He squinted as if that would help him recall the word. "It's just beyond my grasp. Some weird word on the back of this guy's neck. I don't know what it means or whatever. Just a strange memory that popped into my mind when I saw your tattoo. It could mean nothing."

"Or it could mean something."

Rick had a point.

"George, it's not going to be long now before we have an internet connection and the cell service is back up and running. Hopefully, I'll be able to do some digging. Anything you can tell me will be much appreciated. We'll need to get as much information as possible."

Get as much info as possible. Why did Rick's line sound familiar? Maybe because George was a hardened criminal and had been questioned numerous times. The tat again flashed in his mind, but the letters were distorted. "I'm not trying to hide stuff from you," he said. "I honestly don't remember what the tattoo says. I am struggling with my memory. Ask Mariah."

"Yeah, about Mariah." Rick cleared his throat and inclined closer, lowering his voice. "She's like a daughter to my wife and me. She's been through a lot, and doesn't need someone like you causing her trouble."

"I won't cause her any trouble."

"Falling for her will cause her trouble."

"Falling for her?"

Rick narrowed his eyes. "I'm no spring chicken, but I'm not blind. I saw how you looked at her when she was in the room."

How could he deny that? "You don't have to worry about it, Rick."

"Oh, but I do. If you're some kind of corrupt criminal, which you could be, she doesn't need the likes of you messing up her life."

"I wouldn't do anything to mess up her life." *I care about her.*

"See that you don't. See that you mind your 'p's and q's'." Rick puffed out his chest as if making a point that he was a sturdy and strong guy who wouldn't put up with any shenanigans George might entertain.

Not that he entertained any. He would die before he would hurt Mariah. "No worries there."

"Good. Now is there anything else you remember? Anything more about the guy with the tattoo? What it said, who he was, that kind of stuff?"

"No."

Rick stared at him, likely trying to figure out whether or not George told the truth. George held his gaze.

"Keep me updated. I'll be in touch." Rick stood, squared his shoulders, and put the chair back against the wall. "Until next time," he said.

George watched him leave. Why did it seem he was on the man's bad side even though they'd just met?

He heard muffled voices in the hallway between Rick and Linda. "Keep an eye on him."

"He's not mobile yet, Rick."

"Not yet, but he will be soon. We don't know this guy's

history."

There was a pause before Linda answered. "True, we don't, but we can't assume the worst."

"Even before Mariah found George, there had been some criminal activity up here in recent months. While we can't assume the worst, we can't be careless. Besides, he likes Mariah."

"A lot of people like Mariah."

"You know what I mean, Linda. She doesn't need the kind of baggage this guy has."

"Thank you for looking out for us, Rick. We'll keep an eye on him. Here's some homemade potato soup for Carol. Tell her we're praying for her to feel better."

"Will do."

The voices became more distant, and George sat up in his bed, straining to hear Mariah's voice. Did she see him as a threat? He hoped not. Her opinion of him meant a lot.

But what if he *was* a threat?

A vision of a jail cell popped into his mind. Dark. Dank. Isolated. Noise from surrounding prisoners nearby. Someone rapping on the bars. Vile words uttered. Loud footsteps.

Jordan stood beside his wheelchair. "Guess what, George?"

George swallowed hard. Had he been in jail before? Did he deserve to be there now?

"George?"

"Sorry, Jordan. What were you saying?"

"I have a loose tooth. It's my first loose top tooth. See?" Jordan leaned over, and with an exaggerated movement, stuck his top teeth toward George. "It's this one." He wiggled the large front tooth on the right.

"Won't be long."

"If I plan it just right, I can lose both front teeth at once and put a straw right there where my teeth used to be."

"That's a good plan."

"Did they have the tooth fairy back when you were a kid, George?"

George wished he could remember all kinds of details, but whether or not the tooth fairy existed when he was a kid hadn't crossed his radar. "I'm sure she was around and leaving kids money when they lost a tooth even back in the olden days."

"Were you and Abraham Lincoln friends?"

Abraham Lincoln? The name seemed oddly familiar. "I'm not sure. He might be a friend of mine."

"Oh, wow. 'Cause if you were that old, I was gonna ask you all about the Civil War and what it was like."

"All right, time to eat," Linda announced, pouring the milk.

George looked from one person to another in this family that had cared for him. He would miss them when he healed.

Chapter 21

Mariah walked downstairs after putting Jordan and Presley to bed with hugs and prayers. Tomorrow was Sunday, and while she wished they could attend church as they always did, at least they could spend some time reading from the Bible until the roads in Mountain Springs again opened.

George was on the couch in front of the fireplace. He seemed so relaxed, so peaceful. Who and what had caused his life to nearly be stolen from him?

He smiled at her, and she could feel the blush creeping up her cheeks. When had she become so affected by him? True, she was attracted to his kind and patient nature toward her kids and his ability to persevere through pain and difficulty.

Their gazes connected for several beats. Not an awkward moment of silence at all, but rather an introspective one. She had grown to like him in this short amount of time together, despite her reservations and concerns.

She took a seat beside him. "Jordan lost his first upper tooth. A milestone."

"I noticed that."

"They are growing up way too fast. It seems like just yesterday they were babies." Mariah sighed. She wouldn't trade motherhood for the world, but she did wish time would slow, even slightly. She lowered her voice to a whisper. "I hope the tooth fairy remembers to visit. Jordan wants to stay awake late and see if he can see her when she leaves the money."

George chuckled. "Imagine the stories he could tell his sister if he achieved that feat."

"I'm sure with some creative license thrown in for good measure."

"You're doing a great job with them, Mariah."

"Thank you. It hasn't been easy, and I couldn't have done it without my parents. I was born and raised in Briggs. Mom retired recently, and my parents moved to Mountain Springs. It was always Dad's dream to have a cabin in the mountains, and since he was already retired, moving wasn't an issue. Mountain Springs is known for being a peaceful and tranquil town away from the hustle and bustle. It's just big enough with a population of about 700 to be considered a town with some amenities, but far from being like Windfield or even Briggs with a population of about 30,000 people. We go to Briggs about once a week for groceries and the homeschool co-op, but other than that, church, play dates, and quick grocery runs are available here in our humble village."

George repositioned his leg on the pillow. "Briggs?"

Mariah watched George's expression as if he was trying to recall something. "It's about twenty miles away down the mountain. A nice town, but it's really grown in the last several years."

"Every time I hear that name, it sounds vaguely familiar. Not sure why." He shrugged. "Maybe I lived there."

Why was he so easy to talk to? Brandon had never been easy to talk to and rarely cared about anything that concerned her. There she went, comparing George to Brandon again.

And when Mariah did compare the two, George clearly came out the winner.

"I'm so grateful for Mom and Dad. At first, I was hesitant. This was their dream, and they were empty nesters. I didn't want to crash that dream."

"I doubt you crashed that dream. You and your mom seem really close."

"We are. I love my mom to pieces. The three of us have almost always been close, and as an only child, I never had siblings, so..." her voice trailed as she recalled the wish of her heart to have a sister or a brother. "

She reached down and tugged the afghan over her legs. "It has to be hard on you not knowing about your family."

"It is. Just praying I'll someday remember."

"I'm praying for you too." She didn't add that her fervent prayers including praying for— well, actually begging—that George wasn't a hardened and dangerous criminal.

"I don't even know if I'm married or have children."

His words startled her. Just another reason to avoid becoming too attached to him in case he was married.

"How did it go with Rick today?"

"Another interrogation. I don't think the guy cares much for me."

"Rick can be abrupt and brusque when you first meet him. But once you get to know him, he really is great. He cares a lot about people."

"It's clear that he's very protective of you and your family."

Mariah nodded. "He promised my dad he would take care of us if something ever happened. His wife, Carol, is a doll. I hope you get to meet her someday. She's been really sick." Mariah thought again about Rick's offer for him and Carol to move in temporarily were it not for Carol's pneumonia. Perhaps if they'd been able to do so, the threats would cease. "As brusque and gruff as Rick can be, Carol is just the opposite. Soft-spoken, gracious, and sweet. They never had children of their own, so they've become like an aunt and uncle to me and another set of grandparents to Jordan and Presley."

"I'm sure I'll grow on him, but he's quite serious about solving the mystery of who I am."

"As former law enforcement in Florida, he knows his stuff and can't allow a mystery to go unsolved." She laughed. "I asked him to please be kind to you, but I think he's just worried with us not knowing who you really are."

George remained silent, but Mariah wondered if he, too, worried about who he was. She didn't want to think about his true identity. Not right now when she was enjoying their time together. "Rick did a stint in narcotics for several years and some years as a homicide detective. He used to tell my dad all kinds of stories from his time on the force.

"A stint in narcotics?"

"Yes. He told my dad of a time when the Coast Guard seized about 8,000 pounds of cocaine. These drug runners had been smuggling drugs for a long time, and of course, those drugs were filtering into Rick's jurisdiction."

George nodded. "And it's not just the cocaine, but the meth and other hard drugs. Sometimes people are busted with pot and meth at the same time. Just whatever they can get their hands on to sell. Opioids, heroin, and LSD too."

"You sound like you know something about drugs."

"Not sure why I do, but with you talking about Rick's experience, that just came to mind."

"Unfortunately, Briggs has had to deal with a couple of gangs that arrived from other states in recent years from what I've read in the online newspaper. Although Rick is far away from Florida and now in the Rocky Mountain West, he says one can truly never get away from the drug culture."

"I suppose that's right." George paused. "It's odd what triggers a memory and what memories are triggered. Why would I know about drugs?" His voice cracked and he seemed troubled.

"I don't know." Mariah turned her gaze from him and watched the dancing flames in the fireplace. "Maybe you've done research on drugs and that's why you know. You don't have to be on the wrong side of the law to know about things like that." She wanted to convince him, but even in her own ears, her rationale sounded weak. "I know a lot about stuff like that mainly from Rick, and I've picked up some information from the suspense novels—one of the subgenres I edit for a large Christian publishing company—but I've never done drugs in my life, nor do I ever intend to. You could be the same way. Maybe your job necessitated you to know about drugs."

"Maybe."

"It worries me for Presley and Jordan. I have already started telling them age-appropriate things about dangerous substances. The teenage years scare me."

George reached over with his right hand and covered hers. "I have no idea if I have kids or will ever be a dad or am already a dad, but I can imagine things like that would be scary. You're a good mom, Mariah."

She didn't move her hand. Didn't want to. Didn't even want to breathe for fear the moment of closeness would end. Instead, she relished the warmth of his fingers over hers as her heart rate edged up several notches.

George leaned closer, his face mere inches from hers.

"Mommy!"

In an instant, Mariah pulled her hand away, and George did

the same, regret clear in his soft brown eyes.

She transitioned from reveling in the moment with George to motherhood as Presley ran down the stairs, Bibby in her arms and fear in her eyes. "Honey, are you all right?"

"Mommy," Presley said, throwing herself onto Mariah's lap. "I had me a nightmanner."

Relieved that Presley wasn't injured or worse, Mariah snuggled her daughter and allowed her mind to return to George and their broken moment of closeness.

She needed to halt the feelings she was beginning to have for him. For one, she didn't need a second broken heart. For two, she had no idea who he was. And for three, he could very easily be married.

Chapter 22

George watched as Mariah comforted Presley. She was a compassionate and attentive mom. His admiration for her continued to grow.

"You had a nightmare?" Mariah asked, holding Presley close.

"It was so scary, Mommy. There was a mean lion outside and he tried to hurt us."

Mariah kissed the top of Presley's head. "That does sound scary. I'm sorry you had that bad dream, sweetie."

"I prayed that God would help me with my nightmanner and take it away and then I sang 'Jesus Loves Me'." She snuggled deeper into Mariah's arms.

George watched the two interact. While disappointed that the moment with Mariah was broken, he was grateful that Presley had a mom who cared for her.

What was his own mom like?

Presley sat up in her mom's lap and faced George. "Do you ever have nightmanners, George?" she asked, brushing her hair from her face.

"Sometimes, yes." He thought of the dream with the van and the occupants. Or the times he awoke in a cold sweat knowing his mind had concocted a nightmare, but not remembering the details.

"Did your mommy help you when you had a bad dream?"

George squinted, begging a memory to surface—a memory of anything—of a mom or a dad. Surely he had a family. A woman's face flashed in his mind. Short reddish hair and a friendly smile. Who was she? "Yes, I think so," he said, not entirely sure.

"And did you pray that God would take your nightmanners away? And did you sing 'Jesus Loves Me'?"

George pondered her question. For the last several nights, he had prayed to a God he wondered if he knew before the assault. He prayed for the protection that the Psalm pictured in Rick's tattoo promised. He prayed for his memory. Prayed he wouldn't hurt this family that had come to mean so much to him. But he hadn't prayed specifically that God remove the bad dreams. Maybe because that was George's main link to his unknown past. "It's always a good idea to pray," he said.

Presley rested her head against Mariah's chest. "What did your mommy tell you when you had a nightmanner?"

"I remember something about paint."

"Paint? You had a bad dream about paint?"

George chuckled, holding his ribs as he did so. His gaze met Mariah's. "No, it's what I did with the paint when I had a bad dream."

Presley's blue eyes rounded. He had her attention now. "What did you do?"

"Well, I think it might have been my mom who told me this. She said if I have a bad dream, to take a big can of paint and paint all over it and cover it up."

"Cover up the bad dream?"

"That's right."

"What color did you pick?"

George searched his memory. Had he chosen a color? How had this particular memory surfaced? Odd. Or maybe he just imagined it. "I think I probably chose black or dark blue."

"I wouldn't choose those colors. I would choose pink or purple."

"Well, there you go. Pink or purple would work really well to blot out the nightmare."

"I'm gonna try that, George." Presley again snuggled her mom, and Mariah held her daughter close.

After a few minutes of silence, Mariah spoke. "I'm going to carry you up to bed now, Presley. Are you all right?"

"I think so, Mommy."

"Good. Maybe you can dream about the delicious cookies we are going to bake tomorrow."

Presley's eyelids appeared heavy. "Can it be chocolate chip cookies?"

Mariah stood, her daughter in her arms. "Absolutely."

He watched as Mariah carried Presley up the stairs. As all his flashbacks did, the paint memory appeared out of nowhere, causing him to wonder if his memory was reliable or faulty. He supposed only time would tell.

A few minutes later, Mariah returned. He couldn't take his eyes from her as she neared him. He was falling for her, and the sooner he remembered who he was, the better.

She sat beside him. "Thank you for your suggestion for Presley. I think it helped."

"You're welcome." He wanted to reach for her hand again. But the same concerns clouded his mind. He could already have a wife, and if he did, he would never be unfaithful. He could be on the wrong side of the law.

Either way, he had no business falling for Mariah.

"Do you remember anything more about your parents?"

"No, other than that part about the paint popping into my mind and a woman's face. Late fifties maybe early sixties with reddish hair and a smile. It was fleeting. No idea who she is."

"It seems like you are having more flashbacks."

"They are coming at odd times, but yeah, it seems like I'm having more of them."

Mariah leaned back into the couch, a troubled look on her face. Was she wondering the same things he had? Was she worrying about who he was and what he had done?

She finally rose, moving his wheelchair beside the couch so he could more easily climb into it. He could hoist himself into the chair but still needed her help to wheel to his room. Hopefully soon he would be more self-sufficient.

Mariah wheeled him to his room and turned to leave. "Good night, George, and thank you again for your suggestion for Presley."

"Good night, Mariah." He sat for some time in the darkness, praying once again that God would restore his memory.

But he prayed even harder that if he wasn't married and he wasn't a criminal, that he was the kind of man who would be worthy of Mariah.

Chapter 23

Mariah flopped over to her other side, willing sleep to come. Conflicted emotions reigned. The day would come when she would be able to find out just who George was. And when that day came, the answers would change everything.

On a different note, at least Rick was walking the perimeter of the property several times a day. That in itself should make for a better night's sleep. She offered a prayer for his protection and for Carol's healing.

After a sleepless night, Mariah started her morning in a flurry of getting the children settled into their studies, completing a couple of loads of laundry, and baking cookies. Presley and Jordan darted around the kitchen and living room, obviously eager to begin their baking lesson. Mariah opened the bag of chocolate chips. The kids would no doubt love to eat some of the morsels before making the cookies.

Mom pushed George into the living room and assisted him in settling onto a chair at the dining room table. He had changed into one of Dad's old t-shirts. Snug on the shoulders and arms, but fitting reasonably well in the torso. Dad had been a similar size, only shorter in stature and lacking George's firm muscular physique.

Not that she was noticing George's firm muscular physique.

Mom left the room for a moment, and Mariah's and George's gazes met.

How could such kind eyes be those of a criminal?

"You've been doing very well with the exercises I've given you so we'll move on and add a few more. I'm impressed with how far you've come in such a short amount of time," Mom said when she returned.

"I want to be well. Sitting around is challenging."

From George's appearance, Mariah doubted he did much "sitting around". He had the appearance of an athlete.

"At least the infection has cleared," Mom said. "That's a huge praise. How are your ribs feeling?"

"Better every day."

Mariah could hear the smile in Mom's voice. "That's what I like to hear," she said. The woman had been a dedicated nurse for a couple of decades, not to mention the compassionate care she provided Mariah, her dad, and the children when necessary. Perhaps that had been one of the hardest things for Mom when Dad died. So versed in medical procedures and care, yet was unable to save Dad when he had his heart attack.

She could hear the subdued pain in George's groans as he attempted to do the new exercises and stretches Mom gave him.

Jordan and Presley ate several morsels and shared some with George, who determined he liked chocolate chips. They giggled when he made funny faces while eating the little treats.

Mariah watched the scene fold out in front of her. George had a way with Jordan and Presley, and they adored him.

Either he was a good pretender, or he was sincerely a good

and honest man.

Mariah's heart begged for the latter.

With great difficulty, George completed a few rounds of Linda's physical therapy boot camp. While she was right about the essential nature of the exercises, George struggled with the fact that he had so little strength and that so many of the exercises caused him pain on the left side.

Would he ever return to his former self, whoever that was? Something told him he enjoyed working out and staying fit. Maybe he even ran from time to time. And Linda was correct in that the longer he remained unmoving, the stiffer and weaker his muscles became.

At least he could sense God was healing him. The gash on his forehead had become a scab that itched like crazy. His ribs felt a little better each day. His knee was less painful, his shoulder slightly more flexible than before, and his body more able to do simple tasks. A glance in the portable mirror this morning indicated his face featured less bruising.

The reward of freshly baked chocolate chip cookies had been worth any pain and difficulty he'd had to endure due to the exercises. That and the honor of watching Mariah interact with her children. He admired her. Cared about her.

Linda read to Jordan and Presley on the couch, and Mariah took a seat beside George at the table. Should he ask the question plaguing him? He wanted to know, and perhaps it would help him with regaining his memory.

"Tell me about the day you and Jordan found me."

Something in her blue eyes flickered. "Are you sure?"

"Please? I need to start piecing things together."

She nodded and lowered her voice. "All right. Nosy is always so curious about everything, and he had bounded off into the forest." At his name, Nosy's head rose, and his eyes seemed to declare innocence. "At first, I thought he was just chasing an animal. A storm was brewing, so I wasn't sure we should follow him, but Jordan was already after Nosy. A while later, Nosy led us to you. You were by the ravine on your back. At first, I had only seen your foot. I wasn't sure if you were dead or alive. I'll never forget your image that day." Her words stumbled. "I knew that if we didn't try to get you back to the cabin, you would die. But the storm..."

"Thank you." His voice cracked. "Thank you for not leaving me there. It probably put you and Jordan at risk."

She bit her lip. "I prayed so much on the way back to the cabin."

Mariah likely weighed half of what he did. "How did you manage to get me back?"

"I dragged you through the snow. Jordan helped, and Nosy somewhat led the way."

"You saved my life. If you hadn't brought me here—" He owed her everything.

"It's what anyone would have done."

"Not anyone," he countered.

"We weren't sure you were going to make it. It was weird. Usually, we could call 911 in a situation like this, but with the tower down and no way to take you to the ER in Briggs, we did what we had to do. Rick still hasn't been able to get a signal."

George had a feeling he wasn't accustomed to being on the receiving end of charitable acts. Yet, what Mariah and her family had done went far beyond charitable. "Thank you."

"You're welcome."

A wisp of her auburn hair had come loose from her ponytail,

and he gently tucked it behind her ear.

An indiscernible expression crossed her face. She didn't know him.

He couldn't blame her. He didn't even know himself.

———

George wrestled with the covers. No matter what, he could not find rest or relief.

He was running down the alley, Deb beside him and Psycho Eyes in front of him. The flashing lights reflected in the windows of the businesses. "Hurry up!" Deb shouted.

Was she talking to him?

Dawson gained ground then, coming from behind, alerting George to his presence. The skinnier man removed his gun from the small of his back and took a shot at a police officer running after them. George dared to take a look to see if the officer was hit before continuing his escape.

While the marathon down the alley seemed to take a considerable amount of time, George wasn't breathing as heavily as Deb and Dawson were. Instead, his lungs welcomed the night air, as he inhaled the smell of possible rain with each breath.

His long hair blew back in the breeze created by his fast movement.

Long hair?

"Hurry up, idiot!" Alroy's voice rang in his ears and George stepped up the pace, although it was clear Alroy was speaking to Dawson from the way he shoved him forward.

"Stop! Police!"

The voices of law enforcement competed with the shrill sounds of the sirens. Graffiti on one of the brick walls of an alley business reminded George he wasn't in the safest of places. But for some reason, he wasn't fearful.

He fingered his own weapon in a holster at his side, the motion of his legs causing the holster to move slightly against his thigh. A red van circled at the end of the alley, skidding to a stop. Tiny threw open the door, and Psycho Eyes and Deb flung themselves into the vehicle. George dove in, followed by Alroy, then Dawson, whose legs dangled out the door while Tiny put the van into drive and took off down the road.

George leaned on one knee to help Dawson into the van, yanking the man half his size into the middle seat with a quick thrust.

"Shut the door!" Tiny shouted.

Alroy scowled. "Should have just left him there."

George took a place on the seat. Deb, Dawson, and Psycho Eyes gasped for breath. Dawson lit up a cigarette, and Tiny reached for his vape pen.

A box of baggies filled with a white substance on the van's floor became illuminated in the traffic lights. Beside it, three high-powered weapons slid with the motion of the van.

"Drive faster!" demanded Deb.

A glance behind them reaffirmed George's suspicions that they were about to be apprehended.

Was he having a nightmare or was this another key to his past?

———

Mariah couldn't believe she had forgotten. The second her disappointed son arrived at the breakfast table as she served the bowls of cereal, she realized her mistake.

Jordan stuck out his lower lip and slid a bit roughly into his chair at the table. Her eye caught George's in an uncomfortable silence, and he looked from her to her son. "The tooth fairy forgot all about me. I've lost three teeth and this one is the first time she forgot to come. I woked up and there was no money in the wooden box where I put my tooth."

"Sounds like you're pretty disappointed."

"Yes, I am," he pouted.

Mariah held her breath. How would George handle the situation of her accidental negligence? Jordan was looking forward to the tooth fairy money so he could purchase that new set of building blocks he'd had his eye on and for which he'd been saving his money.

"Well," George began. "I think I heard somewhere that there are thousands of kids who lose their teeth each day."

Jordan's eyes widened. "Really? Like millions?"

"How many is thousands?" Presley asked.

George blew out a breath. "Thousands is a lot. Maybe like how many pinecones are in the forest in the summer."

"That's a lot," Presley agreed.

"So, if it's true that there are thousands of kids who lose their teeth each day, then the tooth fairy is quite busy. She cares a lot about kids and it makes her sad when she disappoints them, but sometimes she flies right over a house because she is so busy and in such a hurry."

"Such a hurry to get it all done before it's daytime, you mean," suggested Jordan.

George nodded. "Exactly. She only has the nighttime to make the switch of the tooth for the money. If she doesn't flutter her wings super fast and zip through the night sky, she might not get the job done."

"Do you think she'll remember tonight?"

"Oh, probably. In the meantime, it's always a good idea to

show her..."

Jordan steepled his fingers as though much older than his seven years. "In the meantime, show her grace."

"Very good. Yes. And forgiveness."

"I knew you were gonna say 'grace' because Mom always says to show each other grace when someone is crabby." Jordan tossed a glance at his younger sister.

George chuckled, a nice laugh Mariah would miss when he no longer resided in their home. "Your mom is right. That's a good thing to remember."

"And patience," said Presley. "But Grandma says never pray for patience."

That solicited a round of laughter. "I'm glad you've been listening," said Linda as she poured milk in the children's cups.

"Thank you," Mariah mouthed when George looked her way. He smiled, and the heat rose up her face.

There was no doubt she was falling for George.

Chapter 24

A flashback hit George then with the force of a hurricane. He was in a dank and filthy room, lounging on a sunken couch that had long lost its firmness. Alroy sat beside him, passed out, his acne-covered face tilted back and his mouth open. Track marks marred his arms and his anorexic body sprawled over the brown cushions of the couch. Deb and Psycho Eyes sat perched in the far corner kissing in between drags on some weed. Tiny devoured some potato chips on a dingy recliner next to the couch, and Dawson paced the room, hyper as usual, while he vaped.

Beer cans, baggies of crystal meth, and an impressive collection of firearms lined the opposite part of the room. A pungent odor of a mixture of cigarette smoke, vape, body odor and pot strangled George's nasal passages.

He flipped his long hair over his shoulder and tossed a box of cigarettes on the scratched coffee table in front of the couch.

A loud rap at the door garnered everyone's attention, except Alroy's. He remained in his unconscious condition, a bottle of pills and a can of beer in his lap.

"Finally!" growled Tiny. "Don't everyone rush to the door,"

he said, struggling to wedge his hefty self from the recliner. "Who's got the dough?"

When no one answered, Tiny dug into his pocket and produced a roll of bills. "Got it this time, I guess," he muttered.

The knocking continued until Tiny opened the door. A pimply-faced teenager stood there with two boxes of Brambilla's Pizza. "Hello," the kid said, obviously nervous. He shifted his feet, his skinny arms failing to sustain the boxes' weight. "That'll be $32.04." He handed the pizzas to Tiny.

Tiny, in return, threw a wad of bills out the door. "Go fetch it if you want it," he crowed.

The kid opened his mouth to say something, then apparently thought better of it. "Yeah, okay, then."

Tiny slammed the door. "Stupid kids these days." He tossed the pizzas on a dilapidated table behind the recliner. Opening the lid, he wasted no time reaching for two pieces at once, his beefy hands curling around the crust and his enormous mouth inhaling the pizza.

George's stomach rumbled. He rose to claim a piece of pepperoni thin crust before Tiny ate it all. Of course, if he continued watching Tiny inhale the pizza and chew with his mouth open, he may no longer have an appetite.

Just watching Tiny eat was an appetite suppressant.

George grabbed two pieces and returned to the couch. Deb, Dawson, and Psycho Eyes each took a couple of pieces. Deb's cell rang and she cursed before answering it. "Yeah. Okay. We'll meet you there in a half hour." She clicked off and announced in a quiet voice—quite possibly the only time she was quiet—"They'll meet us in the alley behind the Briggs Pawn Shop in a half hour."

"They want it all?" Psycho Eyes asked.

"Yep."

"Good job, my queen." He kissed Deb hard on the lips and she returned his passion. George nearly gagged on his pizza.

I take that back. Deb and Psycho Eyes are better appetite suppressants than Tiny.

<hr>

A knock on the front door startled Mariah. She jolted from her chair, her mind temporarily sidetracked from schooling Presley and Jordan. An efficient peek indicated Rick standing on the porch, his head on a swivel.

Mariah suggested the children find Nosy and spend some time with him while she, Mom, and George chatted with Rick. Concern crept into her mind at the expression on her neighbor's face.

Rick walked through the door, and she closed it behind him. "So glad it's you," she said.

"I have a few things to tell you. First of all, Carol is doing much better but is still weak with a lingering cough."

"An answer to prayer," said Mom.

Rick nodded. "It is. And now, secondly, I thought we'd have a break from these goons. After all, I hadn't seen anything during my walks around the perimeters of our homes. Not even the sound of a snow machine in the distance. I walked a short distance and passed several of the other houses nearby, and nothing looked suspicious or out of place. I'd hoped they'd given up their pursuit of George." He focused his attention on George. "They're still around."

Mom gasped.

"They took a can of spray paint to your garage door."

Mom's breath shook. "Do I dare ask what it said?"

Rick took his cell phone from his pocket and pressed a few

buttons. "I took a picture of it."

Mariah and Mom stared at the photo Rick had captured with his phone. The words 'U WILL PAY' littered the garage door in bright red spray paint.

"This is obviously a threat. These guys have to be stopped," interjected George.

"I agree." He gazed at his captive audience. "Which brings me to a bit of good news. The cell tower has been fixed. We can now call the police. The bad news is that the road is still closed due to the avalanche."

"At least we can call the police," said Linda. "That's a start."

Rick nodded. "I know it's a pain to have to go to one of the two places on our properties where we can actually get a signal. I was going to call, but I think it ought to be you, Mariah. Obviously to let them know what's been going on, but also to ask if there have been any missing persons reports filed."

The thought filled her with hope and dread both at the same time. "Good idea, but if they see George..."

"Right. I've already thought of that," said Rick. "The closest place nearby for you to get a signal is the far end of your driveway. The other is over behind my house. We'll load George into your car from the garage. Your windows are tinted, but we'll disguise him anyway. You'll be sure your doors are locked and I'll be standing nearby to keep a lookout. You'll need to make this as efficient as possible."

"Do you think it's absolutely necessary that I join in the call?" George asked.

"I thought of that too." Rick stroked the beginnings of stubble on his chin. "I do think it's necessary. They will want to ask you some questions Mariah won't be able to answer. It's starting to snow again and the wind has picked up, but I know the sheriff's office and medical personnel can get here by snowmobile on one of the county trails once the weather improves and the avalanche is cleared."

"Maybe we could also make an appointment for George for next week. The road should be open by then, don't you think, Rick?" Linda asked.

"Could be before that. I know they're working as quickly as possible to restore everything." Rick took his usual stance, feet apart and hands on his hips, and nodded toward George. "Mind if I come back after lunch and you and I can brainstorm? Now that I have the internet, although not fully reliable—but then it never is up here in Mountain Springs—could be that we solve this mystery of who you really are."

"Sure."

Something indiscernible flitted across George's expression. What would Rick find?

George wasn't sure about Rick's suggestion. Seemed risky to him. The thought of Mariah being in what could possibly be the crosshairs of a dangerous gang and not even know it did not sit well with him.

And he, in his weakened and powerless state, frustrated himself. He couldn't even protect the woman he was beginning to care for.

How pathetic was that?

Secondly, if these criminals bent on finding him recognized him, they would come after Mariah and her family and make good on their promise to take revenge if she lied about allowing him to stay in her home.

"Rick, are you sure this is a good idea? So much bad could

happen."

"They won't see you. Not on my watch. You'll sit in the back seat. I honestly think you could provide information to them that could be helpful."

"Even with my lack of memory?"

"Even so."

Chapter 25

It took Mom, Rick, and Mariah to load a disguised George into the backseat of the SUV. Mariah started the engine and backed out of the garage.

Rick surveilled the area from a clump of aspen trees at the end of the driveway.

"This should be the place we get the signal," Mariah said, more to herself than to George. In years past, people had landlines for when cell phones didn't work, service was spotty, or for peace of mind in a storm. She wished that was true now, but landlines had become rare for the most part. If they'd had a landline, the police would have already arrested the three who'd harassed Mariah and her family, and George would have received the medical care he needed.

Mariah put the SUV in park, made sure the doors were locked, and blared the heater. Offering a prayer, she inhaled. This was as good a time as any.

Her heart raced as she reached for the phone and made sure she had a signal. She turned in her seat and faced George. "Are you ready?" she asked.

"Ready as I'll ever be."

Rick suggested that they first contact the Briggs County Sheriff's Department and relay the information about the criminal activity. They should then proceed with calling the Briggs Police Department.

Mariah dialed the number. After explaining they needed to speak to an officer, the receptionist transferred them. She placed her cell phone on speaker.

"Sheriff's Office, this is Deputy Bissell."

"Deputy Bissell, my name is Mariah Holzman. I live in Mountain Springs, and we've had several situations with a group of dangerous people."

Deputy Bissell listened as Mariah relayed the assaults, trespassing, and graffiti. He offered his concerns and a plan. "While the only road in and out of Mountain Springs has been closed by an avalanche, we do have a new deputy—Deputy Rivera— who resides in the community and who just started working for our department last week. I will get a hold of him and have him get in touch with you as soon as possible."

"Thank you, Deputy Bissell. One other thing, have you had any missing persons in Briggs County?"

Mariah could hear the deputy clicking on a computer keyboard. "No, we haven't had any missing persons for at least several decades."

She thanked the deputy and figured she would explain the entire situation about finding George to Deputy Rivera when he arrived at the cabin. The officer could then also meet George and ask him any further questions.

Mariah clicked off and placed the next call, grateful that Deputy Bissell would be sending a deputy to Mom's house soon so they could explain the situation and make a plan of protection, and hopefully, apprehension of the criminals.

She dialed the next number.

"City of Briggs Police Department. This is Officer Wong."

Mariah once again held the phone so George could hear the conversation. "Officer, my name is Mariah Holzman, and I'm calling from Mountain Springs. I was wondering if you have a moment."

"Certainly. How can I be of assistance?"

Mariah held her breath and nodded at George. When he shook his head, she continued, praying for where to start. "Do you have any missing persons in Briggs, Mountain Springs, or the surrounding areas?"

"Not at the current moment. Why do you ask?"

George offered her a reassuring smile that nearly derailed her conversation completely. "My son and I found a man in the forest near our home last week."

"Is he alive?"

"Yes. He was severely injured and we weren't sure he was going to make it. Because of the blizzard and the cell tower being down, we were unable to call 911. However, we did bring him to our home and have cared for him since finding him."

"Interesting. Can you give me a physical description?"

George moved his head closer to hers so he could hear the conversation. She inhaled a pleasant woodsy smell—likely the shaving cream he had used to shave this morning. His closeness nearly undid her, and she prayed for the ability to stay on task.

"Yes. He is about 6'1", blond hair, brown eyes, and..."

"Please continue."

"He has a muscular build." The mention caused heat to warm her face, and Mariah wished she could turn completely from George's scrutiny.

"What age do you estimate him to be?"

Mariah looked at George. Did he even know how old he was? As if hearing her internal question, he shrugged. "I would guess him to be in his late twenties or early thirties."

"So, you and your son found him in the forest near Mountain Springs. What is your exact address, ma'am?"

"Our address is 430 Deer Lane."

It sounded through the phone as though Officer Wong was writing down the information. "Do you feel as though you are in any type of danger from this man?"

"No."

"What is the man's current condition? Was he able to give you a name?"

"He is healing, but my mother, who is a nurse, says he has a traumatic brain injury. He also has some amnesia and other injuries. We've been referring to him as 'George.'"

George knitted his brows together, and Mariah remembered that as far as he was concerned, "George" was his real name. They should have given him a better name, what with all the options these days. "It seems clear to my mother and me—I reside at my mother, Linda's, home, that George had been assaulted and left to die where we found him."

"This is definitely something we will investigate. Do you feel that his injuries require immediate medical assistance?"

"No, sir. However, he needs to see a medical professional. My mom has been able to provide care, but we aren't sure of his long-term prognosis."

"All right. If you felt that he was in need of urgent medical care, I would see what we could do about somehow getting a search and rescue team to your home and bringing him to the hospital here in Briggs, although with the roads closed, including the county snowmobile trail our medical personnel often use..."

Was George healing properly? Did he need to see a doctor sooner rather than later? She looked into his eyes, wondering his thoughts on the matter. He shook his head. "Officer, I think he is fine for the time being, although as soon as the avalanche is cleared and the road opens, he should definitely be seen. My mom has begun physical therapy with him as well, but that's not her specialty. He will require a lot of that."

"The roads are expected to be cleared and open in three days. The avalanche caused an impassable road, so it's taking longer than we anticipated. Do you think he could wait three days to see a doctor?"

"I do."

"And do you think he will be physically able to ride in your vehicle to the appointment, or will we need to send an ambulance?"

"I think he's fine to ride in our vehicle."

"And he has no recollection of his name or any other identifying information?"

George shook his head. "No," answered Mariah.

"When he is able to come to Briggs, we will want to get his statement and question him further. Can you give me more details about his injuries?"

An image of George's wounded body the day she and Jordan found him flashed through her mind. Only by God's grace had he survived all he'd been through. "A blow to the head, some fractured ribs, a knee injury, and..." she paused as a shiver of the terror of what had really happened to this man again entered her thoughts. "And some stab wounds."

"Stab wounds?"

Mariah knew this changed Officer Wong's perception of the incident. She wanted to know if there were any most wanted individuals in the Briggs area. If there was, would George be on the list? She shivered, despite the warmth from the heater blowing on her full blast.

"Yes, and he does have nightmares and flashbacks, but doesn't seem to be able to recall important details. My mom mentioned that a traumatic brain injury can have a highly variable rate of presentation." She could hear something that sounded like a pen scratching on paper. Several beats ticked by before Officer Wong again spoke.

"All right. Please let me know when you plan to have your doctor's appointment, and either I or one of our other officers can either meet you at the doctor's office or we can arrange for you to come down to the station. We'll begin working on this case with the sheriff's office and see if we can help George restore his identity. In the meantime, please feel free to reach out if he remembers anything else."

Mariah caught George's nod in the rearview mirror. "Yes, sir, we will. Thank you. I did contact the Sheriff's Department and they are sending an officer by the name of Deputy Rivera who resides in Mountain Springs to speak with us about that and about some other issues we've been dealing with."

"Sounds good. I will be in touch with Deputy Rivera. Our departments work well together."

Mariah clicked off. She turned and noticed a strange expression on George's face. "Are you all right?"

"Yes. It's just that everything is so hazy. That and from what I could hear of the officer's voice, it sounded vaguely familiar."

She sensed the concern in his tone. "That could certainly mean anything."

"True." His forehead puckered.

Mariah reached toward him and placed a hand on his muscular arm. "At least Deputy Rivera will be arriving shortly."

George covered her cold hand with his warm one but didn't look her in the eye.

What would the deputy discover about George when he

arrived at the cabin?

Chapter 26

As he listened to Mariah relay the information to the officer on the phone, George's mind remained on the woman who'd saved his life. Her proximity to him. Her pretty face. The scent of something flowery in her hair. Her sparkling blue eyes. Her full lips. His growing attraction to her.

All the pain he could cause her due to his real identity.

And even more concerning, the pain he could cause his wife—if he had a wife—if he allowed himself to fall for Mariah.

He should lean away from her. Distance himself. But what his mind dictated, his heart struggled to ignore.

George drew a lungful of air as an awkward moment passed before the sound of the wind whistling through the SUV door again alerted George to reality.

He didn't want to take his eyes off her. Didn't want a break in the moment.

"I suppose we should go inside," he suggested.

"Yes."

Mariah put the SUV in drive and again parked it in the garage. Mariah, Linda, and Rick assisted George into the house and into his wheelchair.

Jordan and Presley rushed toward George, excitement all

over their round faces as they showed him their marshmallow creations.

It wasn't just Mariah that George was beginning to care about, but these two kids who had won him over from the time he built a building block creation with Jordan and was given Presley's doll to help him be brave. If he was the man Rick believed him to be, a man who spent time with characters like Psycho Eyes, then it wouldn't just be Mariah whom George would be hurting when the truth was revealed.

A flashback entered George's mind. Two little boys threw snowballs in a large fenced yard. Laughing as the snow pelted their intended target. The boys hid behind makeshift shields, attempting to block the onslaught of snowballs.

"George? Do you like the snowmen?" Jordan's voice interrupted George's flashback. But he couldn't stop thinking of those little boys. Were they his own kids? Was it him as a kid? Was it he and a brother? Did he have a brother?

Presley was saying something to Mariah, and she was nodding and sharing in the young girl's excitement.

Voices clamored for air space around him. George attempted to retrieve the memory again. What the boys had been wearing, what they looked like, who they were. But nothing came to him.

Rick wandered toward George. As if George didn't have enough things to worry about right now. The man who seemed to dislike him more than George disliked grape jelly was on his way to interrogate him. "Mariah filled me in on the phone conversations with the sheriff's office and police department. Ready for some brainstorming?"

A nap—a long one—sounded more preferable. George was not looking forward to Rick's "brainstorming", a.k.a. interrogation.

George lifted himself awkwardly from the wheelchair onto the couch. He was getting better at the cumbersome maneuver, but he was still a long way from making an easy transition.

Rick sat down next to him on the couch and powered up his laptop. "So, do you remember anything from the last time we spoke?"

The guy didn't waste any time.

"Not much. Just bits and pieces." George wasn't sure he trusted Rick. Yes, the guy wanted to keep Mariah's family safe, but George also had the feeling that Rick could be over-the-top when it came to seeking truth.

Rick typed something on his laptop. "I did some research this morning and looked up the most wanted in our county and state. You didn't show up on any of the lists."

George couldn't stop the sigh that escaped from his lips.

"Surprise you, does it?"

What was with this guy? "I have no idea who I am, so nothing would probably surprise me at this point."

Mariah delivered two steaming cups of hot chocolate, placing them on the coffee table in front of the couch.

"Thank you," he and Rick said at the same time.

Likely the only thing they would ever agree on was hot chocolate.

"There are too many to go through on the national scale, or even in surrounding states, especially without a name. Or should I say, a 'real' name?" Rick took a drink of his hot chocolate.

"Yeah, probably so." What if George was from somewhere far away from the mountain town in which he now found himself?

"So, Mariah mentioned your telephone conversations went well?"

"Yes. We spoke to Officer Wong and will meet with him after my doctor's appointment. He says the road should be open in a few days. Deputy Rivera will be stopping by later today."

Rick placed his cup of hot chocolate back on the coffee table. "Can't say as I know either of them, but I haven't needed to visit the cop shops." He paused. "Did you give him some information?"

"Not much to give."

"Surely you remember something. A name. A place."

"I do have flashbacks, but I'm not sure if they're relevant or not."

Rick's forehead furrowed. "Your elusive tactics take me back to the days on the force. Sometimes I really miss it. And then there are other times that I'm glad to be away from it all."

"I know you'd like to believe the worst in me, Rick, but I want you to know that I want my memory back even more than you do."

"That I believe—unless you have something to hide."

"Nothing to hide."

Rick seemed to ponder George's comment. "Well, I've given you a lot of thought. You're not a drug user. Your eyes aren't glazed over, your teeth aren't rotted or gone, no excessive sweating, stuff like that. Linda says you don't have any signs of withdrawal—dizziness, paranoia, agitation, hallucinations, and the like."

"No, none of those things."

"Or maybe you don't use drugs, just deal them."

"Couldn't tell you." Because he couldn't. "Look, Rick, I've had some memories come back sporadically and at odd times. But you assuming the worst doesn't really give me the motivation to share stuff with you."

Rick had the decency to appear apologetic. "Sorry. It's…yeah, maybe I shouldn't be so hard on you. This family is important to me, but I can see I've probably overstepped my bounds."

Probably?

Rick stood and set his laptop on the couch. He extended a hand toward George. "Can we start over?"

Was the guy for real or just trying to try a different psychological approach?

"All right." George shook Rick's hand. An odd thought hit him that at another time, another place, he and Rick would likely be friends. Could the guy really be serious about starting over or just trying to get information from him?

Regardless, the truth would come out sooner or later.

Might as well cooperate with Rick. Who knows, the guy might actually dig up something that could help George with his memory.

"So, you mentioned some flashbacks. Anything in particular that stuck out to you?" Rick again took a seat next to George and angled himself toward him.

"Well, when the kids were showing me their mellow-marsh snowmen, I had an image of two young boys throwing snowballs at each other. I'm not sure if it was me when I was little and maybe a brother, or if I have children of my own."

"Do you remember if they looked dressed in current clothing? Or anything about the setting?"

"They were dressed in snow pants and coats. It was in a big yard."

"All right. Anything else?"

Should George tell him about the people, especially the men who made an appearance in all his flashbacks and nightmares? Even though their names eluded him? Could he trust

Rick when they had started off so badly on the wrong foot? "I've had some nightmares."

"Go on."

"The hard part is that I don't know if they're real or just bad dreams."

Rick nodded. "I get that. My older brother has bad PTSD from serving time in 'Nam. Sometimes he can't tell if the dreams are real flashbacks or just bad dreams with the same characters and scenarios."

"Yeah. I'm not sure about this one guy who keeps making an appearance."

The image of Psycho Eyes filled his mind. His looming face, crazy eyes resembling something in a horror flick, and a crooked nose...

"Hey, quit staring at me, man," George said. Psycho Eyes' expression creeped him out.

"You mean, like this?" Psycho Eyes leered closer, invading the personal space between them. His intense eye contact with eyes that expressed empty darkness, stared with not even one blink.

"Yeah, like that." George spoke while holding his breath from the foul smell emitting from Psycho Eyes' mouth.

"They don't call me Psycho Eyes for nothing."

"You sound proud of it," George scoffed.

"Oh, I am."

He must know the guy well to be so brazen.

Psycho Eyes. Remember that name.

"George? Earth to George."

George blinked and focused on Rick's hand waving in front of his face. "Sorry."

"Memory?"

"Nightmare is more like it."

"Tell me about it," Rick coaxed and leaned forward.

Was Psycho Eyes involved in the assault on Mariah or the

graffiti on the garage door?

George's muscles tensed as he thought of the assault again. If it was Psycho Eyes or whoever it was, they needed to be apprehended. "In my nightmares, his name is Psycho Eyes."

"Psycho Eyes?"

"Crazy, right? It's a nickname for sure. He's got a tattoo on the back of his neck."

Rick began to type into his computer. "Yeah, I think you mentioned a guy like that before. Not sure I'm going to come up with much, but it's worth a try." He paused and continued to click away on the keyboard. "All that's coming up is the characteristics of psychopaths and information about being able to tell someone is a psychopath by their eyes. Was there any other name?"

George dug into his memory. "There was a woman, but I don't recall her name."

Rick tapped again on his keyboard. "I'm going to try typing in 'Psycho Eyes, a.k.a., arrested.'"

Nothing came up, so Rick added the words "Briggs" and "drugs" to the query.

"I think we got a hit. Is this the guy you saw in your nightmare?"

Psycho Eyes's face popped up on the screen. George's heart rate quickened and a shudder throttled his spine. "That's him."

"Friend of yours?"

"I'm not sure. I hope not."

Rick stared at him for a minute, likely wanting to say something, but instead, he focused again on his laptop.

George read the information below Psycho Eye's looming mugshot. "Daryl Breen, also known as Psycho Eyes, was arrested after police found large amounts of meth, cocaine, other drug paraphernalia, firearms, and large amounts of cash. May be tied to a gang."

The photo and caption indicated a date from nearly five years ago.

Psycho Eyes looked like a dangerous dude with his hooded and angry eyes, one of which pointed forward and the other to the right. His physical description listed multiple piercings and tattoos and a variety of scars, along with his height, weight, age, and ethnicity.

He was exactly the man in George's nightmares and flashbacks. But why had George been with him?

Was he a friend of Psycho Eyes, as Rick had suggested?

George pulled his eyes away from the screen. Rick stared at him, his expression lit with concern mixed with disappointment. "It seems like you know this guy," he said.

"Yeah, but I'm not sure how."

"Well, I'll do some more research on him later. Once I get into this stuff, it takes me a while."

George held back a sigh of relief that formed in his chest and throat. Why would he be involved with someone like Psycho Eyes? Why could he not recall the names of the others in his nightmares?

A knock at the door interrupted his thoughts. Rick stood and placed his hand on his gun. Mariah's face showed one of panic, as she ushered her children to their rooms.

All of this anxiety and nervousness for Mariah and her family because of him.

The guilt engulfed him and refused to let go.

The sooner he was out of their lives, the better.

Chapter 27

Rick rushed to the window. "It's all right. It's a deputy."

Sure enough, Deputy Rivera showed up at the cabin in less than an hour from the time Mariah and George had spoken to him. A young man in his early twenties, he took what appeared to be meticulous notes as Mariah informed him of all that had happened. Mom, George, and Rick filled in the blanks.

"Wow, that's a lot. It stinks that the cell tower was down for so long and you were unable to get a hold of us." Deputy Rivera paused. "When they hired me last week to keep an eye on things in Mountain Springs and the surrounding area, they mentioned dog-at-large calls and maybe a property theft crime or trespassing once or twice in the summer months from a criminally-minded tourist, but..." he sighed. "They never mentioned assaults, destruction of property, and verbal threats."

"It'll be good practice for you. I'm retired Tampa P.D. Anything I can do to help, just let me know."

The skinny deputy grinned. "Thanks. I'm always looking for mentors. Wanted to be a cop for as long as I can remember."

"It's an honorable profession," Rick said.

Mariah watched the exchange, noting that something had crossed George's expression. If he was on the wrong side of the law, it was doubtful he'd find that being an officer was an honorable profession. Could he be law enforcement himself? Or in a witness protection program?

If only he was in the witness protection program like the character in the manuscript Mariah had edited. Someone needing the protection of the police, not someone running from them.

"I'll do my best to catch these guys who are giving you problems," Deputy Rivera was saying. He had turned and nodded toward George. "And to find out your identity."

"Thanks," George finally said. His gaze met hers.

"And I'll be in contact with both the sheriff's department and Briggs P.D. Our departments work well together from what I'm told. We'll catch these guys." He handed Mariah a business card. "This has my work cell on it. Call anytime day or night. I can get here quickly since I'm less than two miles away."

Deputy Rivera took numerous photos of the graffiti on the garage door and other pictures of surrounding areas on the property. He then took statements from Mariah, Mom, George, and Rick.

After he left, relief flooded Mariah. Deputy Rivera had promised to do regular patrols of the area.

Maybe now whoever was after them would think twice before continuing to harass them.

"Was that a real policeman?" Jordan asked after Deputy Rivera and Rick left. He had viewed the happenings from his place at the top of the stairs.

"Yes, it was," Mariah said.

"When I grow up, I think I'll be a policeman," Jordan said. "Do you think I'd be a good policeman, George? I could catch all the bad guys and put them in jail." Jordan's eyes grew large with fascination.

Before George could ponder Jordan's question, he was running. Running fast, Psycho Eyes and Tiny behind him.

The mist in the air and the fog chilled him. He sprinted through the alley past a bar, the sound of his beat-up tennis shoes pounding on the pavement. A glimpse in the window caused him to shudder. Long hair, cap on backward, a navy-blue hoodie, and a pistol tucked in the waistband of his jeans.

He heard Deb's voice behind him. He glanced back to see they were trailing him, Tiny breathing heavily and Deb cursing him or the situation or both. He slid behind the pawn shop, the sound of sirens wailing in the background and the odor of cigarette smoke from the bar they'd passed lingering in his nostrils. The glow from the neon signs tinted the cigarette smoke drifting from the open door with an eerie ambiance.

Moments later, the others followed his lead. The police car flew by the alley. Tiny removed the satchel from across his body, his breathing coming in erratic jolts.

"You stupid idiot. Shut up," Deb hissed. "Your breathing will give us away."

A man cloaked in a black hoodie, sagging blue jeans, and piercing dark eyes stepped from behind the building. He spit on the ground, the phlegm glistening against the dark gray pavement. He pulled a wad of cash from his pants pocket...

George didn't need to have his memory back to know that he'd just witnessed himself involved in a drug deal.

He closed his eyes. It was all so vibrant. So real.

Tiny took multiple plastic baggies filled with a white substance from the satchel, followed by several pistols. The man in the hoodie reached for them, his left hand still holding fast to the wad of cash.

Psycho Eyes blocked his attempt. "Not so fast, Greer. The dough first."

Greer's dark face contorted. Apparently, he wasn't happy with the plan but saw that he was outnumbered. He peeled away several hundreds and handed them to Psycho Eyes. Tiny passed the goods to his customer...

George felt a hand on his shoulder and he jumped. He blinked open his eyes to see Mariah standing over him. He bit his lip to contain his breath that threatened to come out in uneven gasps.

"George, are you all right?"

She brought him back to the present, as did the confused expression on Jordan's face.

"I need to go," he said, his voice barely above a whisper.

But where would he go? How would he prove his identity? How would George change the life he'd been immersed in? *Lord, help me. Help me not be a threat to Mariah and her family.*

Unfortunately, Rick returned all too soon with what he claimed was "new information".

Sure. New information that likely wasn't anything George wanted to hear.

"How are you doing, George?" Rick asked, planting himself next to George at the kitchen table. He powered up his laptop.

"Fine." George closed his eyes and pinched the upper part of his nose. He needed more sleep. Sleep that wasn't fitful and filled with insane nightmares and flashbacks.

"You don't look fine. Your eyes are a little bloodshot. You all right?"

"Yeah. Just tired."

Rick had the grace to appear concerned. "So look, I spent some time doing more searches on Psycho Eyes after I did a walkabout around the perimeter of the property. Here's what I found. This guy has a rap sheet several miles long. Born in California, he was first introduced to the drug scene when he was nine years old and 'hired' by his uncle to deliver drugs. No one suspected a kid delivering the 'goods' he carried in a backpack."

George listened intently to the information Rick provided. Somewhere in the foggy cobwebs of what was referred to as his mind, the tiniest bits of recollection plodded through at a sluggish rate. Delivering drugs? Made sense. Psycho Eyes was in the alley behind the pawn shop that night in the flashback. He was in the shack with the drugs prior to that. The drugs in the van...

George returned his attention to Rick's commentary. "Daryl was born in Las Vegas and first entered juvy at thirteen after hotwiring and stealing a car. At fourteen, he was busted for possession of marijuana then heroin. The next couple of years boasted criminal activity as a minor in possession, assault, battery, and theft. One of the assaults was on a family member. By the time he was in his early twenties, Daryl was a professional. He also had been implicated in his ties with the Florez Gang, who moved from California six years ago to the Briggs area, where Breen was residing before being arrested the most recent time."

Rick paused to take a breath. "This guy is a piece of work. He's an habitual criminal. Been locked up numerous times from the sounds of it. Wonder if he's still in prison. Probably not."

Psycho Eyes certainly belonged in prison. The man had no

morals. His hardened eyes revealed what likely hid within his soul.

Hardened eyes that George had seen more than once during the flashbacks and memories.

"Know anything about the Florez Gang?" Rick asked, interrupting George's thoughts.

The name rang a distant bell. There had been other people in the van in that first flashback. Likely members of a gang. Was he a member as well?

"Well?" Rick prodded.

"You know, the name sounds familiar, but I'm not sure."

"Think you're one of them?"

George abhorred the thought. "I hope not."

"For your sake and the sake of Mariah and her family, I hope not too." Rick's voice no longer held the condemnation it once had, but more of a regretful, honest tone.

"If I am, I'll pay my dues."

Rick said nothing, only stared at him. "You don't strike me as that type, but I've been wrong before." His tone turned light. "Once or twice. Three times if you ask Carol."

George chuckled, himself attempting to lighten the heavy mood that had clouded his afternoon. He needed to pray even harder that when God restored his memory, it was that he wasn't someone like Psycho Eyes or involved with him or the gang.

"You have to know that I would never want to hurt Mariah or the kids," George said.

"At first, I wasn't so sure that I could believe that, but I guess I'm softening to you a little bit. Not sure why, though." Rick's eyes glinted with sarcastic wit.

"It seems like I value right over wrong, but all this up here," George pointed to his head. "It's so fuzzy."

"I'll be praying your memory comes back in time."

"Thank you."

"You know, while in Tampa, I did some prison ministry outreach. Not in the conventional way, but by reaching out to those who really wanted to turn around their messed up lives. I realize I'm over 2,000 miles away from Tampa now, but I still revert back to that ministry from time to time when I hear of someone wanting to change their lives. Maybe God is giving you a second chance."

Mariah walked Rick to the door, and George strained to hear the conversation between them.

"Best case scenario, he's a cop. Worst case scenario, he's a drug dealer, and someone's not happy with what went down during a drug deal, hence the reason they're after him."

"I've been wondering if he might be law enforcement. Or at least hoping he is," said Mariah.

"Hard to say, but we'll keep digging for answers."

"Thank you, Rick. For everything. Please tell Carol hello, and that we miss her."

"Will do."

Rick left the house, and Mariah closed the door behind him.

Could George be law enforcement? He didn't think so, not with the interaction he'd had with the gang in the flashbacks.

His thoughts returned to Rick's comment about prison ministry and God giving him a second chance. If George was a criminal, and if God was giving him a second chance to redeem himself for the stuff he had done, George would embrace it. He wanted to be a law-abiding citizen. And if he wasn't, George would do whatever it took to get his life back on track again.

Chapter 28

Rick's theories stuck in Mariah's mind. The vast difference between a law enforcement officer and a drug dealer and which one George was—if either. She reminded Presley and Jordan about their chores, then took a seat beside George at the table. "How did it go with Rick?"

"I told him about a guy who has appeared in my flashbacks and memories a couple of times. He goes by the name of 'Psycho Eyes.'"

"Psycho Eyes?"

"His real name is Daryl Breen. He's creepy, but we seem to always be hanging out when I have my flashbacks."

Mariah shivered. She had to have faith God would keep them safe and this would all resolve. But there were so many what-ifs. So many unknowns. So many fears. The Lord had been so faithful in keeping them safe. In the shed, the garage, and the house. So much *could* have happened. Chills iced her spine. Thankfully, not only had God protected them from harm, but He'd prevented the children from noticing much was awry, aside from them thinking the intruder was the mail-man and that he was yelling, grouchy, and eating too many cookies.

Mom had been a trooper. This entire tribulation had been more than she needed after recently losing Dad. She'd left with Rick briefly to check on Carol, and Mariah prayed for her safe return.

Awful that even walking between two houses was dangerous.

She returned her attention to George. "Do you remember anything else?"

"Psycho Eyes and I are obviously acquaintances," he said, although more to himself than to her.

If George was an acquaintance of someone with that name, it didn't bode well as a testament to his character. She had no idea what to say in response. Finally, something came to her—something to take her mind off of someone named "Psycho Eyes." She cleared her throat. "Do you think he could be the guy who broke in?"

"What did he look like again?"

"Reddish-brown hair, beard, overweight."

"No, that's not Psycho Eyes." Confusion clouded George's expression. "That's not Psycho Eyes," he repeated, "but I do know who he is. I just can't recall his name."

"There was a woman too, and then the thin man in the shed."

This time, George squeezed his eyes shut as if willing his shattered memory to cooperate. After a few seconds, he reopened his eyes. "They're all together in this, obviously, and they've been in some of my flashbacks. Rick said Psycho Eyes is part of the Florez Gang, but Rick didn't elaborate. My guess is he'll go home and look into who this gang is." He paused, his eyebrows slung low. "Mariah…"

"Yes?"

He placed his hand on hers, his fingers folding gently over

hers.

Mariah's breath hitched and her heart skittered. There were reasons—oh, so many reasons she could not allow herself to fall in love with him. Yet, he'd garnered her thoughts so often. But if he was involved in the Florez Gang, was friends with Psycho Eyes and the rest of them, she would not have anything to do with him. If he was on the right side of the law and was married, she'd never do anything to dishonor the Lord by caring about someone already taken. Then there was the fear of a broken heart again after Brandon's betrayal.

So, so many reasons not to care so much about this man who'd wormed his way into her life and the lives of her children.

His gaze connected with hers, and warmth spread through her.

"I would never want to hurt you," he said, his voice low.

"I know," she whispered.

He squeezed her hand before removing his hand, leaving an emptiness where his fingers had once been.

He was drawn to her, there was no doubt about it. Sitting at the table with her, holding her hands, and staring into her pretty face reminded him just how drawn he was.

When George wasn't having nightmares or flashbacks that he didn't know whether they were a figment of his imagination or real—Mariah consumed his thoughts. He wouldn't act on those thoughts until he knew who he was and if he had a family of his own, but he did enjoy those precious minutes spent with her.

The wind blew, causing the house to creak and groan, and

Nosy yipped a time or two. Somewhere in the house, Mariah and Linda spoke in hushed tones.

George peered at the clock on the nightstand. Ten thirty. He dreaded falling asleep. Dreaded the nightmares that would taunt him with bits and pieces of information. Hated the memories, whether real or imagined.

Rick mentioned his brother had PTSD from Vietnam. Likely George suffered from that as well. He forced his eyes to remain open for as long as he could until finally he succumbed to sleep...

And George found himself darting around a looming gray building, its outline framed against the light of the dusky evening. The sign's faded lettering read "Hughes Industries". Black squiggly letters of graffiti marred the vacant building and a broken window graced the far side of the wall. He inhaled a strong odor—paint perhaps? Whatever it was, it assaulted his nostrils and he instinctively covered his nose and mouth with his left hand, keeping his remaining senses on full alert. He crouched low into a squatting position and peered cautiously around the corner. Gunfire rang through the dark night, reminding George of the battle in which he found himself.

He held a tight grip on the gun in his right hand and eyed the vicinity of the one hidden in the ankle holster beneath his pant leg. He should only need one, but he was thankful for his backup plan.

Psycho Eyes slid beside him, breathing heavily, his eyes screaming darkness in the dimming light. He muttered a string of curse words. "Tiny should be here. Where is he?"

As if on cue, the red van squealed around the corner, as sirens in the distance competed with the van's muffler and the shouts from Tiny as he skidded to a stop. Psycho Eyes waved his gun erratically. "He's too far away. We'll never make it."

George saw the cop cars in the distance. They were getting closer. From the opposite side of the building, he caught Deb's petite silhouette making a run for the van. Dawson followed closely behind her. Without warning, Psycho Eyes ran to the van, leaving George in his now-compromised position near the side of the Hughes Industries building.

Psycho Eyes, Deb, and Dawson piled into the van, just as a bullet hit just above the back right tire. George, as if delayed in his response, rose and sprinted toward the van. "Hold your fire!" someone shouted.

The van took off, leaving George in a fog of exhaust. Police cars trailed the van in pursuit while two officers on the ground appeared to have plans to arrest the ones left behind.

Senses keen and on full alert, George's gaze darted around the perimeter. "What? They left us?" Angry, foul language flew from Alroy's mouth, as he ran toward George from his location behind a rusted vehicle.

The two cops were advancing from both sides. George and Alroy would soon be completely trapped. "I ain't goin' down," Alroy said, his next words emitted in a flow of fluent Spanish.

George's heart pumped heavily in his chest. He didn't want to go down either. "Maybe we should surrender."

"Two against two. We can take them. Besides, I will *never* surrender." Alroy pointed his gun first at his own head, then waved his weapon, his movements sporadic and disordered.

Would the young man take his own life?

"Put the gun down," a cop shouted.

"Never," sneered Alroy. He lifted his gun into position and aimed it at the officer.

"You're surrounded. Put your gun down," the other officer planted himself in close proximity to George and Alroy.

Not quite surrounded. Where was the rest of their backup?

George slowly placed the gun from his hand on the ground and kicked it in front of him in his show of surrender.

Alroy aimed and fired at one of the officers. The man dropped. The other officer's attention focused briefly on the downed officer. His gun then trained on Alroy.

Would the cop shoot Alroy and then George?

He wanted to say he'd go peacefully—was fully surrendering. But it all happened so quickly.

Alroy aimed his gun at his target.

In a millisecond, George withdrew his gun from his ankle holster and fired, eradicating the threat.

———

His breath came in huffs, his heart nearly leaping from his body, as George sat upright in the darkness. A painful pull on his ribs and in his shoulder reminded him that reality was inside the cabin, not at the Hughes Industries business complex.

But...he had shot a man.

Killed someone.

The life seeping from one once alive filled his mind, the image vivid.

"No," George whispered.

It had to be just a nightmare, not a flashback. But it was so real, so intense, so authentic.

He took a few heaving breaths and lay down on his pillow, staring at the ceiling. The scene played over and over in his mind. Why had he fired that shot? Why had he not surrendered like he had planned?

What was he doing hanging around with people like Alroy?

Alroy. He'd have to remember that name.

George closed his eyes tight, willing the haunting memories to subside. He prayed—no, begged—God to remove the images.

Reality struck him and he knew. There was no mistaking it. He was not someone who had any business liking Mariah Holzman the way he did.

The smell of toast wafted into the room. George forced his eyes to open. Exhaustion caused his entire body to feel weighted to the bed. Had he slept at all?

Sun peeped through the curtains, likely welcoming a brisk but sunny winter day. George rubbed his eyes, sat up briefly, then lay back again on the pillow. Weariness shot through every muscle, tendon, and bone of his body. He half expected to see Psycho Eyes hovering in the doorway.

If Psycho Eyes was in the doorway and had any ill will toward George, *I'd be a sitting duck.*

George huffed. Would he ever be well enough again to do more than languish away in a bed while having constant nightmares?

Would he ever discover his true identity?

You killed a man.

The voice that prodded his mind filled his body with tension. A shudder rippled through his spine.

You killed a man.

He'd taken a life. Stolen someone's father, brother, son, friend.

His muscles knotted, and his breathing came in gasps.

He couldn't do this. Couldn't go on not knowing.

Couldn't put this family in danger any longer.

With effort, George rolled to one side and propped himself up on his right elbow. He needed to emerge from his cocoon.

But not on his own he couldn't.

Not without help.

Lord, help me. Help me not be the man I think I am. Please. He knew the Lord, didn't he? He'd placed his faith in Jesus, hadn't he? Could rely on God to remove him from this terror, right?

A knock on the door interrupted George's desperate pleas.

"Come in." His voice shook in his own ears. When had his voice ever wavered?

"Hi, George. It's almost time for breakfast," Jordan announced.

George didn't want to go to breakfast. Didn't want to look into the eyes of those he cared for—especially Mariah.

"Need me to push you to the table, George?"

Jordan's bright eyes and the joy in his voice tugged at George. The kid had been through a lot with his dad, and now he had to deal with a criminal living at his grandma's house.

"Do you need help?" Jordan asked again when George didn't answer.

"I'm not really hungry, Jordan." His stomach revealed the lie when it grumbled.

"You will be hungry when you taste Grandma's pancakes. They're the best. Do you like syrup, George?"

"I probably do."

"I do too. But Mom says not too much because it will rot my teeth out of my head." Jordan laughed. "I'll bet I'd get a lot of money from the tooth fairy if all my teeth fell out and rotted at once. I could buy me the biggest building block set there ever was. Say, George, I've been thinking about things."

The boy was so smart. So capable. So funny and an

all-around good kid. His dad was missing out. George forced the panic from his revelation after the nightmare to subside. *Lord, please let that not be true. Calm my fears.*

Jordan took his place behind the wheelchair. "Maybe we could put some really cool tires on this thing and push you in the snow."

"Like a four-wheel-drive wheelchair of sorts?"

"Yeah. You wouldn't even get stuck in snow drifts."

"You should invent that, Jordan." He could imagine the wheels turning in the boy's mind. "You've got a good mind for creating things out of building blocks. I bet you could create bigger things when you get older too."

"Maybe. And we could build a little side car for Nosy to ride in. Could you help me build something like that, George?"

While Jordan's idea was a bit far-fetched, George would never dampen a child's dreams. Or at least, he hoped he wasn't the kind of person to do so. But he'd not be here much longer to assist Jordan with building such a contraption. He'd be behind bars, where he belonged. Who'd lost a loved one because of him? Why had he gotten caught up with the wrong people?

"George?"

"Sorry, Jordan." He rested his arms on the wheelchair armrests. "We'll see what we can dream up," he answered. Although maybe he shouldn't be promising things. Killers and gang members who hung out with Psycho Eyes and Alroy and shot people didn't assist kids with their dream of building four-wheel-drive wheelchairs. The only place George would be dreaming up things would be between the walls of a prison cell.

Breakfast was a struggle. He couldn't meet Mariah's eye, and the last thing he wanted to do was partake in a conversation with anyone except the One who could remove the thoughts from his mind and perform a miracle that what he'd dreamt wasn't real.

Presley placed a piece of paper in his hands. "It's for you, George."

George peered down at another drawing from Presley. There were five people holding hands in the picture that had been carefully colored with a variety of crayons. "This picture is of you, Mommy, me, Jordan, and Grandma. And there's Nosy." She pointed out each person and her pet in the picture.

"Thank you, Presley."

"We watched church on the TV today, and they gave us a lesson about God 'dopting us into his family. This is a special picture. Even specialer than the last pictures I drawed you. That's because this picture is one of me, Mommy, Jordan, and Grandma 'dopting you into our family like God does."

George swallowed hard at the sentiment behind Presley's picture. They wouldn't adopt him if they knew. "That means a lot, Presley. Thank you."

"You're welcome." She beamed. "When I grow up, I want to be an artist."

"I think you'll do a great job at that."

With a twirl, Presley was off to other ventures, leaving George to deal with the mass of emotions that filled him. He was not an emotional guy—or at least he didn't think he was. He figured he was more based on fact and logic than feelings and emotions. But Presley's picture had done something to him that made him wish he could be "'dopted" by her family. He looked at the drawing again and noted that his nose was quite large and off-centered, but it added to the charm that the little girl had tried so hard to portray through her artistry.

George looked over at Mariah. Would she have welcomed someone like him into her life before he messed himself up?

Once he got himself all straightened out, would he even be worthy of her?

If things were different—if he was different—George might 'dopt this family as his own too.

Chapter 29

Mariah and Mom cleaned the kitchen before Mom headed to the laundry room to do some laundry. Presley and Jordan were playing hide and seek, and Nosy was lounging by the fireplace at George's feet.

George. He'd been standoffish at breakfast. Now he sat on the couch staring into the flames of the fireplace.

"George? Are you all right?"

He said nothing at first, and she thought maybe he hadn't heard her. She sat down beside him. "George?"

"I had another nightmare." His husky voice was barely audible.

"I'm so sorry."

Pain contorted his face. He stiffened and perspiration beaded on his brow. "I shot someone."

"What?" Had she heard him correctly.

"I don't know who I am, Mariah, but as soon as those roads open, Deputy Rivera needs to take me to Briggs."

She instinctively placed a hand on his arm. "Just because you had a nightmare doesn't mean it was real."

"It was a flashback."

"Still, it could have just been a bad dream."

He said nothing but continued to avoid her eye while staring into the fireplace.

"George, we will find out who you are, but I can't believe you'd ever harm someone on purpose. That just doesn't seem like..."

"Like the man you've known for only a short while?" He pressed his lips together in a firm line. "Mariah, you know nothing about me."

His words came out harsh, likely harsher than he'd intended. She nibbled on her bottom lip and fought the tears that threatened. "Rick and I think you might be law enforcement, not even a criminal after all."

"I doubt it."

"We don't know who you are, but we *will* find out."

"And until then, I think it's best I just keep to myself." A muscle jumped in his hard-set jaw.

How could she answer that? If he truly was a man who'd shot someone, there was no way she would want her children, mother, or herself near him. And he could be someone deserving of prison. She truly had no idea. As he'd said, she'd only known him a matter of days.

But that's not what Mariah's gut told her.

But gut instinct could be about as reliable as the internet in Mountain Springs. She'd been wrong about Brandon, after all. Brandon with his charming façade, saying all the right things, pretending to be a Christian, pretending to love her. Until he'd found someone else and dishonored their marriage vows.

Had the traumatic brain injury changed George? Was he a different person than he had been? Mariah recalled a boy she'd gone to high school with who'd suffered a traumatic brain injury that changed his entire personality.

But the fact remained. She knew nothing about George.

Not even his real name.

Her heart lodged in her ribs, an ache moved down her throat, and tears fogged her vision. Having an easy camaraderie with someone, as she did with George, and being attracted to him did not mean he was the man she hoped him to be.

He blinked. "Mariah..."

"You're right, George, but I will keep praying that God heals your memory and that you are not the man you believe yourself to be."

———

George's breath came in hard gasps as he ran on the slick path through the forest. His head ached and his lungs burned. The cold bit through his thin jacket, and he wished for his warm coat. Snow had begun to fall lightly and the sound of an occasional car driving past on the road nearby urged him to continue. He had to get there.

But where?

Taking a quick glance behind him, he noticed Psycho Eyes and Deb following him. Behind them, Tiny. Where were they going? Why?

They called out to him, but he couldn't understand what they were saying. He didn't stop to find out. Instead, he continued to run. Had to get away.

To where, he didn't know.

Within a few minutes, he felt the pain in the back of his head and neck. Then a hit to his face with something. A rock? The blows knocked him off his feet. Psycho Eyes stood above him. Offered a hand. George reached up to take hold of it. Were the police after them? A rival gang? Would they get away in time? Where was the van?

Something connected with his knee. Then blows to his ribs. Crushing pain engulfed him. Saw Psycho Eyes extend a hand again. When they made their escape, would they leave George behind?

And who was hitting him? A rival gang member?

Deb was yelling something indiscernible. She crouched low next to him. Would she help him with the excruciating pain in his head, neck, ribs, and knee?

Tiny pulled a knife. George looked up from his position on the ground to see the blurred figure of someone coming toward them.

A blunt pain in his shoulder. He fought to remain conscious.

Two people appeared to be fighting. Did they want the drugs in the van? *"Just give them the drugs,"* he wanted to tell Psycho Eyes. The pain and torture weren't worth it.

Throbbing pain radiated from his shoulder. A feeling of being dragged across the ground by his feet. His body begged for mercy as he bumped along the icy road.

"Can you take it easy?" he wanted to tell Tiny, whose hands clasped George's feet as he dragged him. But no words came from his throat, only the tortured cries of pain that he recognized as coming from his own vocal cords. Nearly unbearable pain. Crying out to the Lord.

George appreciated the team taking him to safety, but couldn't they at least realize that all of this dragging along the road wasn't doing his aching body any favors?

"Hurry up!" Deb's voice.

"I'm trying. I don't see you helping," Tiny snapped.

"Over there by the ravine. He'll be good there," said Psycho Eyes. Did he over articulate each word or was it the fact that

George struggled to remain conscious?

He wanted to thank them. They could just leave him there and not take the time to make sure he was away from the rival gang. He knew he slowed them down.

Something hit him square in the ribs. Hard. Once. Then twice.

And that's when everything went black.

George opened his eyes and willed himself to remember that this was just a nightmare. *Or a memory.*

Wednesday morning came all too quickly. George waved to Jordan and Presley. Rick and Carol, who'd improved, would stay with them for the day. George hoped no matter what happened, he would see them again.

The road opened late yesterday from the avalanche and George's doctor's appointment remained scheduled.

A large part of him wanted to avoid the entire trip to Briggs, especially now with the latest turn of events.

He would miss Mariah. Their talks, their camaraderie, her easygoing personality, and her pretty smile. He would miss Jordan's and Presley's enthusiasm, their hilarious antics, building creations and listening to Jordan read, and the pictures Presley drew for him. George would miss Linda's patient instruction as he did his physical therapy exercises, and he'd miss Nosy's snuggles. He would even miss Rick's cantankerous mannerisms.

His life was about to change and he knew not one ounce of what his future held.

But God did. And he would have to rest in that, as difficult as it was.

George sat disguised in the passenger's side of Linda's SUV. The wind blew the existing snow across the road where it swirled on the pavement.

Unsettled, just like his thoughts.

The nightmare from the other night continued to haunt him. Even though it was a risk to step foot inside the police station, George knew it was the right thing to do. Justice needed to be served, whatever that looked like, even if the thought of spending time in prison horrified him. He wasn't so completely naïve and forgetful that he couldn't imagine what that life would be like.

Yet both Mariah and Rick indicated that they doubted he was involved in criminal activity. Mariah's faith in him meant more than he could ever articulate.

Linda maneuvered the SUV slowly around the corners of the winding road. George peered out the window, searching for anything that triggered recognition. The blowing snow combined with the massive number of trees made it difficult to see.

Silence filled the vehicle. The awkwardness of fears realized, things left unsaid, and uncertainties looming in the future compounded his worries.

As they drove down the hill and toward Briggs, the wind alleviated some, and George was able to view the beauty of the drive. He'd been on this drive before—likely many times. For sure he must have been a passenger in the van the night he was assaulted. He sought familiar landmarks.

A yellow farmhouse stood to the right. It boasted a large front porch and smoke coming from the chimney. Dormers lined either side on the second floor. As Linda drove slowly past it on the icy roads, George stared at the house. Bare trees lined the long driveway.

The house seemed familiar.

George craned his neck, flinching at the pain it caused while doing his best to get a full glimpse of the house. A barn stood not far from the house.

Did he know that house?

As they entered Briggs, a green sign indicating the town's population of 30,043 greeted them. George glanced out either side of the SUV at the snow-covered town. While there appeared to be some accumulation, it definitely had been nothing like Mountain Springs.

They passed several businesses—grocery stores, new and used car lots, the courthouse, real estate offices, restaurants, and a pharmacy. They drove through the bustling downtown area with its multitude of shops and eateries, then turned onto a main thoroughfare and proceeded up a hill.

All the while, little whispers of recollection edged on the perimeter of his memory.

Chapter 30

Mariah pushed George into the Briggs Memorial Clinic and Hospital. He'd been quiet all the way from Mountain Springs.

As they entered the clinic, the first door on the right housed twenty-six primary care doctors and physician's assistants. Mariah pressed on the blue automatic door button. "Would you like me to tell them you're here?" she asked George.

"Yes, thanks."

Mariah parked George next to a row of three chairs and informed the receptionist he was here for his appointment. It took a while to explain that George didn't have a known last name or birth date. After some confusion, the receptionist was able to access Dr. Hines's patient list for the day and locate George there.

She returned to sit next to George. Dark circles underlined his brown eyes. Likely he hadn't slept well last night.

Mariah placed a hand on his arm. She wanted to let him know he wasn't alone in this.

But so many unknowns...

"We'll get through this," she whispered.

A teenage boy and woman entered. When the boy glanced in their direction, a recognition seemed to light his eyes. Mariah watched as he sauntered toward George. "Hey!"

"Hi," said George.

"What happened to you?"

"Bad accident."

The teenager nodded. "Man, are you all right?"

"I will be. How are you?"

"Doing good. Just here for a follow-up on my stupid asthma." The boy rolled his eyes.

The woman joined them a few seconds later. "Did I hear you say you were in a bad accident?" she asked.

George nodded.

"Well I hope you feel better soon." She extended her hand toward Mariah. "I'm Loraine Johnson."

"Mariah Holzman."

"Grant here was so helpful when my son was struggling. We owe him so much."

Mariah attempted to hide her surprise at the woman's revelation. What exactly was George's profession? And was his real name "Grant"?

George appeared as puzzled as Mariah was. He recovered well and smiled at Loraine and her son. "You're welcome," he said, as more of a question than a statement.

"George?" a tall nurse with a clipboard in her hand called from the far corner of the room.

"That's us," George said.

As Mariah pushed George toward the nurse, she heard Loraine say to her son, "I wonder why they called him 'George'?"

The nurse led them to a patient room down a long hall and to the left. She followed them into the room and introduced herself as Sybil.

"Would you like me to stay?" Mariah asked.

"Yes," George answered, but the expression on his face was

unreadable.

Mariah took a seat in the chair opposite from where George sat. She hoped she would be more of a help than a hindrance.

"I was reading through the notes. You've been through quite a lot, George." Sybil reached for the extra-large blood pressure cuff and wrapped it around George's muscular bicep. She then placed an oximeter on his finger. "Your blood pressure is good, as is your oxygen. The doctor will be in here shortly." With a smile, she left the room.

"George, I can leave if it makes you more comfortable," Mariah said.

"Actually, you'll remember things I won't, and you know my condition when you and Jordan found me. So, I'd like you to stay if that's all right."

"Absolutely." She leaned back in the uncomfortable chair. "Loraine and her son recognized you. Did it trigger any memories for you?"

"Nothing that's coming to mind, although they both did seem familiar."

After a knock on the door, Dr. Hines entered the room. A middle-aged woman with black curly hair and kind eyes, Dr. Hines listened patiently as George and Mariah reiterated George's symptoms.

"I'm going to do a physical exam, and then we'll do some follow-up tests. Dare I say that you are lucky to be alive?"

George nodded. "I realize that."

Mariah squeezed his hand. So much could have happened that could have caused George to lose his life to his injuries.

When George returned Dr. Hines's smile, she nodded. "Excellent. Your smile is equal and symmetrical." She asked him to open his mouth and stick out his tongue. "I'm checking to be sure your uvula isn't deviated to one side or the other, which it is not." Dr. Hines then shined a light into his eyes. "I'm checking for pupil responsiveness," she explained. "I'll order a CT scan, and we'll do some x-rays on your ribs and knee." She checked the stab wounds next. "These look to be healing well. In addition, I'd like to do CBC and CMP blood draws. Sybil can arrange each of those tests for you today if that will work with your schedule."

Thank you. That would be great."

"After we receive the results, I'll have you return here to discuss the findings. Do either of you have any questions for me?"

"Do you think I have a pretty good prognosis?"

Dr. Hines smiled. "Traumatic brain injuries can have a highly variable presentation. That said, I do believe you have a good prognosis, and I will know more after we receive the results. The Lord was certainly watching over you."

Mariah and George met Dr. Hines in the examining room three hours later.

Dr. Hines opened her laptop and viewed the results. "The good news is that you have no infection due to the stab wounds. You do have a couple of fractured ribs that are healing. You suffered a severe contusion on your left patella, which is also healing. Another bit of good news is that you did not suffer any damage to internal organs. I am going to prescribe breathing exercises and some pain medication for the ribs. The thing we will have to watch for is that you don't develop pneumonia. I'll also refer you to a neurologist and a mental healthcare professional for the PTSD, and I'll also write you a script for both physical therapy and occupational therapy."

Mom parked the SUV in the Briggs City Police Department parking lot. "I'll meet you two inside," she said, giving them a moment of privacy.

Mariah took her place in Mom's seat after she had vacated it. "How are you feeling?"

"Tired. This all-day doctor stuff has really worn me out."

"I'm sure. It's been a lot."

"Look, Mariah..." He cleared his throat. "Whatever—whoever I am, I've enjoyed getting to know you and your family. Whatever I've done, I will pay my debt to society. That's my promise."

"I know." Tears formed in her eyes. "We'll stay in touch." But would they? If his criminal history brought to light even worse things than they had both imagined, would she still *want* to maintain contact? The answer was a resounding no.

George reached over and brushed a tear that had slipped down her cheek. "Thank you. For everything."

Mariah swallowed hard. While the SUV's heater produced more than enough heat, a chill enveloped her.

"You're cold. Here." George reached one arm around her shoulders and his injured arm around her waist. "Come here."

She leaned into him. Heard the sound of his beating heart. Inhaled the scent of the soap he'd used earlier that morning. Saw the anguish in his brown eyes.

He kissed the top of her head. "It's all going to be all right."

She hoped so. For George, for herself, and for her children. Everything *had* to be all right.

"I recognize this place," George said. The smell, the sights, the sounds.

Mariah didn't congratulate him on this recollection. How could she? It wasn't every day that a guy remembered clearly the foyer of the police station.

George's right leg shook as Mariah pushed him through the doors. Was he a normally nervous guy or was this just a case of nerves because of the situation? He prayed for the hundredth time that whatever he found out today wouldn't be painful to Mariah and her family. He could take whatever was thrown his way, but for Mariah to be hurt by his actions—

That would crush him.

Linda sat in a chair in the waiting room, and just as he and Mariah entered and Mariah sat down beside him, an officer came around the corner. "I'm just checking to see if my 3:00 is here," he said to someone behind the desk.

The man appeared familiar.

Mariah pushed George toward the meeting room. "Would you like me to go with you when they call for you?" she asked, interrupting George's scrutinizing of the officer.

"Please." He didn't want to do this without her.

"MacGuire?"

George looked up to see the officer walking toward him, an incredulous expression lining his face.

"Is that you, MacGuire?"

The man appeared familiar, although George couldn't say why. And who was "MacGuire"?

Chapter 31

"I can't believe it's you." The officer led George and Mariah down a hall to a room on the right.

He took a step toward Mariah. "I'm Officer Wong. Please, have a seat."

"Mariah Holzman. We spoke on the phone."

"Yes. But I had no idea the injured man you rescued was MacGuire."

Mariah watched George's expression. Nothing about the name "MacGuire" seemed to register any recollection. She directed her attention to Officer Wong. "Thank you for agreeing to see us."

"Sure. I have been in touch with the sheriff's office, who mentioned they have two deputies keeping an eye on your place and looking for the people who have been harassing you."

"Thank you. The sooner we find them, the better." Mariah cringed at the thought of criminals visiting again, even though there had been no sign of them in recent days.

"I agree. And as for you..." Officer Wong leaned forward in his chair toward George. "We send you on a much-needed two-week vacation to your parents' remote cabin in the wilderness and you get yourself beat to a pulp. What's up with that?"

"A two-week vacation to my parents' cabin?"

"That's right. Ms. Holzman mentioned you had a traumatic brain injury and amnesia. Sorry about that. Did the doctor give a good prognosis?"

George nodded. "Overall it was good, for which I'm grateful. There may always be things I don't remember."

"Are you telling me that George is a police officer?" Mariah asked.

"He is," said Officer Wong. "And not just any police officer, but one of Briggs's finest detectives. Transferred here from Windfield."

Her jaw went slack. Could it be that she had worried for nothing these past several days? "He's not a criminal, then."

Officer Wong laughed. "No. Far from it. MacGuire is about as justice-oriented as you can get."

"And my name is MacGuire?" George asked.

"Yes. Grant MacGuire."

"Not George Washington?"

Officer Wong chuckled. "No. Not George Washington. I can't even say there is a resemblance. You're Detective Grant MacGuire of the Briggs Police Department."

Grant. That was what the boy had called George at the clinic. The pieces of the puzzle were beginning to fit together for her. All this time of worry and fear of who he may be and his connection to the people who insisted on harassing her and her family was thankfully for naught. Relief flooded her. *Thank You, Lord!*

She wanted to jump up and embrace George—Grant—upon hearing the good news. Instead, she returned her focus to Officer Wong. "But he has these flashbacks with this gang, and we believe one of them broke in and assaulted me."

Officer Wong tossed her an encouraging look. "There's a lot to this story. We'll be able to share some of it soon. But for now, we'll take MacGuire home and see that he recovers."

So this was goodbye. So many emotions tucked into the span of five minutes.

George—Grant—would she ever become accustomed to using his new name?—glanced over at her from his wheelchair. "Mariah," he said, his voice low. "Thank you again."

"You're welcome."

"The sheriff's office will be in touch with you, Ms. Holzman. In the meantime, please be sure to take extra precautions. As I mentioned earlier, Deputies Rivera and Bissell are patrolling the area, and the sheriff's office is looking for the suspects who broke into your home. I understand they've taken your statement."

"Yes, sir."

"If you have any questions or concerns, please don't hesitate to reach out to them or to me."

"Thank you," she said, in a voice that didn't sound like her own. "I better go then." Mariah stood. Her gaze lingered on Grant. If only they had a few minutes of privacy to say goodbye.

While she knew she would miss him when she returned home, the gratitude that filled her heart to the brimming point outweighed any sadness.

George, aka Grant, was not a criminal.

———

Mariah shared with Mom all that she had learned about

George during their drive to Mountain Springs, including his real name and employment status. Mom had been just as shocked as she was.

And relieved.

Somehow relaying it to Mom made it seem all the more real. Although Mariah almost called the police station to ask Officer Wong if she'd heard correctly.

"Where's George?" Jordan asked when they arrived home. "Did you forget him at the store, Grandma?"

Mom laughed. "No, we discovered George lives in Briggs."

"He does?" Presley's eyes grew round. "Will he come for a visit? Nosy and Bibby will really miss him."

Mariah enveloped her children into a hug. "I know, sweetie. We will all miss him. Why don't you two get ready for bed and then we'll have a late surprise snack that Grandma bought for you at the store."

Any complaints about getting ready for bed were quickly quelled by the promise of a surprise—one to eat, no less.

"Was everything quiet here?" she asked Rick and Carol after the children headed upstairs.

"Yes. Nothing unusual at all. Rivera stopped by and said that the sheriff's office was sending a couple of deputies to find these jokers. I think there's more to the story than we think. On that note, I heard you mention that George lived in Briggs. Did you find out anything else about him?"

Mom ushered Rick and Carol to the couch and put a coffee pot on the burner. "There's something we need to tell you," she said. Mom met Mariah's eye and nodded.

"George's real name is Grant MacGuire."

"Hold on" Rick reached into his pocket and pulled out a tiny spiral notebook and pen. "Spell his last name for me. I'm going to do some research when Carol and I get home."

"There won't be any need for that, Rick."

"Oh?"

Mariah shook her head. "George, or Grant, is a detective for the Briggs Police Department."

Rick quickly recovered from his shock. "I wondered about that. To be truthful, I never really did think he was a criminal." He puffed out his chest. "The evidence actually contradicted it."

Carol rolled her eyes. "I'm so thankful he's not a criminal." She placed a hand on Mariah's arm. "A definite praise."

"Yes," Mariah said, recalling that she'd thanked God at least a hundred times on the way home for the favorable outcome of Grant's identity.

"Now we can focus on solving the mystery of who assaulted him and if they're connected to whoever's been stopping by paying us visits," said Rick.

Mariah hoped that in the midst of discovering the answers to those questions they would all remain safe.

Chapter 32

With effort, Grant wheeled himself to the couch. So, this was his home? Not too shabby. It was dark when Rory, a fellow officer, delivered him here, so he hadn't been able to see much of the outside, but from the limited amount he saw of the inside, it was what he might expect if he remembered himself at all.

Now that he knew he wasn't a criminal.

How many times had he thanked God for that just in the past few hours?

Grant leaned his head back on the cushion of the brown sectional couch in the living room. With the light glow of the floor lamp, he could easily fall asleep. The day had caught up with him, and his eyelids grew heavy.

Having a fellow officer posted in the front in a patrol car relieved him of what could happen if Psycho Eyes or anyone in the gang in which he belonged discovered Grant was still alive. In his sad shape, he knew he wouldn't be able to fight off anyone that meant him harm.

Something inside him stirred. All of those nightmares and flashbacks about Psycho Eyes and his cruelty. The attack. The rap sheet of this man and his cohorts. The assault and harassment Mariah and her family had endured from helping him. Grant would make it his mission to see to it that this gang was put away for good and would never harm anyone else.

He thought of Mariah. What was she doing right now? Could he now entertain thoughts of more than a friendship with her? Would she be open to pursuing a relationship with him?

A scan of the room indicated he wasn't the worst house-keeper—or the best. In the dimly-lit room, he noticed a flat screen TV, a recliner, a gas fireplace insert, and a narrow bookcase. What did he like to read? Maybe tomorrow when he had some strength, Grant could wheel himself over and peruse the books that lined the shelf. What movies did he like to watch? What were his hobbies?

So frustrating that he knew none of those answers.

As Dr. Hines had said, his memory would likely come back. Most of it, anyway. In time.

But Grant had a feeling patience wasn't a character trait he possessed.

An afghan was draped on the end of the couch. It would do little to keep out the cold of the night. At some point, Grant would have to wheel himself to his room, wherever that was, and crawl beneath what he hoped was a stack of blankets. Thank goodness the floors were hardwood. Maneuvering the wheelchair was difficult enough, let alone on thick carpet.

A question arose in his mind. Did anyone else live here?

Just then a knock at the door sounded. "Grant?" The voice sounded oddly familiar, but Grant couldn't place it.

"Yes?"

An officer opened the door and three people walked in. "Your family is here to see you."

His family?

"Grant!" a woman with short red hair and glasses rushed toward him. She plunked down on the couch next to him and wrapped her arms around his neck, nearly squeezing the life out of him. "We were so worried about you!"

"Mom?"

She pulled away from him and placed her hands on his face. "Praise God you weren't killed." Tears filled her eyes. "How are you feeling?"

"Better every day."

She sighed. "Praise God! I never envisioned when you wanted to enter law enforcement that you would be injured within an inch of your life. When you decided to take the transfer from Windfield to Briggs, you assured me that Briggs was a safe community and that you would only be dealing with crimes that wouldn't threaten your life."

Grant wished he knew what types of things he dealt with during a day on the job. But he had no clue.

A tall older man with broad shoulders and graying hair stood beside the couch. "Glad you're all right, son. You gave us quite a scare."

"Dad?"

The man nodded. "Rory told us what happened. We had no idea."

Another man stood behind his dad, a man about the same age as Grant. "I'm your brother, Graham."

He had a brother?

Could this be the same boy who was building a snowman in his flashback?

Mom's face mirrored concern. "We never even thought that you could be missing. We figured you were enjoying your vacation at the family cabin for two weeks."

"Wong had mentioned something about a remote family

cabin."

"Just past Mountain Springs on Highway 68," answered Dad. "No cell service, no internet, just some time for you to relax."

"We won't stay long because I know you've had a long day, but we did bring you some chicken noodle soup, and tomorrow I can stop by and get a list of things you'll need at the grocery store."

"Thank you, Mom."

"Sure, sweetie."

Grant wished he recalled more about his family. From the sounds of it, he was a lucky man.

Dad placed a firm grip on Grant's right shoulder. "Is there anything you need before we go?"

"I'm good, Dad, thanks."

"All right, then. Call if you need anything. I'll write down our number on the way out."

Graham sat down on the couch after Mom and Dad left. "Wow, man, from what Rory told us, you're lucky to be alive."

"It was quite an ordeal. You should have seen me at first. The family who took me in didn't think I'd survive."

"Rory only told us you'd been beaten up and left for dead. So, a family rescued you?"

Grant recounted the story Mariah had told him.

"Incredible. Well, I'm glad you're all right. You're the only brother I've got."

"So it's just the two of us and Mom and Dad?"

"And my wife and three kids."

Things were slowly coming together. "A wife and three kids, huh? So, am I married?"

"Married?" Graham laughed.

"Is that funny?"

"For you, it is. You're like a workaholic. You wouldn't have time to be married."

Interesting. "Do I put in extra hours at the station?"

"That and you volunteer for an at-risk youth program."

"Can you tell me more about me? I virtually know nothing. I couldn't remember Mom, Dad, or you, or this house, or...anything."

"Sure. We grew up in Windfield, but we've all been looking at moving for awhile now since the housing prices there have skyrocketed. Mom and Dad moved first, then me, then you transferred to Briggs PD. You're fourteen months older than I am, and we were practically like twins growing up. You've always teased me that not only am I the younger brother in years, but also the smaller brother." Graham shook his head. "Unfortunately, you got Dad's tall genes, and I got Mom's short genes."

"What else?"

"As I mentioned, I'm married and have two twin daughters and a son. They adore you, and between you and Mom and Dad, they are totally spoiled. Dad and I are both electricians. Mom works at the library."

"So, there's no one special in my life?"

"As in a girlfriend? No. You're too much into your work and the volunteer program to make time for much fun. That's one of the reasons we persuaded you to take a trip to the cabin. That and all that you had been through in the past year. All of us are regretting that now, though, with all that happened."

"Tell me about that vacation." Weariness clouded his mind, but Grant needed to know. Needed to discover who he was.

"You were supposed to be going there to relax and recharge. A kid at the at-risk youth group that you mentored died of a drug overdose. It really shook you, understandably so. You'd also been working on a case, but couldn't tell us much about that. I guessed it might have been something undercover, but you never confirmed it."

His life was far more exciting than he imagined it to be. While he may not remember anything else, he'd never forget the relief he constantly felt at being on the right side of the law.

"Because you were supposed to be at Mom and Dad's rustic cabin in the mountains with no phone service and just the basic utilities, we all thought you were there vegging and snowshoeing."

"That sounds like the perfect vacation. Guess I was supposed to be, but I'm not sure how I came into contact with the gang who tried to kill me."

"No idea. That's a puzzle for you and your coworkers to solve. We wouldn't have missed you for a few more days."

Grant blew out a deep breath. "Wow. This is just all a lot to take in."

"I bet."

Mariah's face flashed through his mind. He already missed her. "So, there is no one special in my life?"

Graham shook his head. "Nope. As I said, you're just too busy to have time for a relationship."

"Good."

"Good?"

"I met someone, and I wasn't sure if I was already married or in a relationship."

Graham slung his arm over the back of the couch. "Okay, so let me get this straight. You were nearly killed, and you somehow meet someone. How does that work?"

"It's Mariah, the woman who found me."

"Good thing she doesn't know the 'real' you. She might

make a run for it."

Grant chuckled. "Very funny." He paused, attempting to take in all that Graham had told him. "Am I a Christian?"

"Your faith is important to you, but in the past couple of years, it's taken a back burner, much to Mom's concern. You used to make sure you attended church, but your priorities have been a bit skewed in recent months."

Not cool. Grant would have to change that.

"What else can you tell me about myself?"

Graham leaned his head back and stared at the ceiling. "Let's see here...you're bossy, get irritated by those less motivated, and you're stubborn."

"Is there anything good about me?"

"Sure, but you'd have to ask Mom."

"Can't think of any, huh?"

Graham chuckled. "Actually, you're not that bad. You've always been on this mission to save the world, hence becoming a law enforcement officer. You take your job seriously, excel at it, and are dependable, hardworking, and dedicated. You're not content to just sit around. How's that?"

"A lot to take in."

"Yeah, so on that note, I'm going to let you get some sleep. Anything I can do to help?"

Before he left, Graham pushed Grant down a hallway, past two other rooms to Grant's bedroom. Finally alone with his thoughts, Grant stared at the ceiling, attempting to fall asleep. But his mind raced as it sought to process all he had learned tonight.

He was grateful to be alive. Grateful that the Lord saw fit to send Mariah and Jordan to rescue him. He was thankful he had a family, worked for the PD, and owned a home.

And Grant was relieved he could pursue a relationship with

Mariah. As he closed his eyes, her beautiful face filled his thoughts.

Chapter 33

Grant limped to her side of the table and pulled out her chair. Mariah was impressed, but not surprised by his chivalry.

"Thank you."

"You're welcome."

Her gaze connected with his, and her heart flip-flopped in her chest. Just the fact that she was able to fall in love with Grant without any concerns made their time together even more special.

Now if she could toss aside any fears of her heart being broken again, Mariah could fully embrace the freedom of a new relationship with the man who had stolen her heart.

Grant looked handsome tonight in his jeans and long-sleeved red henley shirt. The color of his shirt brought out the deep brown in his eyes. Mariah had missed him, having only spoken to him by phone in the past couple of weeks.

"You look pretty tonight," he said, reaching a hand toward hers across the table. He covered her hand with his, and she relished the comfort of it.

They commenced with small talk about Jordan and Presley, Mom, Rick, and Carol. "How is the therapy going?" Mariah asked.

"Slow. Way too slow and still no driving yet. Rory brought me here tonight. Felt like I was a teenager again before I had my driver's license and Mom and Dad had to drive me everywhere." He chuckled, that pleasing laugh that Mariah had grown accustomed to. "How's the editing?"

"I've been keeping busy with work and homeschooling the kids."

"Glad things are getting back to normal. Has there been any sign of unwanted guests?"

Mariah shook her head. "No. I'm so grateful. Deputy Rivera's presence has helped tremendously."

"Deputy Bissell told me yesterday that he's been in touch with you and that they haven't located the individuals yet."

"That's correct. It's scary not knowing where they are or when they could strike next, but at least there are people watching now that the roads are open and assistance would arrive quickly if needed.

"I'm thankful for that. If they're the ones we think they are, they're extremely dangerous." Concern lit his brown eyes and he gently squeezed her hand. "I don't want anything to happen to you or your family."

His thoughtfulness drew her to him all the more.

Grant and Brandon were nothing alike

"Tell me about work," Mariah said, taking a sip of her soft drink that the waitress had just brought to the table.

"They aren't letting me do much. I was off that entire first week, and then Chief allowed me to come back for limited desk duty, mainly because I whined about going stir-crazy at home. Right now, my life consists of medical appointments, appointments with the department psychologist, work, and calling you in the evenings, which is the highlight of my day."

It was the highlight of her day as well.

The waitress brought some chips and salsa and placed them on the table. Grant reached for a chip and doused it with salsa. He took a bite. "My memories of loving salsa are coming back to me."

Mariah took a bite and savored the taste. "This place has the best salsa. I think that's why people from miles around come here."

"Who would have thought Mountain Springs with its small population would have such a popular Mexican restaurant? I'm glad the waitress gave us two bowls of salsa. Something tells me we're going to make good use of them."

Mariah had always appreciated how easily the conversation flowed between them, and tonight was no exception, even though they hadn't seen each other in a couple of weeks. "You mentioned that Rory brought you?"

Grant stared in the direction of two men sitting in an opposite corner of the main dining area. Mariah followed his gaze. She recognized Rory, but not the other man. "There's a story behind that, but yes, Rory did bring me."

Before he could elaborate, the waitress returned at that moment and took their orders. "I'll take a number twelve, the chicken enchilada with rice and beans."

"And for you, sir?" the bubbly waitress asked.

"I seem like the kind of guy who would like the beef fajitas on corn tortillas with extra guacamole," he said, a teasing glint in his eyes.

The waitress tossed him a confused look, but wrote down his request. "That'll be right out," she said, collecting the menus before moving to the next table for their order.

"You're hilarious, Grant. You 'seem like the kind of guy'?" Mariah appreciated his sense of humor.

"Well, I'm not sure if I like beef fajitas or not, or even

guacamole, but I probably do. Guess my memory will return when I take that first bite. I've been remembering more and more each day, but the neurologist says there's no way to know when or if my traumatic brain injury will heal completely."

She respected him for the fact that instead of dwelling on and becoming down about his condition, Grant instead chose to make light of it the best he could.

They sat in silence for a moment before Grant continued. "So, you had asked about Rory. It's a long story, but you should know because it could indirectly affect you."

"How so?"

Grant nodded toward Rory and another gentleman. "Chief wanted Rory and Randall to accompany me here tonight."

"Randall is an officer as well?"

"Yes. They're known at the precinct as 'the two Rs.'"

Mariah followed Grant's gaze to Rory and Randall. The two men were dressed in everyday clothes and seemed to be nothing more than fellow patrons. They didn't even return his gaze as they maintained their own private conversation.

"That's nice of them to bring you. I could have met you somewhere in Briggs."

"That's just it. I don't go anywhere in Briggs except for work and medical appointments. My mom and the ladies from church even bring me groceries."

"Because of your injuries?"

"No. I'm getting around fairly well. It's more due to the attack."

Mariah recalled the day she and Jordan had found him. She shuddered. If it had not been for the healing from the Great Physician, Grant would not have been sitting in front of her today.

Thank you, God, for allowing him to survive all that he went through.

The restaurant filled with more people, and Grant lowered his tone. Mariah was grateful that he had requested a table in the far corner, away from the other patrons. She leaned forward.

"I have permission to clue you in on a few things because it likely does affect you. Most of it is public record, so what I'm telling you isn't a secret."

Why did Mariah feel like she was living inside one of the manuscripts she was asked to edit?

"About four years ago, a gang from California made its way to Briggs, which until then, hadn't seen much in the way of violent crime. We have had our petty thefts, a few automobile thefts, a burglary here and there, some arson and, unfortunately, some assaults and domestics. We had a couple of murders, especially the one year that a man, high on meth, decided to take the lives of four of his former coworkers. That was a trying time for the department. But never did we have the level of crime like we did after the Florez Gang invited themselves to Briggs."

"That's frightening."

"Very. And that's just the beginning of it. Our department worked tirelessly to try to bring these guys down. They were ruthless, invincible, brutal, and calloused, even for as young as they were. You can find out just about all you want to know by looking at online articles for *The Briggs Daily,* but I'll give you a quick briefing."

"Why do you think the Florez Gang chose Briggs?"

Grant leaned back in his chair as the waitress returned with their meals. "The plates are hot," she said, placing the meals in front of them. Grant led them in prayer and continued the conversation, as he loaded his corn tortilla with steaming beef strips.

"I think they chose Briggs because sometimes criminals think our guard is down in small towns. Which is true. We tend to become more complacent. 'Oh, things like that never happen in my town', that sort of thing. People get more lax on keeping an eye on their kids, locking their doors, turning their car engines off when they run into the store to get a quick item. I grew up in Windfield, a town of 75,000. Big enough to have its share of problems. Even people on the outskirts there didn't lock their house doors at night or when they left for work, especially ten to twenty years ago. But things have changed." Grant took a bite of his fajita. "I transferred here and they put me to work undercover in the hopes we could apprehend the Florez Gang and maybe even the dealers above them in the food chain. The police department always uses law enforcement from other counties so they aren't recognized. In this case, it was convenient that I'd just transferred."

Mariah thought of how her own parents had always taught her to be cautious. She cringed to think that the Florez Gang was still on the loose. "Did they target random people?"

"Not so much as a certain demographic. Although in looking through their records at work the other day, I was reminded of how sadistic they are. They wouldn't hesitate to commit a brutal crime against someone if they saw an easy victim." He cleared his throat. "Their main M.O. was to sell drugs, especially meth and fentanyl, that had been siphoned in from California via the Mexican border. While the mileage between that state and ours is a lengthy distance, there is a pipeline and the Florez Gang is only a mere part of it. Again, you can find all of this information online. They're fairly well known."

"Wow." Her knowledge of drug running was limited.

"Yeah. It's an impressive network, but a dangerous one. I

think about our fellow officers in highway patrol and who they may encounter just in a day of work." Grant paused. "So, the Florez Gang was selling their drugs, committing some random burglaries, especially to steal firearms, and beat up a couple of people who got in their way. They were quite successful in opening up a whole new door of illicit drugs for the people of Briggs and the surrounding area. We've seen graffiti increase in rundown areas, and thefts have skyrocketed as well. Stealing provides funds for drug addicts. Not saying this uptick is all due to the Florez Gang, because it's not, but they are a large part of it."

"I bet it was challenging having to read up on all of this again."

"It was. I remembered very little of it, but once I started digging, which was one of the things Chief has me busy doing during my time of desk detention, things started coming back to me." Grant looked up and did a sweep of the room, something he had done many times since they started dinner. When the door opened, his attention focused on those entering. "Sorry. situational awareness training. Once Rory reminded me of it, that part of the training came back to me. Always should be on the alert."

Mariah knew she'd been privy to only a meager amount of what was really taking place. From what Grant said about the Florez Gang, her family was very fortunate to have survived their interactions with some of its members.

Chapter 34

Grant gazed across the table into the eyes of the woman he was growing to love. The freedom to date her without fear of being on the wrong side of the law or being married had rejuvenated him.

There was so much he wanted to tell her about the circumstances, but so much of it was confidential. Still, he would do his best to keep her safe—whether doing so himself or via his fellow officers.

She had no idea just how dangerous the Florez Gang was, and that at the height of their crime spree, several law enforcement agencies had become involved. They'd caught a break from an informant and had been able to capture most of the gang.

He'd learned much over the past few days. How Psycho Eyes had a rap sheet longer than the distance between Mountain Springs and Hawaii. How Grant had worked undercover to find out all about the Florez Gang's movements, their employees, and their future victims. The cache of firearms like one he'd never seen, suspected as coming from Mexico and South America and many times stolen from unsuspecting victims in Briggs who didn't think twice about locking their houses or leaving their firearms in unlocked vehicles.

Up until that one fateful night, the Florez Gang had had no idea Grant wasn't one of them. He'd been effective posing as a criminal.

No wonder he had figured himself on the wrong side of the law after the attack.

"You need to be especially vigilant right now, Mariah. I know we have eyes on you, but you and your mom still need to be aware that these guys are dangerous."

The fear in her eyes was almost his undoing. He wished he could move back to the cabin and offer protection for her family.

Grant reached across the table and squeezed her hand. "I'm sorry. I don't want to scare you. This should be an enjoyable date, not a safety plan."

"No, you're right to tell me what you know. I just wish this was all behind us."

"Me too."

He wished it for many reasons, the chief one being that he could then more actively pursue a relationship with her.

"Officer Wong mentioned you were going on a vacation when you were attacked. How did all that happen?"

The question came out of nowhere and it took him a minute to regather his thoughts. "Right before the attack, a kid I was working with—I work with a group of high-risk kids in an afterschool program—lost his life due to a drug overdose. He'd come so far and was doing so well." Sorrow clenched his throat. Could he have done more to come alongside the young man? "The drugs he was using had come from the Florez Gang."

Mariah gasped. "Oh, Grant, I'm so sorry."

"It was rough. I read through some of the notes and that

was a huge struggle for me."

"Understandably so. I should have guessed that you worked with kids."

A weight settled in his heart. "I had to talk to the department psychologist about that and some other things that are still fuzzy to me. Chief suggested I take a few weeks off. I was due for vacation time anyway. He suggested I go somewhere totally off-grid. Spend some time snowshoeing and just being in nature. My parents have a remote hunting cabin up past Mountain Springs. I was on my way there when the Florez Gang found me. Apparently, before I even left the Briggs city limits. No one in my family or in the department thought anything because everyone was content to let me have some time away. But little did they know how deadly that time away was."

"I am so thankful they didn't kill you."

"They wanted to. Just one or two of the injuries, or even just the hypothermia alone should have done it. God is good."

"Yes, He is."

The waitress returned and removed their plates. She bid them a good evening, left the bill, and tended to her other customers.

"With the Florez Gang still at large, will you be safe?"

"I've got round-the-clock police protection." Grant smirked. "Weird being on this end of things, but seriously, there's always an officer by my side, and there's a cruiser parked at my house whenever I'm home. Make no mistake, the Briggs law enforcement agencies, along with the state crime unit, are exceptional. The Florez Gang won't give up until they find me, but they're up against the best of the best."

They enjoyed the rest of the evening with her talking of anything except the Florez Gang and the danger they posed.

He only hoped he hadn't put her and her family in more danger than he already had.

A woman approached the table then. "Hi, Mariah," she chirped.

"Hello, Tracey."

Tracey grinned at Grant. "Who do we have here?"

"This is my friend, George."

Tracey extended a hand, "Nice to meet you, George. I'm Tracey. I work at the convenience store down the street."

Grant took her hand. "Nice to meet you as well."

Tracey winked at him. "I never pass up the chance to meet a handsome stranger. Well, I better go. Nice to see you, Mariah, and nice to meet you, George." She kept her focus on Grant as she spoke, even when she referred to Mariah.

"You have to watch Tracey. She's always on the hunt for a date," said Mariah after Tracey left.

"Well, she needs to move on because the only woman I want to date is right here in front of me."

A rosy shade colored Mariah's cheeks.

"Well, thank you."

"Good job in telling her my name was George. Was that a slip-up or intentional?"

"Intentional. I figured if she thought 'George' was your name, she couldn't tell anyone she met a hunky guy named 'Grant.' Who knows who she interacts with."

"Hunky guy, huh?"

She blushed again and he grinned, thinking he'd better change the subject before he embarrassed her further. "I'm impressed with the whole 'George' thing. Spoken like a true undercover detective."

"Or maybe just someone who has a crush on an attractive detective."

"A crush, huh?"

A glint touched her sparkling blue eyes. "Yes, a crush."

Grant and Mariah headed toward her vehicle in the parking lot. "We're going to follow you home," he said, checking her backseat when she clicked the fob to unlock the vehicle.

"Thank you. Do you think I should be worried?"

"Not worried. But vigilant."

They stood for a moment in the cold night air. He embraced her, not caring that Rory and Randall looked on. He leaned into her, catching a whiff of her coconut-scented shampoo.

She was so pretty tonight. But then, when had she not been pretty?

Grant's lips met hers and he kissed her thoroughly. Sure, Rory and Randall would rib him, but it would be worth it. He reluctantly released her and brushed her cheek with his thumb. "I'll miss you," he whispered in her ear.

"I'll miss you too.

"Until next time."

He held her again, pulling her close to him as she buried her face in his chest. He could hold her like this forever but reluctantly stepped back after a few minutes. He captured a wisp of her hair that blew in the breeze and kissed it. "Until next time."

Next time couldn't come soon enough.

Grant had hated leaving Mariah behind. As they left the cabin, he'd craned his head to watch as much as possible, for any signs of suspicious activity. Deputies Rivera and Bissell were keeping an eye out, but Grant wanted to be the one protecting Mariah and her family.

During the first several minutes of the ride to Briggs after they'd followed Mariah home, Rory and Randall did, in fact, rib Grant about his affection for Mariah. Afterward, Grant took some time to reflect and ask questions. His mind was still so unclear that he constantly craved clarity. Had he been scared when he'd gone undercover? Or had he been brave? He seemed like a brave guy, but when things got rough, what stance did he take?

"Was the undercover job somewhat successful?" he asked.

"It was," said Rory. "You were in constant contact with me, Randall, Ned Wong, and the Chief. Although when it did go down, it wasn't what we expected. Do you remember anything about the night things went awry?"

"Some of it's coming back to me, and I've had what I believe to be flashbacks."

Randall kept his eyes on the dark road ahead. "You had earned their trust. Developed the streetwise attitude, looked the part with the long hair and beard, and had rehearsed answers to the questions they'd likely ask."

"In the end, an officer was shot by one of the gang members, Alroy Florez. Do you remember Alroy?"

Grant searched his mind. "Vaguely."

"Short skinny wiry guy all doped up with buzzed-cut black hair."

"Yeah. I think I remember him."

"Well, he and his twin sister, Deb..."

"Deb? I've had flashbacks about her." Grant closed his eyes. The petite woman with an anger issue the size of Texas. Yeah, he remembered her.

"Deb and Alroy were twins and were a force to be reckoned with, as the saying goes. Deb was like this with her twin brother." Rory crossed his fingers to indicate the twins' closeness.

"They were out for revenge after you killed Alroy. He shot one of the two responding officers. Fortunately, the injured officer pulled through after an excessive stint in the ICU, although the only explanation for that would be a miracle."

A scene flashed before Grant's eyes. He'd thrown his weapon in front of him on the ground as a show of surrender at the officers' request. Alroy's face registered shock when Grant reached for his second weapon. His eyes blazed in the dark night, his movements erratic and compulsive.

"Alroy was so high on fentanyl-laced meth at the time that no one could guess what was going through his mind," said Rory. "He then aimed the gun at Wong. This is where you came in."

The sound of a gunshot reverberated through Grant's mind as if it happened at that very moment in the car on the way to Briggs. "I'm just grateful it wasn't an officer's life I took that night like I formerly thought."

"No," both Rory and Randall said at the same time.

"In doing what you did, you saved the lives of two fellow officers." Randall's voice echoed through Grant's mind. "Alroy would have killed Wong and the other officer had it not been for your quick action."

"Yes. You saved both of their lives," agreed Rory.

Only by God's grace was he even functioning after all that had happened.

"Unfortunately," said Randall, "the Florez Gang got away that night. After an extensive investigation, which is standard procedure, the State Crime Unit cleared you of the shooting. Chief sent you on vacation for some R&R after that."

Grant whistled. "A lot to take in."

"Any of it coming back?" asked Rory.

"Bits and pieces."

"The Florez Gang decided revenge on you was their ultimate goal. You never made it to your parents' cabin."

Grant inhaled to ease the pressure in his chest. It was all coming together.

Randall thrummed his fingers on the steering wheel. "They found you out and made good on their promise to take revenge for shooting Alroy. We don't know all the details and hopefully you'll be able to provide them for us as your memory gets clearer, but one thing is certain. They meant to kill you in a slow, torturous way by leaving you to die with injuries in a remote location."

It again dawned on Grant that had it not been for Mariah, he wouldn't be having this conversation.

Chapter 35

Mariah opened the email from Grant.

Attached are the wanted posters for two men and a woman. Can you please let me know if these are the ones who paid you a visit? Also, please let Deputy Rivera and me know immediately if you see any of them.

Can't wait to see you again.

Grant

Truth was, she couldn't wait to see him either. The police chief mentioned that it would be best for she and Grant not to see each other for the next couple of weeks. That would give the police a chance to locate the gang and for things to settle down a bit.

Not see Grant? Easier said than done.

She waited to open the email, hovering her finger over the mouse before clicking it. So many emotions ran through her mind as she processed the fact that the people who nearly killed Grant were still on the loose. Grant said it was unlikely they would come back and harass her with the police presence, but that she should be aware they could still be in the area.

Gooseflesh covered her arms.

Would she and her family be safe? Would Grant be safe?

Her mind wandered to the most recent date with Grant at the Mexican restaurant and the subsequent kiss. She never thought she'd fall in love again after Brandon, but Grant had captured her heart.

Mariah returned her thoughts to the email. She clicked on the link to the website, *"Wanted in Briggs County and Surrounding Areas."* Her hands shook as she scrolled to the first name on the list, complete with a photo.

```
Name:   Stan Timmons
Alias: "Tiny"
Sex: Male
Race: Caucasian
DOB: June 21, 1990
Hair color: Auburn
Eye color: Hazel
Height: 5'10
Weight:  305
Markings: Numerous  ear  piercings  in  the
left  ear,  clean-shaven  or  possible  beard  and
mustache
Criminal History: Violent history of crimi-
nal activity including more than one instance
of aggravated battery, aggravated assault,
possession of a controlled substance, sale of
a controlled substance, possession of stolen
firearms, felon in possession of a firearm
```

Mariah cringed as she stared at the looming photo of Tiny. His eyes were hard, and his thin lips were drawn into a hateful grimace. His head appeared almost misshapen with a slim top portion and progressively growing wider from his cheeks to his neck.

She would recognize those eyes anywhere.

Yes, he'd been the one who had assaulted her.

She scrolled to the second one on the list.

```
Name: Dawson Faas
Sex: Male
Race: Caucasian
DOB: February 26, 1992
Hair: Lt. Brown
Eye Color: Green
Height: 6'0
Weight: 135
Markings: flesh tunnel earring in left ear,
eyeball tattoo on upper right shoulder,
   may have a mustache and/or goatee
Misc: severe acne, missing teeth
Criminal history: possession of controlled
substance in liquid and crystal form, more than
one instance of aggravated assault, aggravated
battery, felon in possession of a firearm,
possession of stolen firearms, burglary
```

Mariah would bet money it was Dawson Faas who had broken into the shed. The last and final mugshot and wanted information was for the woman.

```
Name: Deborah Florez
Alias: "Deb"
Sex: Female
```

```
Race: Hispanic
DOB: December 19, 1990
Hair: Brown
Eye Color: Brown
Height: 5'1
Weight: 102
Markings: High-arched diagonal eyebrows,
skull with frizzy hair tattoo on right wrist,
red necklace tattoo around neck
Criminal history: violent criminal histo-
ry including assault with a deadly weapon,
cruelty to animals, possession and sale of
controlled substance, possession of stolen
firearms, burglary
```

This one was a little more difficult. The woman had been bundled up in winter gear when Mariah saw her, but the high-arched diagonal eyebrows had stuck in Mariah's memory.

She quickly emailed Grant.

Yes, these are the people who came to the cabin. Is there anyone else I should be on the lookout for?
Miss you,
Mariah

Moments later, Grant sent her another email.

If you see this man, please also let us know as soon as possible. He is another member of the Florez Gang. Miss you too. Hopefully soon this will all be over and we can see each other on a regular basis. I'm looking forward to that.

Grant

This mugshot was far more chilling than the other three, if that was even possible.

```
Name: Daryl Breen
Alias: "Psycho Eyes"
Sex: Male
Race: Caucasian
DOB: April 12, 1989
Hair: Blond
Eye Color: Blue
Height: 6'
Weight: 150
Markings: multiple piercings, "danjruss"
tattoo on back of neck, serpent tattoo on left
forearm.
Criminal history: Violent history of crimi-
nal activity including more than one instance
of aggravated battery, assault, robbery, do-
mestic assault, cruelty to family member,
possession, sale, and delivery of controlled
substance, possession of stolen firearms
```

While she didn't know him and had, to her knowledge, never seen Psycho Eyes before, he seemed to be looking right at her from his mug shot.

What must Grant have gone through at the hands of these vicious thugs? It was likely he wasn't remembering near all what they had done to him.

Unease permeated every fiber of her being. She bowed her head and prayed once again for safety for her family and for the man she was growing to love.

And that she would never again cross paths with anyone from the Florez Gang.

Chapter 36

Officer Ned Wong stopped by Grant's desk with an armload of files. "Denberg wants to see you in his office."

"Sounds serious."

Wong nodded. "Could be. He said he was going to call a staff meeting later today." He shuffled the folders in his arms. "Hope to get through some of these files first."

"Looks like a job that'll take a while."

"Yeah. Want to help?"

"Nah, I'll stick with the Florez Gang investigation. Kind of personal, you know?"

Wong chuckled. "Well, if you need any help, let me know. I could use a diversion."

"Will do."

"By the way, I know I've told you this a million times, but thank you for saving my life that day."

"You're welcome."

Wong looked like he wanted to say more, but instead nodded and exited the room.

Grant hobbled toward Chief Denny Denberg's office. He had come a long way from using the wheelchair at Mariah's house.

Mariah.

She was never far from his mind. To say he anticipated seeing her Friday at her mom's house was an understatement. It had been far too many weeks spent only hearing her voice.

Grant longed to see her again. To hold her.

When he reached Denberg's office, he saw his boss's head bowed over some paperwork, phone in hand. He knocked lightly on the door.

Denberg both motioned and mouthed to him to come in and take a seat. Grant did so, wondering if later might have been a better time to meet. But the chief held a finger up to him that he'd be only a minute. Grant settled into the worn chair at Chief Denberg's desk. As he did every time he entered his boss's office, Grant glanced around the interior. Numerous plaques lined the walls, including a prestigious "Police Officer of the Year Award". His desk was littered with files, paperwork, several photos of his family, and a coffee mug that had seen better days. While not the most organized person, Chief Denberg was the perfect example of someone to emulate in law enforcement.

Chief Denberg held a burgundy-colored pen in his hand, which he clicked on the end of while he listened to the caller on the other end. Grant could almost bet that the pen was one of the ones from Briggs Community Church where Denberg also served as an elder.

Finally, the chief hung up the phone. "That was a long and tedious call." He shifted back in his chair and clasped his hands behind his bald round head. "So, how are you doing?"

Grant arched a brow at Denberg's question. Usually, a call to his office didn't necessitate discussing niceties. Denberg preferred to do those over coffee in the "coffee corner" of the station. "I'm getting there."

Denberg nodded, a smile crossing his ebony face. "Good to know. Physical therapy going well?"

"It is."

"And you're keeping up with your meetings with the department psychologist?"

"I am, much to my annoyance at having to discuss my feelings on an ongoing basis."

Denberg laughed and placed his hands on the desk in front of him. "It's good for you, MacGuire."

"Or so they say."

"Right? How's the memory coming along?"

Grant would never take his memory for granted again. "Slowly, but each day I'm remembering more. My mom and dad came over this past weekend. I think my dad put out his back carrying the 452 photo albums Mom had him bring into my house."

Denberg's low rumbling chuckle filled the room "What a sacrifice for your dad. But did it help with your memory at all?"

"You know, actually it did. But the going is so slow. It's frustrating."

"I can imagine. And the pain?"

"Getting better all the time. I can't wait to be out in the field again. It's depressing being stuck on desk duty. Feels like detention in school."

"Well, we principals have to make sure our pupils behave."

It was Grant's turn to chuckle. Denberg would have been an excellent principal.

"And are you clinging to the Savior?"

"Yes, sir."

"Good. It's been nice to see you back at church, by the way, even if you have to attend with police protection."

Grant thought of the irony of the situation. He was a cop

himself, but couldn't even attend church without other officers protecting him. "It's good for Randall to attend church."

"Yeah, praying Randall won't be an atheist for too much longer after listening to Pastor's sermons." Denberg quickly sobered. He stood and closed the door to his office, indicating the importance of the situation.

He returned to his seat. "Look, MacGuire. I think we have ourselves a situation."

"Oh?"

"Yeah, so, this came out in today's paper." Denberg reached across his desk to a covered pile and unearthed a newspaper. He opened it, folded it in half, and placed it in front of Grant.

Grant sucked in a deep breath as he read the headline: "Local Officer Saves Baby During Traffic Stop." He glanced up and met Denberg's concerned expression. "Why is this coming out just now? This happened nearly a year ago in Windfield. Was it a repeat of the prior article?"

"That's what I thought at first, but apparently it's a follow-up, and someone figured out you're the same cop. Look, MacGuire, I join everyone in saying how proud of you we all are for performing CPR on that little one and saving his life during the traffic stop. But this was not the time for reporters to write articles about you. This alerts the Florez Gang that you are still alive. The last sentence mentions that, as of today, you have been a member of the Briggs force for seven months. Just what we needed."

"Any idea who offered the tip on this story?" Grant recalled the day like it was yesterday, interestingly enough since his memory failed him on so many other recollections. A tiny unbreathing infant. A frightened mom. A dad begging him to help. Grant's racing heartbeat and unending prayers as he performed CPR while waiting for the ambulance to arrive.

"I had Randall look into it. Seems that the baby turned one today and this was a way of celebrating both the fact that he survived and the fact that we have excellent law enforcement in Briggs and Windfield."

"Both true, but as you said, this isn't the time."

"Exactly. I appreciate the sentiment, as I'm sure you do, but with your looming face gracing the front page and a quote from local people mentioning what a great cop and your involvement with at-risk kids, it won't take long for someone in the gang to realize who you really are and that you are still alive."

Grant released a stifled breath. They didn't need this right now. They were so close to closing in on the whereabouts of the Florez Gang. "We sure don't need them finding me before we find them. And worse yet, paying another visit to Mariah and her family."

The latter caused ripples of protectiveness to rise in his chest. He would do anything to safeguard and shield the woman he was growing to love.

"Not good for the investigation, for sure." Denberg sighed. "And that's not all." He pulled a file from his organized chaos. "Remember DeShawn Korfanta?"

Grant didn't recognize the name. He searched his blurry memory. "Can't say as I do."

Denberg flipped open a two-inch file. "We've known DeShawn since he was about fourteen. He decided to live on the edge and see if he would get caught stealing his grandma's prescription drugs."

Grant stared at the photo of a young man with an angry expression. Close-cropped dark, black curly hair topped an ebony face that was marred by a scar on his left cheek. It registered some vague familiarity.

"That started DeShawn's history with crime. They sent him to juvy for a while. He got out and enrolled in the Project New Start program, of which you volunteer your time to work with troubled young people."

"Yes." Grant did vaguely remember that he was a volunteer there. "But I don't remember him."

"I don't believe you ever worked with DeShawn. Anyhow, for a time, this young man seemed earnest in turning his life around. Then last year, he thought he should form a gang at the age of nineteen."

"What happened that he slipped up?"

"Not sure. His grandma said it may have had something to do with his uncle dying of cancer. Apparently, they were close. Anyway, DeShawn had a few more minor skirmishes with the law that landed him on probation. Randall did some digging, and there has been some connection between DeShawn and the Florez Gang."

"Seriously?"

"Seriously. You know how Psycho Eyes and Deb are always on the hunt for more recruits? DeShawn seemed to fit the bill. Lost, angry young soul in search of something to make him feel worthy. You know the type." Denberg paused and huffed a frustrated breath. "An informant told Randall that DeShawn and Dawson had been seen together at a local hangout."

"And just when we thought Briggs was still a safe community."

Denberg nodded. "Exactly. And Briggs was and is still considered a safe community, and even safer once we get the Florez Gang off the streets. Transplanted here from another state in the hopes that we aren't quite as aware of crime and won't notice their grand plans of drug dealing, firearm thefts, robberies, assaults, and the attempted horrific murders of two of our own."

Grant remembered that night. Had relived it too many times to count. And was now in counseling due partly to it. The night the officer was shot and Grant killed Alroy in self-defense. The PTSD might never go away completely, his therapist said. Add to that the revenge of the Florez Gang on him and their attempts to end his life.

What did people do without the Lord to get them through the crazy, evil times of the present culture?

Grant returned his attention to Denberg. "So what's the plan?"

"I'm glad you asked. We up your protection. County is continuing to do rounds in Mariah's neighborhood. They discovered just yesterday that the Florez Gang was hiding out in the home of some snowbirds spending their winter in Arizona. Unfortunately, by the time the sheriff's office discovered their whereabouts, the gang was long gone, although not without extensive damage to the home they were squatting in." Ridges etched the flesh above Denberg's eyes. "We believe they have returned to Briggs and have some leads on their whereabouts. My suggestion was that we hustle the investigation a bit quicker if possible. The Sheriff's Office and the State Crime Unit are on board. There shouldn't be any reason we can't find this gang and bring them in. They can't be that elusive."

"Could they instead be in Windfield?"

Denberg steepled his fingers. "It's a possibility. That would be under the radar. I'll get Windfield PD on it. Watch your back, my friend. Be more alert than ever. I understand that you and Mariah have arranged to meet this Friday. It doesn't sit well with me, as you know."

"I know that, sir. It's just that I do miss her."

"Haven't you heard that absence makes the heart grow

fonder?"

Grant doubted anything could make his heart grow fonder for Mariah. Yet, just the thought of such a crazy romantic notion made him roll his eyes. A romantic he was not, or at least he didn't think he was.

"Be careful when you meet with Mariah."

"Yes, sir. Rory will be with me."

Denberg arched a thick bushy brow. "I know you hold your partner in high esteem, but he isn't superhuman. Besides, why isn't Randall going along too?"

"He had something come up at the last minute, but remember Deputy Rivera patrols the area and we do have the retired cop next door."

"Just remember this is risky."

"Understood. If you'd rather I didn't go, I will change the plans."

"I'd pray long and hard about that," said Denberg. "It's not like the Florez Gang will read the paper, but they will go online given Tiny's research skills. Ultimately the decision is up to you, but we don't want to do anything to put Mariah and her family at more risk. Maybe have dinner with her, get it out of your system, and then take a break from seeing her again for a while until we nab these perps."

"I'll do that." He would do nothing to put the woman he loved at any type of risk. Now or ever.

Chapter 37

"I'll be right back," Mariah said, planting a kiss on Jordan's and Presley's heads. She waved to Mom and locked the door behind her. A hurried glance at her fitness watch indicated she had less than two hours before Grant would be arriving for dinner.

She couldn't wait to see him again.

Mariah called Deputy Rivera and let him know that she would be taking a quick jaunt to the convenience store. He reminded her to be careful and that he would be keeping an eye out for her return.

She whispered the first of several prayers and drove down the curvy roads of the town toward the convenience store. The late March winds blew through the trees, alerting the residents of Mountain Springs that spring would, as usual, be a late arrival. But although the springs and summers were short and the town small and without many modern amenities, one thing that Mountain Springs did have going for it was the ease of grabbing a few items at the convenience store less than two miles away. That and the gorgeous scenery, which, as far as Mariah was concerned, was unparalleled.

Mariah attempted to put out of her mind any fears she had

that the gang would attempt to harass her...or worse. Perusing the mug shots, descriptions, and detailed depictions of the crimes they had committed had seared into her mind just how dangerous these criminals were.

But as both Grant and Deputy Rivera mentioned on more than one occasion, the gang had not been seen in Mountain Springs in at least a month. They were likely in Briggs or elsewhere.

It was also likely that they wouldn't venture too far from the town that was home to the police officer they'd attempted to kill.

So, should she worry about grabbing some grocery items at the convenience store? Should she have asked Rick to come along with her? Mariah did her best to ignore her erratic heart rate and focus on the task she set out to accomplish. Surely just this hasty trip would hold no frightening excitement, and she should shove any trepidation aside.

Right?

Mariah pulled past the gas pumps and parked near the front doors of Osgood's Corner Market. When she'd set out to make lasagna for dinner, she hadn't anticipated being out of two critical ingredients. Sure, she could have made something else for the special meal, but knowing that lasagna was one of Grant's favorites made the decision easy.

There were no other customers in the store, yet an eerie shiver rippled down her spine.

"Hello!" called Tracey, one of the clerks, interrupting Mariah's apprehension.

"Hi," Mariah answered. For a town the size of Mountain Springs, Osgood's Corner Market had an impressive variety of items, and Mariah glanced down each one of the six aisles on her way to her destination. She then averted her focus to the back of the store where the refrigerated items were found. She reached for a tub of cottage cheese and wound her way to aisle six for two cans of tomato sauce, all the while keeping a vigilant eye on her surroundings.

Just in case.

"Wow, I totally did not know that that guy you were with at the restaurant the other night was a cop," said Tracey, flipping her long thin dark hair over her shoulder.

"I'm sorry, what?" Mariah placed the items on the counter and unzipped her purse. Had she just heard Tracey correctly? And if so, how did Tracey know?

Play it cool, Mariah.

"You know, that hot guy you were with at the restaurant? There's a huge article about him in the paper. I just had no idea he was a cop." Tracey plunked a copy of *The Briggs Daily* in front of Mariah. "See? He's right here on the front page." She pointed at a photo of Grant with her claw-like manicured nail.

Mariah's breath caught as Tracey continued. "This is from yesterday, but we always keep a couple days' worth of previous papers. It's actually been worth it for once. This one has been a huge seller." She paused. "Totally amazing, so he just like saves this baby. Sounds like you found yourself a winner, hon."

Mariah scanned the article, her eyes roving over the print. Grant had performed CPR on a baby and saved his life? "Was this recently?"

"No, it was sometime last year. Great picture of him, though."

The picture was obviously before Grant's assault. No scars on his handsome face. "Yes, it is."

Mariah took a covert glance around the store and out the doors to the parking lot. *Be aware of your surroundings.* For some reason, the article in the newspaper had added to her anxiety level tenfold.

Something didn't feel right.

The sooner I get back to the cabin, the better.

When Mariah returned her focus to Tracey, the woman stared at her and snapped a piece of bubble gum. While Mariah figured the woman to be about her age, Tracey dressed like a teenager in her tight-fitting mini-sweater and skinny jeans. "He must be a popular guy."

"What makes you say that?"

"Yesterday I had this chick come in and ask if I'd seen him in town."

Mariah's heart thudded. "What did she look like?"

"Oh, no need to get jealous, hon. She wasn't as pretty as you. Probably a couple of years younger, though. Short dark brown—and I mean really short—hair in a pixie style, a necklace-like tat on her neck, a nose ring, and super petite, like majorly short. She had kind of a tough look, you know, like she'd had a life of hard living."

Mariah dismissed the thought that Tracey's appearance indicated a life of hard living and focused on the concern that had ramped up her heartbeat. "This was yesterday?"

"Yep."

"And what did you tell her?"

Tracey tossed her an incredulous look. "The truth, of course. I told her that yes, I'd seen him here in town at the Mexican restaurant just the other day and that I thought he was dating a gal who lived just off Fish Hatchery Road."

"You told her that?"

"Well, yeah. She wanted to know, and besides, that's one of the things people value about me working here. I have all the info."

Mariah needed to relay the message to Grant that the woman known as "Deb", whom he had shown her a photo of, could be looking for him. "Did she say why she wanted to know?"

"I never pegged you for the jealous type." Tracey regarded her. "She just said she was trying to reconnect with him and that they'd been friends years ago. Just between you and me? I think she had a crush on him, but it seems she's not the only one. She'll probably need to stand in line." Tracey released one of her annoyingly shrill laughs.

"What did she say after that?"

Tracey rolled her eyes again. "For hardly ever really talking to me, you're mighty chatty today. It's almost like I'm under some type of interrogation or something."

"Seriously, Tracey, what did she say after that?"

"She asked if I knew your name and what your house looked like. Said she really wanted to see him again and that she still had his class ring from school that she wanted to return to him. She seemed pretty peeved that he had a girlfriend. So, I told her your name and that your house was the two-story cabin with the green roof and double car garage off of Fish Hatchery Road on Deer Lane. Why the twenty questions?"

Mariah did her best to contain her temper. "Tracey, you really shouldn't be telling people private information."

Tracey's generous eyebrows melted together. She scanned the cottage cheese. "It's not like she's going to steal him from you. I could tell he was really into you. Do you want a copy of the newspaper too?" Tracey moved with the speed of a snail as she next scanned the tomato sauce.

"Sure." Mariah subconsciously tapped her fingers on the counter in an effort to hurry the lethargic and dramatic clerk.

"You sure are impatient, Mariah." Tracey scowled and

dropped the three items in a bag. "That'll be $8.52."

Mariah handed her a ten. Someone entered Osgood's Corner Market, causing the bell on the door to jingle and Mariah to startle.

Phew. No one in the gang.

"Wow, little jumpy are we?" Tracey stopped what she was doing and tossed a flirtatious "hello" to the man in the leather jacket who had stepped into the store.

Seconds ticked by before Tracey returned her focus to the task at hand. "Here's your change."

Mariah simultaneously grabbed the bag, the change, and waved "goodbye" to Tracey, all in one fell swoop before bolting out the door.

With the ridiculous amount of details Tracey had offered, the Florez Gang had more than likely figured out her connection to Grant and that she had been lying about his whereabouts after his attack. What would they do with that information? Once again come after her and her family? Sit and wait for Grant to show up at some point for a visit? Had they already attempted to stop by, only to be deterred by Officer Rivera's presence?

It wasn't the brisk air that caused Mariah to shiver, but the realization that many lives could be in danger at the hands of a careless clerk.

The dusky and chilly early evening hour invited mischief, and Mariah bemoaned her lengthy visit to the convenience store. She needed to call Grant and get home. As Dad had instructed her when she'd begun driving, Mariah checked the back seat of her SUV, underneath it, and finally hit the fob to unlock the doors. Sliding into the cold vehicle, she locked the doors and reached for her cell phone.

At first, a weak bar on her cellphone lit. *Phew! A signal!* But it was short-lived. There were spots along the way where she could snag a signal, but it would be faster just to call him from the driveway. Hopefully she could catch him in time. If not, Mariah would have to let him know the moment he arrived. She mentally reminded herself to inform Rick as well.

The drive back to the cabin took longer than ever on the icy roads, and Mariah constantly checked her rearview mirror for signs of anyone following her. At one point, an unfamiliar dark gray, newer-model truck pulled in behind her. They maintained a closer-than-safe distance.

What would she do if they continued to follow her? She fumbled with her phone to see if any bars indicating a signal popped up. None did.

The gray truck edged closer, its lights nearly blinding her.

Mariah squinted into her mirror and could make out a tall figure in the driver's seat. Were they following her or merely just going in the same direction?

No one else traveled the icy and vacant roads.

The truck rode her bumper. If she had to slam on her brakes for a deer or slow around a corner, the vehicle would slide right into her.

Should she head straight to the cabin? Take a detour to throw off the person following her?

Before she could decide her next course of action, the truck veered left off of Fish Hatchery Road in the opposite direction of the cabin.

Mariah breathed a sigh of relief, watching as her breath fogged up the driver's side window. What-ifs filled her mind. She'd be sure to mention the truck to Grant, Rick, and Deputy Rivera, even if it had just been a fluke that it was following her.

When she reached Deer Lane, she scanned the area around

Mom's house, wishing just this once that there were not a zillion trees surrounding the property. Seeing no one, not even Deputy Rivera's vehicle, she pulled over at the edge of the driveway where she had a signal. She called Deputy Rivera, whose phone went to voicemail. She then texted Rick, waited briefly for a response, and when she received none, steered her SUV into the garage and bolted into the house.

"Is everything all right?" Mom asked.

Mariah quickly relayed the information while grabbing the landline. She dialed Grant's number, but it went to voicemail. Should she leave a message? "Grant, this is Mariah. Please call me as soon as you get this message. The Florez Gang knows you're alive and they know my name and where I live. They may have made the connection that you were here at the cabin all along."

Now all Mariah could do was pray and do her best not to worry.

Chapter 38

The concern over the information Tracey had shared with Deb and the close-following dark gray truck remained a constant in Mariah's mind. Why had Tracey been so eager to reveal the information? Lack of discernment? Wanting to appear important and "in the know"?

She wished she could have seen the driver in the truck more clearly. Had he or she been a member of the Florez Gang? If they knew to follow her the minute she stepped out of the Osgood's Corner Market and into her SUV, had they been stalking her?

The questions zipped through Mariah's mind with no signs of ceasing.

Good thing preparing for Grant's arrival would create the diversion she needed.

After preparing the lasagna, Mariah put on her earrings and ran a brush through her hair. She hadn't seen Grant in some time, and he mentioned that this could be their last time meeting in person until the Florez Gang was apprehended.

The realization of her feelings for him had struck her unexpectedly.

Focusing on Grant, she tried her best to set aside the fear

that permeated her heart after talking with Tracey at the convenience store. Surely the Florez Gang wouldn't come to Mom's house again, would they?

"Mommy, you look pretty." Presley stopped beside Mariah and snuggled Bibby in her arms.

Mariah leaned down and planted a kiss on the top of Presley's head. "Thank you, sweetie."

"A kiss for Bibby too," she said, lifting her doll toward Mariah, and Mariah obliged. "Bibby and me have missed George. I mean Grant."

"I have too."

Jordan appeared then, a building block creation in his hands. "Do you think Grant will like my new creation? It's a spaceship."

"I think he'll really like it. Very creative, Jordan."

Jordan beamed and examined the spaceship. "I kinda wish Grant still lived here so we could build more creations. That was fun."

"Maybe if there's time after dinner, you two can build something."

"Really?" Jordan's eyes lit up. "You know, Mom, it's hard to call him 'Grant.' For so long we called him 'George.'"

"Yeah, Mommy, why did he change his name?" puzzled Presley.

Jordan rolled his eyes. "He didn't change his name. George was just a nickname." He whispered to Mariah. "Little kids get confused so easily."

Mariah laughed at Jordan's insinuation that at seven years old, he was no longer a "little kid." She welcomed the diversion Jordan's humorous statement caused. Much better than focusing on trepidation that caused a round of anxiety in her stomach.

The aroma of lasagna filled the house, and Mariah opened the oven to check dinner's progress. Mom was busy chopping lettuce and tomatoes for a fresh salad.

Darkness had fallen outside and the temperature had dropped. Even though it was nearly April, Mountain Springs wouldn't be seeing spring temperatures for almost another month. A loud bang captured Mariah's attention, and she turned from the stove to the front window. "Did you hear that?" she asked Mom. Nosy began to bark, his tail wagging and his eyes focused on the front door.

"I did." A look of concern crossed Mom's face. "Hopefully the wind didn't come up again. After the winds two nights ago, I worry about another tree falling like the one that fell on Rick and Carol's house."

At a record speed, the winds had landed a tree square on Rick and Carol's roof. Mariah squinted into the night, scanning for the American flag that hung from the garage indicating Dad's love for his country. "The flag isn't moving."

Her heart stopped for a moment and her imagination kicked into place. Was the Florez Gang lying in wait for Grant to arrive? But how would they know he was coming tonight? Had someone been in the Osgood's Corner Market during her conversation with Tracey and Mariah hadn't realized it?

Even so, Mariah hadn't said anything about Grant arriving for dinner.

No, there was no way they could know. But they did now know that Mariah and Grant were dating and that it was *likely* that Grant would pay her visits in the course of their relationship.

"Hopefully it was nothing," she said, simultaneously trying to comfort herself and Mom.

"Could have been an animal," suggested Mom, joining

Mariah by the window.

"You know, we haven't reminded the kids about the 'hide and seek emergency' game for a while. Maybe it's time to do that."

Mom pressed her face close to the window. "Good idea. We have about fifteen minutes before Grant is due here and the lasagna is done. Let's give them a brief rundown."

A few minutes later, Mariah had called a family meeting in the living room. "Do you remember when we learned about the game 'hide and seek emergency'?"

Presley bobbed her head and Jordan offered the commentary. "It's when we go to the pantry and lock the door behind us. It's where we go if there's an emergency like a tornado or something. We have to be real quiet so no one can hear us. It's like a game."

Mariah marveled at Jordan's memory. While tornadoes were rare in Mountain Springs, there had been one several years ago that flattened rows of timber just eight miles away. Conifer trees, as well as wooden snow fences were torn apart on Mountain Springs Pass. She shivered at the memory. They often headed that way when going on hikes. Thankfully, they weren't in the vicinity that day.

"It is like a game," Mom was saying, "only more serious because we absolutely cannot make a sound."

"I like that game. It reminds me of when George Washington and his soldiers had to be really quiet so they wouldn't alert the enemy." Jordan's eyes grew large. "Can we play it again someday?"

"We will be playing it again soon," promised Mariah. And when they did, she hoped it was only a practice and not for a real emergency.

Mariah had removed some plates from the cupboard when

she heard another noise, this time, the sound of squealing tires. Nosy again went wild with barking, his tail flipping back and forth at ninety miles an hour. "Mom, did you hear that?"

Once again, she and Mom went to the window. A vehicle without headlights appeared to be coming down the driveway. It did an abrupt turn around near Rick's driveway before spinning its tires and reversing its travel away from the cabin.

Strange.

Neither Mom nor Mariah could ascertain the make or model of the vehicle, only that it appeared to be a pickup truck.

Mariah returned to the kitchen and unloaded the plates from the dishwasher and stacked them on the counter to be used for tonight's dinner. She couldn't shake the realization that something was wrong.

Jordan and Presley ran around the living room, obviously excited that Grant would be visiting. The thought put a smile on her otherwise stressed countenance. Her family was fond of Grant too.

The timer went off and Mariah removed the lasagna from the oven. It was then that she heard another noise. Was Grant here? The sooner he and Rory arrived and were safe inside the house, the better. She walked to the large front window and gazed out into the darkness.

But it wasn't Grant and Rory that she saw.

It looked to be a man in the front yard coming toward the house.

Her heart stopped and her feet refused to move. Who was the man? Had he gotten lost? Where was Grant? Had Rick seen the man? Where was Deputy Rivera?

Three other people emerged from the shadows, all walking toward her house.

The door handle rattled.

A noise that sounded like shattered glass rang through her ears.

And that's when Mariah knew. The gut feeling about forthcoming danger that she'd experienced earlier was coming to fruition.

Someone—or several someones—were attempting to break into the house.

She leaned toward Presley and Jordan. "Hide and seek emergency!"

"What?" Jordan asked.

She repeated herself, reaching an arm toward each of her children. Mariah passed Mom coming out of the laundry room. "Hide and seek emergency," she repeated herself, willing her heart rate to remain at a somewhat reasonable level.

The door handle on the front door clicked.

Lord, please let Rick be aware of what's going on. Let Grant be on his way. Let Deputy Rivera be in the vicinity. And please, please keep my family safe.

Mariah, Mom, Jordan, and Presley ran toward the pantry. She wanted to call to Nosy, but the dog had disappeared. Would he give away their location?

She prayed not.

Closing the door behind them, Mariah clicked it to a locked position.

"Why are we in here?" Presley asked.

"Sshhh," Mariah said. "Remember? Hide and seek emergency. We can't talk. We have to be very quiet."

"Like we are undercover agents for the FBI," said Jordan, patting his sister on the head.

Presley snuggled Bibby. Mariah could see the fear in her eyes.

They hid behind the large rack that held a variety of pantry items. Not only was Mom good at keeping the pantry stocked, but she was also good at stocking it strategically. Toilet paper and paper towels lined much of it, followed by dog food on the lowest shelf, and cereal boxes, pasta, and cans on the higher shelves. All of which provided the perfect camouflage for anyone opening the door and peering inside.

Mariah stretched on tiptoe to reach the top shelf where she'd set the 9mm loaded and ready for use. Her eyes connected with Mom's in the bleak lighting.

They crouched low in the pantry, Mariah willing her heart rate to calm to less audible levels. She could hear voices in the kitchen.

A minute amount of light filtered through the crack where the door and the floor met. It provided just enough light to barely see the scared faces of her children.

"I wish I could warn Grant," she mouthed to Mom, doubting her mother could read her lips in the near darkness.

Mom bowed her head and Mariah followed suit.

She prayed the Lord would keep them safe and that He would keep Grant and Rory safe as well. Because she knew that if this was the Florez Gang, they wouldn't stop until they achieved their ultimate goal of taking the lives of those who had crossed them.

Chapter 39

The voices echoed throughout the house. Mariah shivered at the harshness of their tones. "Hey, let's eat before we do some damage," a man's voice thundered.

She could hear clanging dishes and more voices. That would be the only logical explanation. Just how many people were in the house?

And where were Grant and Rory? Would they walk into this? Had Rick seen anything?

Presley snuggled against her. Jordan's eyes were round and frightened. Mom, always capable and prepared, shifted. Had she had the chance to grab her own weapon?

If there was one thing Dad had insisted upon, it was that his girls could defend themselves. Countless hours at the gun range helped reassure him. Lives in danger at the hands of violent criminals.

In their own home.

A teeny whimper left Presley's pressed lips. Mariah shook her head, held a finger to her lips, and then placed an arm around her daughter. *Please, Lord, please don't let them hear us.*

She had an idea then, and she leaned to the level of the children. In her softest whisper, she spoke. "Presley and Jordan, I need you to do me a favor."

The fear in their eyes broke her heart, but Jordan responded with a firm, "Okay."

Mariah took a deep breath. "I need you both to hide under the cabinet right there. You are spies during the American Revolution. George Washington is your commander, and he has ordered you to spy on the Redcoats."

"Ooh. Patriots, we are!" Jordan exclaimed, almost too loudly. "Can I be Paul Revere?"

Mariah loved his enthusiasm but feared he might be heard. She pressed a finger to her lips. "Yes, you can. And, fellow patriots, this is very important. Don't utter even the tiniest noise or move from your spy camp—under the cabinet—until I call the special code."

"What's the special code?" Presley whispered.

Jordan crawled beneath the cabinet and extended his neck toward Mariah. "How about the British are coming? That can be our code word."

"Are the British *really* coming?" Presley asked.

"No, it's just pretend. You must stay very quiet and spy from underneath the cabinet until I call out that the British are coming. This is very, very important. Even if Grandma and I leave the pantry. Do you understand?"

Jordan made a mock salute. "Ay, ay, Mrs. Washington."

Mariah hid a smile. She caught Mom's eye, and Mom gave her an appreciative nod.

She offered a prayer that the intruders hadn't heard any of the conversation. And more importantly, that she and her family would get out of this alive.

More dishes clanged, along with voices—some using crass words. Mariah wanted to cover her children's ears, but there was more to fear at this moment than foul language. She hoped that by being wedged beneath the two-foot-tall cabinet, they wouldn't hear the worst of the conversation.

"Hey, I get first dibs on the girlfriend," said a loud male voice.

A string of curses uttered by a woman's voice followed. "Just eat the lasagna and let's get back to business."

"I could eat the whole pan," a familiar voice offered.

"You always eat too much, Tiny. Save some for the rest of us."

Tiny. The name sent off alarms throughout Mariah's brain and confirmed what she already suspected—that this was indeed the Florez Gang.

"Yeah, well, it's better when it's food I don't gotta pay for."

"Check out the fridge. There's all kinds of food in here."

"Hurry up and eat so we can get down to business."

"Revenge will definitely be sweet, eh, Deb?"

"Oh, yeah. This time we'll make sure that cop doesn't live. No sloppy business like last time, Dawson."

"What? Why is it always my fault?"

"Because you've got the smallest brain, you idiot."

"Enough with the fighting. So there's the girlfriend, an older woman, and two kids. They can't have gotten far."

"Yeah, I saw her in the window. Pretty stupid to look out of a lighted house and into the darkness. We could see her perfectly."

"Even I'm not that dumb.

"I wouldn't go that far, Dawson."

"My bet is they're still in the house."

Mariah's stomach lurched. What would they do to her family? Would Grant and Rory walk into this as sitting ducks?

Her eye met Mom's again. What would they do if the members of the gang decided to break into the pantry?

"Well, well, look who decided to join us," Deb's voice sneered.

Mariah's heart stopped. Was it Grant? Her question was soon answered.

A loud male voice echoed outside the pantry door. "It's about time you joined us, DeShawn."

"Hey, this place ain't that easy to find, you know."

DeShawn?

Grant hadn't mentioned someone with that name.

"Was anyone out there?"

"Not that I could see. This place is kinda hidden and hard to find. I parked my car back on the main road and walked. Hope that's okay."

"It's all good. So, this is your orientation. To see if you can join the Florez Gang." A couple chuckles followed the male voice.

A clearing of a throat. DeShawn's? "No worries, man. I'm good. What do I need to do to pass the test?"

"You got your biscuit?"

Biscuit?

"Yeah. Right here. Loaded and ready for action."

The realization struck Mariah that "biscuit" must be a code word for "gun". Tears squeezed her throat, and her windpipe clamped. How would they ever make it out alive?

She glanced in Mom's direction. Mom's eyes were closed and her head bowed. Only God could remove them from this lethal situation.

"Yo, Tiny, quit eating up all the food." Another male voice.

"Have you seen what's in this fridge? Maybe I'll just move in. There was a lemon meringue pie in there. Emphasis on *was*."

"Do you ever stop eating?" Deb sneered.

A spiteful chuckle. Tiny. "No. Not when there's food to be eaten. Besides, I need food to give me the energy I need to get back at that cop. Isn't that what this is all about, Deb? To punish that cop for killing Alroy?"

"Nothing gets past you, does it?" Deb's voice was hoarse and bitter. "Of course, that's why we're here. But first, we'll make him suffer."

A cruel laugh. "I like how you guys think."

"Good, DeShawn, then watch and learn."

"You got it, man."

After what seemed like a lengthy eternity, the rowdy voices ceased. Maybe the gang changed their minds and left the house.

Wishful thinking.

A thundering order rang out. "Let's find them!"

Mariah held up a finger to her lips again. The kids could not make a sound. *Please, Lord. No coughing, no sneezing, no whimpering. Let us all be so quiet that they have no idea we are here. Keep us safe, Lord. Protect us, and protect Grant and Rory.*

"Psycho Eyes and DeShawn, you take the upstairs, I'll take the downstairs. Dawson and Tiny, you go outside and make sure that nosy neighbor isn't wandering around. If you see him, take care of him. Remember when—and it's a 'when' not an 'if'—we find the girlfriend and the rest of them, we wait until our cop friend knows we've got them. I've got his number on speed dial." An evil laugh punctuated Deb's words.

Mariah's stomach churned. Why hadn't she called the police from the driveway when she had a signal? And poor Rick and Carol. She inwardly begged Rick to stay inside his house.

"We meet back here in five minutes, got it?" Deb asked.

Loud footsteps rang out overhead. Doors opened and slammed. It would only be a matter of time before Deb or someone else tried the pantry door, found it locked, and forced their way inside. Mariah fingered the SIG that was in her waistband. She would never want to shoot someone, but if it meant protecting her family...

The pantry's wood door was slimmer than all the other doors. That could work in their favor if the gang believed it was a coat closet and not somewhere someone could effectively hide. Looks were deceiving, so when they opened it, they would be surprised to see how spacious the pantry really was.

After a few minutes had passed, voices again thundered throughout the house. "Anyone out there?" Deb asked.

"No." A male voice.

"Good. Dawson, stay out there and keep watch. Take DeShawn with you and, Tiny, you come back in. The rest of us can handle searching the house. They have to be here somewhere."

"Dude. Can I have a bite to eat first?" Tiny.

Silence, then Tiny's voice again. "Okay, okay, Deb, cool it. Take a joke."

"Nothing here is funny until we do what we set out to do. This is for Alroy, remember?" Deb sounded as though she spoke through clenched teeth.

"Way to tell him, Deb."

"Thank you, Psycho Eyes."

Obnoxious kissing sounds before stomping footsteps. Doors slamming. Yelling. Vile words.

These people would have no mercy on them.

Someone tried the doorknob to the pantry. "It's locked!" Seconds ticked by before what sounded like multiple feet began kicking the door. Someone jimmied the lock and the door flung open.

They'd been found.

Chapter 40

Grant stared into the night. While not yet pitch black, it did get dark early, especially in the mountains. He couldn't wait to see Mariah.

"You're quiet," said Rory, maneuvering his truck slowly on the icy roads. "You must be thinking about a certain woman."

Grant chuckled. "You know me too well." He sobered and turned his attention to his friend and coworker. "Since you're this old married man, how did you know that Kayla was the one?"

"Old married man at thirty-two. Yeah, sure. So, I actually knew from the beginning. Corny, I know. But when we met that night at the mission trip fundraiser, I knew. I just knew. Now if you tell anyone that I said anything that sounds remotely romantic like that, I will use some of my tactical skills on you."

"My lips are sealed, man. I'd never want you to use any of that fancy Judo or whatever other tactical skills you have on me." Rory might be small in stature, but the guy was a powerhouse. He had earned a black belt in Brazilian Jiu-Jitsu and Kodokan Judo. He was one guy you didn't want to mess with.

"Good. You keep it that way. So, you thinking Mariah is the 'one'?"

"Too soon to know, but we just click, and I'm hoping when this is all over, we can spend more time together. But she's godly, pretty, sweet, full of compassion, and an amazing mom. I think I found a winner. And don't you let on that I'm getting all mushy or I'll use *my* tactical skills on you."

Rory laughed. "Not scared, dude. You may be a much better shot than me, but even though you're about seventy-five pounds heavier, I can take you down in one move."

"I knew I should have listened to Dad and taken some martial arts as a kid. Who knew football wouldn't do me many favors as an LEO?"

"Yeah. Who knew?"

Grant appreciated the easy camaraderie he had with Rory. Appreciated that they had each other's backs.

They rode in silence for a few more minutes until they rounded a corner by the fish hatchery. "Take the next left."

Rory maneuvered his truck around the curve and turned on his turn signal. Linda's house came into full view. The place was lit up like a Christmas tree.

"Wait. Stop here a minute and kill the lights."

Rory stopped the truck. "What's up?"

"Something's not right."

"What do you mean?"

"Her house."

"Yeah, lots of lights, so?"

"No, the front door is open." Grant leaned forward in his seat.

"You're right, but just a little bit. Maybe one of the kids left it open."

Grant shook his head. "Not at 7:00 at night. Not under Linda's watch. She wouldn't allow the front door to remain open even a little bit, not with the cold temps and not with Nosy potentially escaping." Grant scanned the area surrounding Linda's house. He focused on Rick's house. Nothing seemed out of the ordinary there. "I don't like this. Something isn't right."

A second later, Nosy bolted from the house and someone shut the door. "There's the dog," said Rory.

"That's not normal either. Mariah would never allow Nosy to be out here by himself. He's too curious and would run off after the first animal he sees."

"Well, someone didn't want him in there."

"The question is who?"

Rory put the truck in reverse, parked behind some trees, and killed the engine. "Isn't county supposed to be keeping an eye on things?"

"That's what Denberg said. Maybe they were called to another emergency."

"Unfortunately, that's the problem with Mountain Springs. Nice place with like zero crime. Well, until your attempted murder case came along."

Grant couldn't shake the uneasy feeling that had settled over him. "Deputy Rivera is the new full-time deputy they hired for Mountain Springs. I'm surprised he's not out doing some rounds."

"You mentioned the neighbor is a retired cop.

"He is."

"Do you remember how to use your weapon?"

Grant rolled his eyes. "That is something I have not forgotten."

"Good. You might need it. Check out the guy in the shadows."

Grant squinted. He could make out a skinny figure smoking in the far corner by the garage. "He looks familiar." Grant begged his memory to come through for him. "That's why. It's Dawson. One of the Florez Gang." He hit his hand on the dash. "They're here."

Rory cracked his neck and popped his knuckles. "And look, there's another guy hiding over there."

Grant followed Rory's gaze. He didn't recognize the other guy. Stupid faulty memory.

"How much can we rely on the neighbor?" Rory asked.

"He's highly competent."

"But can we rely on him?"

Grant could answer that with one-hundred percent certainty. "I'd stake my life on it."

"Good. We're going to need him. You up for this?"

Grant offered a prayer for Mariah and her family and for the ability to function the way he needed to in what appeared to be a dangerous situation. "I hope so. We need to call for backup from Rick's phone. Maybe we can get Rick's attention and brainstorm. It's doubtful he even realizes something's going on." Although the thought of that did seem a little off—Rick was highly observant. How had he missed the fact that the gang had arrived and entered Linda's house?

Nosy began to bark and head toward Rory's truck. "No, Nosy," Grant muttered under his breath. The dog coming toward them was the last thing they needed. Nosy seemed to have understood, but upon closer examination, Grant saw the dog run after something into the woods.

But it was too late to maintain their cover. Dawson had looked up from his cigarette and seemed to be zoning in on Rory's truck. "I don't think we camouflaged ourselves well enough. Dawson looked our way. We need to make a move and run for Rick's house. Will you cover me?"

"Got your back, partner."

Grant touched the holster on his hip. "They aren't going to win this time."

———————

From the meager space between the box of cereal and the pillar of soup, Mariah could see someone enter the pantry.

From the wanted pictures that Grant had shown her, she recognized the man as Psycho Eyes. Bile climbed up her throat and settled uncomfortably there.

A little hand pulled on her pantleg. She couldn't stoop to see what her child needed. Couldn't ask.

Couldn't even breathe.

"Nice pantry. Don't let Tiny see it."

Another face. Smaller, shorter, female.

Deb.

Mariah watched as they scanned the rows of food and household goods. Would they see her and Mom hidden behind the stacks of supplies?

Would Presley or Jordan forget about the "hide and seek emergency" game and blow their cover?

"I don't see them in here. Maybe there's a crawl space beneath the house or something. Let's go see."

"We could send Tiny," Psycho Eyes looked over at Deb.

"Very funny. We need someone who can actually fit down there."

They slammed the pantry door and Mariah and Mom both let out a simultaneous breath of relief.

"That was close," Mariah mouthed.

Mom nodded.

A little hand tugged on her pantleg again. This time, Mariah dropped to her knees. She held her finger to her mouth as she kneeled.

"Are the British here yet?" Presley whispered.

"Not yet. Remember, you can't talk or move until I give the code word."

"Okay."

Mariah gave Presley a love squeeze on the arm and stood again. How long would they have to remain in the pantry?

And, more importantly, where was Grant?

Chapter 41

Grant limped behind the tall lodgepole pines toward Rick and Carol's house. This was one thing that had resurfaced in his otherwise deficient memory—how to handle remaining covert in a dangerous situation.

Funny how some things came back to him while other things remained long gone and far from his reach.

Dull pain seared his shoulder, and his left knee begged him to sit down and stay awhile.

Why did the physical healing of his body seem to take its own sweet time?

Doing his best not to create more noise, Grant hobbled as quietly as he could toward the back of the cottage. Rory had his back, and there was no one he trusted more, except maybe Denberg.

The moonlight, combined with the well-lit yard due to Rick's, and probably Mariah's dad's, tenacity in providing safety to their families, was both a blessing and a curse.

A blessing to be able to see where he was going and to see the two men who were likely tasked with keeping watch. A curse because they could see him too.

Thoughts rushed through his mind on what could be happening inside the house. A partial curtain in the front window was pushed to the side, but besides that, Grant could see nothing of the ongoings inside. He saw Nosy sniffing around in the front yard and mentally begged the dog not to come his way. To do so would for certain give away his location to Dawson and the other gang member. Strange how Nosy didn't seem to mind the visitors.

He prayed for God's guidance for the hundredth time and that the Lord would keep Nosy far from him.

Grant heard the cabin door open and saw Psycho Eyes poke his head out into the night. He looked to the left, then to the right. Nosy slipped in through the door. *Thank You, Lord.*

Grant continued on his journey toward Rick's cabin. Dawson and the other gang member engaged in conversation, oblivious to their surroundings and likely high on their drug-of-the-hour. If only the entire situation was as easy as dealing with people like Dawson. Memories of the young man with far too many brain cells killed off by drugs flashed through Grant's mind.

He turned and gave Rory the hand signal that he was going to make the final, and most dangerous, stretch to the house. Unshielded by trees, Rory's protection would be the most important during this stretch.

Rory gave the appropriate signal back to Grant, and Grant made a beeline for the house. Ignoring any pain that tempted him to retreat, Grant made his way to the back door. He knocked quietly, but quickly.

No answer.

He stood on tiptoe and peered into the house through the blinds.

Seemingly vacant.

He knocked again.

Still no answer.

After a few moments Grant realized a disturbing truth.

Rick wasn't home.

———

Now if they could just be kept hidden until Grant and Rory arrived. They would know what to do, and if they enlisted Rick's help, together, they would be able to overtake the gang.

But just as quickly as her optimism gave rise, Mariah's heart fell. Rick had taken Carol out to dinner tonight in Briggs. It could be hours before they returned.

Her legs fell asleep due to standing in the same still position for so long. She could only imagine how cramped and uncomfortable her kids were. *Lord, please let them stay quiet and please, please let us get through this.*

Mariah heard Nosy bark, a deep excited bark. She could envision his tail wagging. Nosy's barking grew louder, followed by even louder voices.

"Shut that dog up!"

"Can I do the honors?"

Would the gang hurt their pet? They seemed ruthless enough to do anything. "Wait a minute...this could work to our favor."

"What do you mean?"

"I bet this mutt could lead us to the girlfriend and her mom."

Mariah's heart fell. Nosy could absolutely do that. And then what? *Lord, please don't let him lead them to us.*

"It's worth a try. They're around here somewhere. They weren't in the crawl space, weren't upstairs, aren't on this floor. They couldn't have just disappeared. How do we have the mutt lead us to them?"

"No idea. Just saw it in some dumb movie one time. Maybe if we wait long enough, he'll lead us to them."

Several laughs arose. Mariah flinched. Nosy began to growl. It wouldn't be out of the realm of possibility for him to wonder where his people were and to sense that something was awry.

Time passed. She wasn't sure how much. She heard a quiet rhythmic snore. Jordan had fallen asleep under the cabinet. She was so grateful Mom was here too. She reached for Mom's hand and together they bowed their heads and prayed silently. Letting go of Mom's hand, Mariah again pondered their options. If only Dad was here. He would know what to do. He had always been fiercely protective of his "girls." With Dad, Mariah had always felt safe. Emotion seeped into her anxious soul. The good news was that one day, she would see Dad again.

She just hoped it wasn't today.

A familiar sound brought Mariah back to the present. A thump-thump against the door. Wop, wop, a cadenced strike sounding against the hollow wood door. She swallowed hard.

Nosy was right outside the pantry.

"Hey, look, the mutt's by that closet door."

Mariah heard footsteps pounding toward the pantry. She shared a frightened look with Mom.

The door flung open, causing light to flood the pantry. She willed Nosy to stay outside the room or to forget about them altogether.

But her inner dialogue with the dog proved useless. Nosy wound around behind the cabinet, his tail wagging, and planted a dog kiss on her arm. She shook her head. "No," she tried to whisper.

"Well, what do we have here?"

Too late.

Tiny stood a mere six inches from her face. "Hey guys, I found the girlfriend."

Psycho Eyes and Deb stood behind him, attempting to peer around his oversized frame. Psycho Eyes sneered. "Good. Bring her out."

Tiny yanked Mariah's arm so hard she feared it would become disconnected from its socket. She winced. His breathing was labored and his breath foul. Like too much garlic and onions. Probably too much of her lasagna.

Lasagna meant for a special event with her family and Grant.

"So, we meet again, do we?" Tiny hissed. "I plan to pay you both back for spraying my face with that bear spray. Trust me, revenge will be sweet."

Mariah cringed. Tiny's eyes were red rimmed and swollen. Was that the remaining effects of the bear spray or from the drugs he likely partook in?

Psycho Eyes reached for Mom and tugged her behind. Thankfully, Nosy followed them, rather than go back to the pantry for Jordan and Presley. *Thank You, Lord.*

"We are going to stay here until the British come and they aren't here yet," announced Mariah.

"Wow, not only a pathetic excuse for a human being by dating a cop, but also as crazy as someone in a psych ward," muttered Deb. "The British? Really?"

Mariah prayed that Jordan and Presley would understand her statement. They likely could hear the cruel voices and had seen the way their mom and grandma had been snatched from the pantry. Her heart broke at the trauma they would likely remember for years to come.

"Where are the brats? Tiny, didn't you find out that there

are two brats?" Deb asked.

"They are at their dad's house. He has visitation this week." While an overt lie, Mariah would do what it took to keep her kids safe.

"Oh, right. Visitation. I remember those days." Tiny shoved her to the ottoman and Psycho Eyes did the same with Mom before binding their wrists. Tiny's piercing beady eyes bored into her. "My dad was supposed to have visitation with me. Do you think he ever did? No, he was always conveniently busy. Too busy for his son."

Mariah feared the rage that lit Tiny's face. Red dotted his cheeks, nose, and forehead. His receding hairline seemed to recede even more. He seethed for a moment, glaring at her. Then, as if a switch had been turned off, he calmed. "But then the strangest thing happened. He had an accident and died."

Psycho Eyes howled. "Yeah, a *strange* accident," he said, putting air quotes around the word "accident".

Tiny perched on the barstool in the kitchen and faced Mariah, Mom, and the rest of the gang. He took a bite of lemon meringue pie. Grant's favorite that Mariah had made for *him*, not Tiny.

A breeze came through the partially open door and Mariah shivered. Deb reached over and slammed it. "Start a fire, someone," she snapped. "It's stinkin' cold in here."

Psycho Eyes sauntered over to where Mariah sat on the ottoman and plopped between her and Mom. He ogled her with cold eyes before reaching a thumb with a chewed nail and stroking the side of her neck. "Hey, pretty lady."

Bile rose in Mariah's throat, and she fought the urge to vomit. Psycho Eyes, true to his name, had even crazier eyes up close than from a distance. His eyes never blinked, his perusal of her calculating as his lips drew back in a snarl.

Mariah cringed and closed her eyes. Sweat trickled down her spine as the fear threatened to paralyze her.

"You are about the only good decision that worthless cop has ever made. Too bad he won't be able to make good on that decision any longer." He caressed her neck with his thumb, his ever-enlarging pupils contrasting with the abundant whites of his eyes. "There's just something about you."

Dread twisted her gut. Mariah noticed Mom's expression from the corner of her eye. Mom would do anything to protect her daughter, but even if she did make a move, they would have no chance against the gang. Mariah knew they were heavily armed, not only on their person, but some larger guns were resting on the counter.

She thought of her own pistol. Would there be an opportune time to use it? Could she free her wrists from the tight restraints? She and Mom were outnumbered— would she even gain freedom by using her pistol? The stakes seemed impossibly high.

Out of nowhere, Deb appeared. Petite, but with a large presence, she seemed to loom over Psycho Eyes. "Get up, loser."

Psycho Eyes threw back his head and laughed. He winked at Mariah and stood. "Now now, you know you're my queen, Deb. You're the prettiest thing there is. Don't be getting jealous on me." He planted a passionate kiss on Deb's lips, one eye remaining open and focused on Mariah and Mom.

Deb pulled away from him. "You better keep it that way."

"Oh, I intend to. Since she's only a temporary, what's the harm in a little flirting?"

Only a temporary? Mariah's entire body began to shake.

"True." Deb stood on her tiptoes and planted another kiss on Psycho Eyes. "I am prettier, right?"

"Absolutely, my queen."

"Hey, the mom ain't bad lookin' for an old gal," said Tiny, his mouth full of food.

Mariah could imagine Mom cringing at the term. She always hated being called "old", and at fifty-four, she was far from it. But that was the least of their worries.

"We need to get on with business here," growled Psycho Eyes. "I've got the cop's number. Let's give him a call and bring him up here. Anyone ready for a shoot-out? Oh, that's right. It's not a shoot-out when there are five against one."

Tiny laughed. "Gonna have me some cottage cheese first." He pulled open the lid from the remaining cottage cheese and scooped a big bite into his mouth. "This is good stuff. Where'd you get this, Mom?" he asked.

Mom narrowed her eyes toward Tiny but didn't answer.

Deb rolled her eyes. "Enough eating, Tiny. Get Dawson and DeShawn in here and let's make the call."

Mariah held her breath. Then remembered to breathe again.

Grant would be walking right into a dangerous situation. The only good thing? They would never reach him with the lackluster cell service.

Then too, there had been no way to warn him.

Would she awaken soon from this nightmare?

Chapter 42

A flash of lights veered down the driveway. Rick's SUV rounded the corner and toward the garage. Would Dawson and
the other guy take Rick and Carol out when they exited the
vehicle?

Not on my watch.

Grant focused his gaze on the criminals when the lights lit
up the area where they stood by the house. Then a dawn of
recognition slammed into him.

The other man was DeShawn Korfanta, the young man who
wanted to join the Florez Gang and was likely going to have
to prove his allegiance.

Grant didn't want Mariah and her family, Rory, Rick, Carol,
or himself to be sacrificed for DeShawn to meet that goal.

He hid from sight and watched as Rick pulled into the
garage. Nodding toward Rory, they both discreetly filed into
the garage. Fortunately, both Dawson and DeShawn had their
heads bent toward their cell phones. Some watchmen they
were. Whatever their preoccupation with their phones, it
worked to Grant's and Rory's advantage.

Rick killed the engine, but he didn't step from the vehicle
immediately. Instead, as an obviously trained professional,

Rick surveyed his surroundings, then surveyed them again. Grant stepped into his line of vision slowly and carefully. No sense in coming face to face with a bullet from Rick's Sig. He waved. Rick squinted and then waved back. Grant held a finger to his lip. Too easy for Dawson and DeShawn to hear any additional noises and blow the entire plan.

What plan?

Right. Grant didn't have a plan yet, but he would as soon as they put their minds together and figured out a way to rescue Mariah, Linda, and the kids.

Rick heeded Grant's nonverbal cue and nodded toward the house. He opened the door for Carol, and she, apparently accustomed to reading Rick's mind after all their years of marriage, said nothing when she saw Grant, instead heading to the door that connected the garage to the house.

Grant signaled to Rory and kept an eye on the unobservant Dawson and DeShawn. Both continued to keep their heads down, staring at their phones. From the devoted attention given to their devices, the guys were likely playing games that didn't necessitate a signal. Good. They needed to be distracted.

Grant and Rory followed Rick and Carol into the house and closed the door behind them without so much as a sound. Rick closed the automatic garage door.

Had Dawson and DeShawn heard the door close? Or had they been too wrapped up in their phones to notice?

"What's going on?" Rick demanded. Grant rubbed his freezing hands together and ignored the ache in his shoulder.

"The gang is here."

The vein in Rick's forehead pulsed. "Yeah, I figured that. Saw the two guys on the west side of the house on their phones. They gave us all of two seconds of their time when we pulled into the driveway. How many are there?"

"Likely five of them. Rick and Carol, this is my partner and friend, Rory. Rory, this is Rick and his wife, Carol."

After a quick greeting, they returned to the seriousness of the situation. "First thing we need to do is call the sheriff's office and get some backup," Grant said. "Then we call Rivera."

"My thoughts exactly," agreed Rick.

"It'll take them about twenty minutes to get here, maybe longer given the slick roads. But at least they'll be on their way," added Rory.

Rick pointed at the cordless phone.

"You have a landline?"

"Newly installed. Should have heard the shock in their voices when I called and requested it. Gonna convince Linda to get one too. Should have done it a lot sooner given the poor cell service here."

Grant dialed 911 on Rick's landline.

"911 what is your emergency?"

"This is Officer Grant MacGuire. I'm off duty, but have encountered a situation at 430 Deer Lane in Mountain Springs that requires backup."

"Please explain your situation."

Grant explained the best he could, trying to be patient with the operator for only doing her job. But time was of the essence. There was no telling what Psycho Eyes and Deb had planned.

After he clicked off, Rick called his attention to the front window. Someone had opened the blinds in the living room at Linda's cabin. "This doesn't look good."

Grant followed the direction of Rick's gaze. In Linda's living room, Mariah and Linda sat on the ottoman. Psycho Eyes was touching the side of Mariah's face.

His blood boiled and his pulse sped. He gritted his teeth. "We need to get over there." Grant took a step back from the window and clenched his fists. If Psycho Eyes did anything to hurt Mariah...

"That's what we're fixing to do," said Rory, laying a hand on Grant's shoulder. "Let's talk a plan."

They needed a plan, all right. This was personal.

Lord, please keep them safe and please restrain me from acting on impulse.

"Grant, I know it's tough to keep your mind on the task, and the Lord knows I'd handle it half as well as you if it was my Carol over there in the clutches of some creep, but you've got to keep your head in the game," said Rick.

"You're right. I'm just...I know how these guys operate."

"Yeah, and that's why we're going to shut them down." Rick paused. "Carol, I want you locked inside our room with your pistol in case you need it."

Carol nodded, gave her husband a quick kiss, and retreated.

Rick turned to Grant and Rory, his expertise and experience clearly shining through the intensity of the circumstance. "All right, men, what's the plan? And give me a quick rundown of what to expect with these delinquents."

Grant peered through the window twice more. Deb and Tiny were in the living room as well. As small as she was, she was likely either as evil or more evil than Psycho Eyes. "As you know, they all have serious criminal pasts. Psycho Eyes is the ring leader, but Deb pretty much runs the show. She's out for revenge since I killed her brother, Alroy. She'll be ruthless. According to police reports, she tested high on the sociopath chart. She also knows some form of martial arts and is small and quick. Psycho Eyes wants to please Deb, so couple that with the fact that he has no conscience, and he's a dangerous dude. Don't let Tiny's obesity and lethargic movements fool you. The guy is strong and tough. The two outside are Dawson, who has had more brain cells killed by drugs than anyone I've ever dealt with, and DeShawn, a young kid seeking the approval of the Florez Gang to join their ranks."

They discussed a few options, but none sounded feasible. One wrong move could place Mariah's and Linda's lives in further jeopardy. "Where are the kids is what I'd like to know," Grant mused aloud.

"Hopefully protected somewhere," said Rory. "You said Mariah has a good head on her shoulders. Perhaps she was able to keep them away from the gang."

Rick briefly gazed upward. "That's what we'll be praying for."

"We need to get over there ASAP," Grant muttered. He'd always had a clear head when doing the job of a law enforcement officer, but the thought of Mariah being in danger threatened to cloud his thinking.

"Patience, my good man," said Rory, trying to be serious and lighten the mood at the same time.

Grant nodded. "All right, let's incapacitate them one at a time."

"Starting with the wimps outside," said Rick. He pulled his gun from his holster and double-checked the magazine. "We can tie them up in the garage while we take on the other three."

"And not leave them freezing out in the elements like what they did to Grant?" Rory asked, a smirk lining his oblong face.

They formulated the plan, prayed, then decided to act.

The lights of Rick and Carol's SUV lit the driveway.

"Who's that?" Tiny sneered.

Psycho Eyes stood and walked toward the front window. "That would be the neighbor. Might need to have a few extra bullets on hand." He removed his gun from his waistband and stroked its black barrel. "You won't let me down now, will you?" he asked, planting a kiss on it.

"Just remember that you don't get all the fun," said Tiny. He ambled to the refrigerator and fixed his gaze on the top of it. "You know, I'm feeling like some cereal."

Mariah watched in horror as the gang member poured Nosy's kibble from a clear oblong container into one of the kids' plastic bowls with a built-in straw. Tiny then poured milk over the kibble and took a heaping bite.

"Kinda crunchy, but not bad."

He scooped more into his mouth, milk dripping down his bearded chin. "I gotta get some of this next time we go to the store."

"Can we get back on task, Tiny?" Psycho Eyes growled. He held his pistol in front of him, admiration in his eyes. "Can't wait to put this thing to good use tonight."

"Yeah, well, there's only two shots I'll be firing tonight." Deb's high-pitched squeal bordered on hysteria.

Tremors coursed through Mariah. Deb planned to kill her and Grant. What would become of Mom and the kids?

Her wrists were raw from the ropes used to tie her hands. She tried not to worry, but fear had clouded every area of her mind and heart.

Fear for Mom that all the stress would make her borderline high blood pressure worse.

Fear that Jordan and Presley would make a noise and be found.

Fear that Grant would walk right into this mess, not realizing that he'd walked into a landmine.

Fear of being shot and killed.

Fear of what they would do to Mom and the kids.

Fear of Grant being shot and killed.

Fear that...

"Peace I leave with you; my peace I give to you." She inwardly recited the words from John 14:27. But how could she have peace when so much was at stake? She wanted to argue, wanted to insist that no way could she possibly experience peace at a time like this.

"Let not your hearts be troubled, neither let them be afraid."

How could she not be afraid at a time like this? Yes, Mariah had full confidence in where she'd spend eternity since she'd long ago placed her faith and trust in Christ Jesus. But her heart *was* troubled. She *was* afraid. Afraid of what these horrible people would do to her children, to Mom, to Grant. To her.

Mariah meditated on the words and willed her breathing to become more normal, rather than the ragged huffs it had become.

She closed her eyes for but a mere second and again surrendered the situation to her Heavenly Father.

The Lord was faithful.

Hadn't He rescued Grant via Nosy by sending Mariah and Jordan to find him?

Hadn't He allowed Grant to not only survive, but heal?

Hadn't He kept the kids safe, even when they could have been so easily found?

Hadn't He prompted Rick and Carol, for whatever reason, to return home sooner than they had originally planned?

God was faithful.

That much was true.

Now Mariah just needed her heart to relay that critical

message to her mind.

Chapter 43

Dawson, as expected, was an easy target. Grant snuck up behind the aloof man and whacked him on the side of the neck. Dawson went down quickly. Instead of DeShawn fighting, shooting, or calling attention to himself, as they had expected, the young man ran, his ebony face full of fear.

So much for meeting the expectations of the Florez Gang. DeShawn didn't stand a chance of being initiated into their ranks.

Rory tied Dawson's hands and feet, giving a glimmer into his former life of high school rodeo days. He and Grant dragged him into the garage via the small door that led to the outside so as not to call attention to themselves.

Grant watched DeShawn run—right into Rick's thick-barreled chest. "Going somewhere?" Rick hissed.

DeShawn opened his mouth and Grant feared he might yell or cause a commotion. But Rick's reflexes were quicker than DeShawn's would ever be. The older man connected his own bald head with a hard hit into DeShawn's. DeShawn staggered backward from the hard and unexpected hit and toppled to the ground in a wiry heap.

Rick yanked on DeShawn's arm that had been tucked beneath him during the fall. He then hoisted DeShawn over his shoulder, and crouching to avoid being seen, jogged toward the garage. He reminded Grant of a military officer carrying a load of cargo through the war-infested jungle.

DeShawn was tied up at the opposite corner so neither he nor Dawson could see each other.

"Guess we'll see who's next," said Rory.

"The only one who will be a little harder is Deb. Hard to attack a woman." Much as she deserved it, Grant would struggle with ever hitting or hurting a woman.

"Maybe she'll be the last one in there when backup comes," suggested Rick.

That could work in their favor or against, as Deb had the most to gain.

Rick slithered across the snow and threw a pinecone against the house. He then edged his way back to their location behind the corner of his house. From there, they had a direct view into the living room, but it was likely that view wasn't returned from their opposition.

Grant watched as Tiny's head jerked up from his position sitting on the barstool with a bowl of food. While he couldn't hear his words, it appeared that Tiny was asking about the noise.

A bark came from inside.

No, Lord, please don't let Nosy come outside.

That dog definitely was a blessing and a curse.

Tiny slowly removed his meaty self from the barstool. Nosy continued to bark, and Tiny pounded on the counter.

No, Mariah, don't say or do anything. Nosy will be all right.

Mariah seemed to listen to Grant's unspoken words, but he could see her face twisted with pain for what could happen if Tiny took out his anger on Nosy.

Tiny opened the door and stepped out into the freezing night. "Dawson! DeShawn! Where are you?"

When there was no answer, he glanced back at the house. Would he go back for reinforcements?

But Tiny didn't go back inside the house. Instead, heightened in readiness, he scanned the area, gun drawn.

Rick had emerged from the garage and had taken his place not far from Grant and Rory. Tiny didn't have the agility and speed of Deb or Psycho Eyes, but he was burly and weighed 305 pounds—a considerable percentage of those pounds in his rotund gut. Nevertheless, he *could* and *would* be taken down.

Maybe the big guy wasn't as aware as he thought, which was proven when he tripped over the rope, just out of sight of the front window. He landed with a thud while uttering profanities.

Grant, Rory, and Rick launched into action before Tiny even had a chance to recover. Grant jumped on his back and yanked his thick arms behind him while Rory and Rick waited for their cue. Tiny gave a shove and was on his back in an instant. He socked Grant squarely in the jaw and knocked him over. Jolted by the unexpected attack, it took Grant a second to recover. In that second, Tiny had a firm grasp on his gun and pointed it directly at Grant's head.

"Should have finished you off the first time."

Dizziness enveloped him. *No, I have to stay in the game. Lord, please give me strength.*

He stared up at Tiny and an image of a knife finding its way into his shoulder clouded his vision. It had been Tiny's hand that wrestled the knife into his flesh.

No, stay with it. His muscles cramped and threatened to yield in defeat. *No. Don't let him win. Distract yourself.* In the dim outside lights, Grant could see the food particles that made their home in Tiny's full, unkempt beard.

The gun's cold barrel rested against his temple. "How does that feel?" he gloated. Tiny looked toward the house and scowled. "Oh, yeah, I forgot. Deb wants you to see us take revenge on your girlfriend and her mom first."

Grant would survive to protect Mariah and her family.

"Might just have to let you live and knock you out until we need you," Tiny sneered, continuing to point the gun at Grant's head.

Let him live? Now there was a novel thought.

Grant weighed his options. He remembered from his extensive training how to remove himself from this situation. Tiny hadn't seen Rick and Rory lurking in the shadows. Grant could wait for them. Wait for Tiny to make another move, or react.

Tiny continued to speak, his breath a foul mixture of garlic, dog food, and stale cigarette smoke. "I knew you'd come up here to see the girlfriend, but I didn't expect it to be today. How convenient. We thought we'd have to call you. But hey, now that you're here, why don't you come and see what Psycho Eyes and Deb have planned for your woman and her mom?"

While the words rattled him, Grant could not afford to let emotions overtake him. He remained calm and quiet, with the exception of a silent prayer for wisdom. One wrong move could jeopardize everything.

Tiny laughed, his foul breath wisping from his mouth in a rush and exposing nubbed teeth that were in desperate need of a cleaning. He finally lowered the gun and glanced toward the house.

Could Deb and Psycho Eyes see him from their position in the living room?

Likely not.

Tiny's heavy breathing made clouds of white in the cold air. The guy might be strong, but he was the furthest thing from being fit and healthy.

That would play into Grant's favor.

In an unexpected move, Tiny took a swing at Grant.

Grant squirmed out of the way and returned the swing, connecting hard with Tiny's nose.

He didn't wait for Tiny to react.

Instead, Grant pushed through the pain, lunged to his feet, and threw several more punches toward his adversary, each one connecting with its intended target. Each hit causing more pain to sear him as he delivered the hits.

Tiny winced and bent over, the gun falling from his hand.

Grant simultaneously kicked Tiny's pistol aside while grabbing Tiny's head and bringing it to meet his knee. If they were going to rescue Mariah and her family, they needed to incapacitate the members of the gang until backup arrived.

A much more merciful plan than the gang had prepared for Grant.

Tiny fell to his knees.

Rory and Rick, seeing Grant's signal, joined the area, all three of them alert for any signs that the remaining gang members had seen them.

Grant watched as Rory practiced some type of Brazilian Jiu-Jitsu on his pudgy victim until, finally, Tiny lost consciousness.

They'd just dragged Tiny from view when Deb opened the door.

"Tiny!" she yelled. "Dawson! DeShawn!" Her spiteful tone echoed through the night. She spouted a few swear words. "Where are you?"

The door to the house slammed, and Deb returned to the

living room, but Grant knew it wouldn't be long before she or Psycho Eyes searched for their missing gang members.

"Hurry, get him to the garage," whispered Rick.

"Kind of hard to hurry with this guy," muttered Rory as he tied Tiny's thick wrists together.

Rick leaned over and began to pull Tiny through the snow. "Let's get his happy butt to the garage."

Grant chuckled as he assisted Rick. It was doubtful Tiny would be happy once he discovered his predicament.

"You okay?" Rory asked.

"Yeah. I'm good." Grant ignored the pain in his shoulder. He'd been through worse.

The snow started to fall, blown slightly sideways with the wind. Not good. They needed backup here as soon as possible, and this weather would only hinder their travel.

Rick checked on Dawson and DeShawn before they formulated their next plan. It was likely that Deb would be the one who would emerge from the house first. This definitely had its pros and cons.

Grant rubbed his hands together. The weather had gotten colder. Rick tossed an old army blanket on each of their captives.

Once again, more mercy than Grant had been shown when he'd been left in the elements to die.

The snow outside had begun to fall. Was Grant out there somewhere injured from the gang members who were sent to guard the perimeter of Mom's house?

Nosy continued to bark, obviously angry from being trapped inside Mom's craft room where Psycho Eyes had placed him.

Were Jordan and Presley still hidden beneath the cabinet? It was a lot to expect two little children to remain there for such a long period of time.

How much time had passed?

Mariah glanced at the mantle clock. She'd been sitting here on this couch for nearly an hour. Surely Grant and Rory would have arrived by now.

Mom didn't look well. Worry lined her face. She'd already lost Dad so recently. Would she also lose the rest of her family and her own life as well?

"Hey, someone is out there," hissed Deb. "Tiny didn't respond when I called him. Something must have happened." She paused. "I don't like the way this is going. Let's kill them and get it done and over with. Then we go outside."

Psycho Eyes walked to the large front window. "Someone is out there all right. Probably that worthless cop. But could he really take down all three of our guys?"

"If he has help."

"But how would he know we were here?"

Instead of an immediate answer, Deb trotted over to Mariah and backhanded her hard on the cheek. "Probably because of her. Did you find a way to reach your boyfriend?"

Mariah's cheek stung, and she choked back the tears. She shook her head.

"Yeah, right you didn't!" Deb shoved her, causing Mariah's neck to snap back against the edge of the ottoman.

Mariah struggled back to a sitting position. Her vision blurred and her face throbbed.

"Untie her," demanded Deb.

Psycho Eyes took out a knife and cut the ropes from Mariah's hands and feet. Anxiety rippled through her. If they killed her, what would happen to Jordan and Presley? "Anything else, my queen?"

"Oh, there'll be more. We'll make this good. It's the least we can do for Alroy." Her voice took on a shrill laugh, even as her facial expression didn't change.

"Stand up," Psycho Eyes demanded. But Mariah's legs were heavy, as though someone had attached heavy barbells to her ankles. She found it difficult to move, let alone stand.

Psycho Eyes loomed, his face so close to hers that his two evil eyes became a blurred image of one. "Stand up!" he shouted.

Foul breath entered her nostrils and Mariah gagged. But she willed herself to obey his command. Legs begging otherwise, she stood and teetered, praying she wouldn't fall into him.

Her head throbbed and her arms shook. A brief perusal of her arms proved her assumption correct—the tight rope had rubbed raw marks into her wrists. Thankfully, he hadn't cut her when he'd removed the ropes.

Psycho Eyes grabbed a handful of her hair and yanked, hard. More tears burned her eyes, and Mariah struggled to keep them open. "Guess you should have thought twice about getting mixed up with the cop, eh?"

Deb laughed again. "Hey, save it for when we bring him in." She squinted out the window. "It won't be long now."

Chapter 44

The three were starting to rouse from their unconscious states. When would backup arrive? There had to be a good reason for the delay. Briggs had one of the best sheriff's offices in the state.

Maybe just the weather alone had been enough to cause a postponement.

And where was Rivera?

Rick and Rory stood guarding the three men. Who should keep the three in line and who should go inside and remedy the situation with Deb and Psycho Eyes?

Grant had hoped that Deb would emerge from the house so they could incapacitate her as well. But she'd rushed back inside. Grant held up a signal and relocated. From his new position, he could see through the window. Psycho Eyes had untied Mariah and was standing face to face with her. He watched as the vicious man yanked a fistful of her hair.

His pulse sped and, despite the cold air, heat radiated up his neck and into his face. His blood boiled.

He had to save Mariah before Psycho Eyes did something worse.

At that moment, DeShawn struggled to his feet and started

hopping away. Rick stopped him, blocking his path until Tiny rolled over and used his bound legs to trip Rick.

Calamity ensued.

And Grant was torn.

Help Rick and Rory get the gang members under control or go inside the house and rescue Mariah and Linda?

He tossed the question nonverbally to Rory. After a signal that meant to proceed, Grant gave a swift nod of his head and bolted toward the house.

He lurked in the shadows, watching as Psycho Eyes and Deb appeared to taunt Mariah. Linda sat on the ottoman, likely doing all she could to maintain her composure at watching her daughter being threatened.

Somewhere in the house, Nosy barked. Was he detained in one of the rooms?

And where were the kids?

Sliding his back against the house, he could hear voices inside. He willed Nosy to quiet his rambunctious barking.

As if on cue, Nosy ceased—for the time being.

Come on, memory, kick in, Grant begged. He needed every single one of his tactical skills to win this war. Psycho Eyes and Deb were no ordinary criminals. Experience, added to perverse and hateful natures and being under the influence of drugs, created forces that Grant did not want to oppose alone.

Good thing he wasn't alone.

Lord, help me.

He cautiously peeked into the window. Psycho Eyes shoved Mariah toward Deb. Mariah stumbled before Deb shoved her back.

Almost like a cruel playground joke.

But it would get worse. Much worse.

True to his premonition, Deb punched Mariah in the stomach. He watched as the woman he loved doubled over in pain.

Adrenaline coursed through him. Common sense threatened to flee.

He needed God's assistance to maintain his composure, to think this out rationally, and to wait until just the right moment. Or else all would be for naught.

Mariah was athletic, fit, and strong, but she was no match for the volatile and malicious Deb.

Booming voices with fully articulated words rang through the frigid night.

"Tell you what, my queen, why don't you take care of the girlfriend, and I'll go out and find the cop. Sound good? But leave her alive—just barely—so we can get the revenge for Alroy that you want."

"Yes! It's for Alroy. The cop will pay for what he did!"

Grant crouched low in the shadows. When Psycho Eyes did come outside, there would be a present waiting for him.

***

Mariah likened the shoving back and forth to a rag doll being tossed to and fro. How could she remove herself from this situation? And more importantly, how to make sure that she, Mom, and the kids were safe?

The punch to the abdomen caught her completely off guard. It knocked the air out of her, and she clutched her stomach and fell to her knees. Torrential pain trundled through her. She looked up just in time to witness Deb launch another punch. She dodged it and stepped aside, right into Psycho Eyes. His manic laugh chilled her to the core and ramped her pulse into a thundering panic.

What would they do next?

"Don't think she liked that," Psycho Eyes crowed, his un-blinking stare taunting her.

A noise at the door captured the attention of both Psycho Eyes and Deb. Mariah followed their gaze. The door stood open, but no one was there. "I'll go see who it is. Probably that cop," said Psycho Eyes. He stepped outside and slammed the door behind him, causing the windows to shake.

Deb gripped Mariah's forearm and squeezed. "Don't even think of making a run for it."

The thought hadn't crossed Mariah's mind, but other thoughts had. She directed her attention to Mom. If only her mother could get loose from the binds. Two against one would be to their advantage.

"Are the British here?" a tiny voice squeaked.

Mariah's heart froze midbeat.

No, Presley. Stay in the pantry.

"Not yet, honey," Mom's shaky voice answered her grand-daughter's question. Little footsteps shuffled away from the living room.

Deb released a feral snort. "They're with their dad, huh?" The woman appeared torn between finding where Presley had gone and finishing her work with Mariah.

Mariah had to distract her from Presley.

She wrenched back to release the grip Deb held on her.

Deb's grip tightened.

The woman was about five inches shorter, twenty pounds lighter, and faster than Mariah, but Mariah had Someone more powerful on her side. *Lord, please, give me wisdom...and strength.*

Mariah yanked again. Deb's face contorted as she shrieked her disdain in Spanish. She lifted her foot and kicked Mariah hard in the kneecap. Mariah staggered, the pain excruciating. In a burst of adrenaline, Mariah returned an elbow punch, connecting with Deb's cheekbone.

Fire blazed across Deb's face, and she balled her fists. Goosebumps pricked Mariah's skin.

What now?

She couldn't just leave and run for help.

For there was no help.

If Grant, Rory, and Rick were outside, there was no guarantee Mariah would reach them before the Florez Gang took out their fury on Mom and the kids.

But Mariah couldn't just stand here and contemplate.

Deb's nostrils inflated and contracted with her heavy breaths. Reminding Mariah of a bull fixing its wrath on its target, Deb's eyes narrowed, and she pressed her lips into a thin line.

Mariah reached into her waistband and retrieved the 9mm just as Deb rushed her. Mariah's head hit the floor hard as Deb, in a fit of drugged-up rage, wrested the gun from her. As she swayed and attempted to stand, Mariah kicked a leg beneath her adversary causing Deb to fall.

With the agility of a cat, Deb was again on her feet. Mariah dashed into the kitchen as fatigue flooded her legs and debilitating pain seared through her kneecap. Mariah wavered, nearly falling before gaining her balance.

Deb was right behind her.

Mariah circled the island counter and ducked as Deb fired a shot with Mariah's gun.

Deb cornered her and held the 9mm to her head.

Her pulse pounded in her ears, drowning out all other noise.

Would this be how it would end?

Mom screamed.

The door opened.

And in that fraction of a second when Deb's attention turned to both noises, Mariah took action.

The 9x13 glass lasagna pan, empty thanks to Tiny's overindulgence, became the closest weapon. In one expedient motion and with strength that surprised Mariah, she lunged for the pan and swung it hard, down on Deb's head.

The woman fell to the floor, crumpled in a heap as blood spurted from the gash in her head.

Horror mixed with relief consumed her.

But it wasn't over yet.

Deb stirred and reached for the gun. Mariah slid beside the woman, snatched the gun, and pointed it at Deb. The woman blinked, then spit a curse before going still.

Mariah limped toward Mom. Remembering the brevity of the situation and that Psycho Eyes was still a threat, she knew she must act quickly and free Mom from the ropes on her wrists.

How long would Deb remain unconscious?

Her focus fixed on her tormentor, Mariah assisted Mom with untying the ropes.

"Psycho Eyes is still outside," Mom said, rubbing the raw skin.

"He can't know about the kids."

Mom agreed, gave Mariah a quick and comforting hug, and suggested they form a plan.

━━━━━

Grant had caught Psycho Eyes by surprise, but the leverage didn't last. The man was the same height as Grant, but Grant had sobriety and a fifty-pound advantage. They wrestled in the snow, Grant imploring his aching body to perform a miracle.

The cold only served to numb his extremities, but he ignored it.

Thoughts flashed through his mind. Was Mariah all right? Her mom?

Where were the kids?

Where was backup?

Where was the strength he once had?

Psycho Eyes reached down and clamped his hands around Grant's neck. Grant hooked him into a lock with his legs, and Psycho Eyes pressed harder. Blackness blurred Grant's vision. *No, stay awake!*

He poked his finger into the eye of his enemy, clawing and scraping. Psycho Eyes reeled back in pain. Grant went for the nose, groin, and throat.

But there was yet another disadvantage for Grant.

The meth enabled Psycho Eyes to have more strength, and he again wrestled Grant to the inferior position and he once more went for Grant's throat.

Fingers and thumbs pressed on his neck, attempting to snuff the life from him.

Grant gasped for his breath to return as the darkness threatened to overtake him. His breath came in spurts, as cold air entered his lungs.

Getting a second wind, Grant reached for his pistol, his hands fumbling against the holster and his mind uttering prayers that God would enable him to defend himself.

Psycho Eyes removed his hands from Grant's throat for the briefest of moments and wrestled Grant for his weapon. Grant knew the man had one of his own, but he also knew that in the time it took Psycho Eyes to retrieve it, Grant would have finished the altercation.

Grant held tight to the gun, willing his numb hand to cooperate with the task before him. Psycho Eyes, bleeding from a wound, pushed and wrestled harder and more fiercely.

"I will kill you!" Psycho Eyes screamed.

What happened to Deb being the one to take the revenge?

Not caring about the hierarchy of the gang and who decided what, Grant prayed for one last surge of adrenaline.

God answered his prayer.

Shoving as hard as he could with his left hand, Grant thrust Psycho Eyes off of him and onto his back. At the same time, he trained the gun toward his enemy.

Psycho Eyes again lunged toward Grant, landing atop him. Evil and darkness glowed in his eyes.

A shot rang out and ended the brawl as Psycho Eyes toppled to his death.

A flurry of emotions clouded Grant's mind—relief, fear for Mariah, disgust that Psycho Eyes had fallen on him...

No time to ponder anything other than protecting and rescuing the woman he loved and her family. Grant shoved Psycho Eyes off of him, struggled to his feet, and stumbled toward the house, just as sirens sounded in the distance.

He inhaled and exhaled, deep and full breaths, thankful he could breathe at all.

Chapter 45

Mariah ran to her children and embraced them. "The British are coming," she whispered, tears flooding her vision.

"I thought I heard a movie or something out there. It was loud." Jordan's eyes grew round with curiosity. "Was it a movie? And why are all the police here?"

"Why don't we go into your room and read a story," Mom suggested, walking with Presley toward Mariah and Jordan.

"Aww, Grandma, this is way too exciting to go upstairs and read a story. Can we wait?" Jordan asked.

Mariah smiled at her son's inquiry. So much could have happened tonight. She could have lost her family, Grant, and even her own life.

But God had protected them.

"What's wrong with your face, Mommy. You have an owie. Do you want to hold Bibby?"

Mariah planted a kiss on the top of Presley's head, ignoring the pain that surged through her at bending down toward her daughter. They were all alive. That's what mattered. "I'll tell you what. Why don't you, Jordan, and Grandma take some special treats upstairs with you and have a picnic in your room."

"Ooh. We never eat food in our rooms," Presley squealed. "Can we have cookies?"

"Yes, you may."

"Mommy, did you hear me all the way? Cookies for dinner?"

Mariah embraced both children in a group hug. "Yes, cookies for dinner."

"Yes!" exclaimed Jordan. "Come on, let's go to the pantry and find some."

Mariah was thankful they couldn't see Deb toppled over on the floor on the other side of the counter. With God's mercy, her children hadn't seen any of the violence. And what they'd heard, they believed to be a movie.

Father, thank You. Thank You for Your protection. For saving us.

She dared not think of the alternative outcome.

———

Grant's limbs were frozen and his stomach growled. But it didn't matter. Mariah and her family were safe, the gang was incapacitated, and he was still alive. Rick and Rory had experienced a few skirmishes of their own in the garage with Tiny, Dawson, and DeShawn, but had maintained the upper hand, although Rick had succumbed to some minor injuries. Deputy Rivera's wife had gone into labor, hence the reason for his absence.

Deb, Dawson, and Tiny would never see freedom again. DeShawn would do some time, although it was likely he'd be released since it was his first offense. Perhaps the young man could be rehabilitated.

And Grant? He just couldn't wait to see Mariah. To hold her. Kiss her. Tell her he loved her.

Chaos ensued around them, but Grant could only think of one thing—to check on the family who'd come to mean a lot to him in recent weeks. He stumbled through the doorway. Mariah met him halfway and toppled into his arms.

If he held her for an eternity, it wouldn't be long enough. Grant kissed the top of her head before framing her bruised face and gazing into her eyes.

"Is everyone all right?"

She bit her lip and nodded as tears glistened on her cheeks. Emotion engulfed him. So much could have happened at the hands of the Florez Gang—the reality that, were it not for the Lord's protection, he would not be standing here with her in his arms.

He could have lost her.

Grant gathered her to him again and gently rocked her back and forth, keenly aware of how she felt in his arms. "Mariah," he whispered. "I'm so glad you're okay."

Mariah tilted her head and looked into his eyes. "I was so worried about you. They were here, and I had no way to warn you."

He wiped a tear from her cheek. "When I saw you through the window and what Psycho Eyes was doing…" the memory was too vivid in his mind. A memory he *wanted* to forget. He cleared his throat. "And the kids and your mom?"

"They're fine. Thankfully, Presley and Jordan didn't see or hear much. It could have been—she choked out a sob. "It could have been so much worse. I'm so grateful you were here."

"Me too. Proud of you with that lasagna pan."

Pink stained her cheeks, and she offered one of her gorgeous smiles.

Nosy propped his forelegs on Grant's pants. It reminded him that something good *had* happened through the midst of the attack, the loss of his memory, and the terror Mariah's family had experienced.

"Thank you, Nosy," he said, removing one hand from Mariah's waist to pat the dog's head. "Thank you for finding me that day."

Epilogue

A gentle breeze blew through the pine trees surrounding Mountain Springs Lake. Mariah gazed up into the blue cloudless sky. Could the day get any better?

Grant paused from rowing the canoe. "Deep in thought?" he asked.

So much had happened in the past year. The remaining Florez Gang had been sentenced to prison, Grant had recovered most of his memory, and was back on the force full-duty. Presley and Jordan had advanced another year of homeschool, and the best thing of all?

She and Grant had married two weeks ago. Not only that, but Brandon relinquished his parental rights to Presley and Jordan, and plans were underway for Grant to adopt them. Mariah knew he'd be a wonderful, loving, and doting father. They'd settled on residing in Briggs, with frequent visits to Mountain Springs.

Now back from their honeymoon and skirting the lake in Dad's canoe, Mariah couldn't think of anywhere she'd rather be. "Just loving it that I'm here with you."

"Is that so?"

Mariah inhaled his woodsy scent and looked into his brown eyes. "Yes, it is. I happen to have a little bit of a crush on you." She held up her finger and her thumb to indicate her words.

He laughed and leaned forward. "Want to know how I feel about you?" he asked.

"As a matter of fact, yes."

But Mariah already knew. And when Grant wrapped his arms around her and kissed her with a passion and warmth she'd never tire of. She offered a silent prayer of gratitude. Who knew a forgotten identity could lead to a happy ever after?

———

If you loved *Forgotten Identity,* turn the page to read a sneak peek from *Unexpected Witness,* a Christian romantic suspense novel in the new Mountain Justice Series.

DON'T MISS THIS SNEAK PEEK

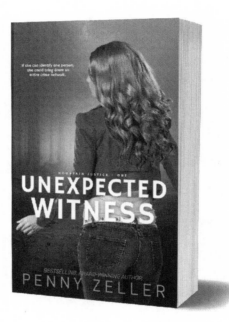

If she can identify one person, she could
bring down an entire crime network.

MOUNTAIN JUSTICE - BOOK ONE

Unexpected Witness

The day couldn't get any worse.

Mila charted the information from her last patient, relishing the silence after what had been a chaotic eight hours. Dr. Burch left fifteen minutes ago, and after she tended to a few more tasks, Mila would be on the road home as well. Her legs throbbed from little downtime, and a headache formed at her temples, courtesy of the challenging patients who collectively decided to make today their day for an appointment. Add to that the pungent stench of vomit still lingering in the air from an earlier patient, despite Mila's best attempts to sanitize the area several times. Thankfully, within the hour, she'd be on her way home where leftovers, a new book she'd borrowed from the library, and a hot bath awaited her.

She jumped as a loud banging on the front door interrupted the silence. The light above the door gave just enough of a clue as to the visitor's identity. That and his trademark worn-out red tennis shoes.

"What's he doing here again?" Brittaney Mead, the administrative assistant, stalked to the door she'd locked only moments before. "He's already been here once today." She cracked open the door and glared at the visitor. "You," she hissed.

"I gotta be seen."

"No, you don't. You were already seen today and besides, we closed twenty minutes ago. It's a Friday night. Go home."

"But..."

"No, go home. You got what you needed."

Mila started toward the door. "If he needs—"

"He doesn't." Brittaney shut the door and locked it again, waving away the man. "Besides, he can come back Monday."

Mila hated turning anyone away, even if the patient was a hypochondriac who stopped by nearly every day with a new ailment. She watched as Troy Pollard limped into the darkness. Mila finished charting, then emptied the trash cans while Brittaney resumed tending to a matter on her phone.

"There's Antonio," Brittaney said as car lights shone upon the outdoor steps. "Gotta go."

Antonio, Brittaney's boyfriend, pulled up alongside the clinic in his larger-than-life four-wheel drive truck with a massive lift kit. He honked the horn not once, but four times.

Brittaney grabbed her belongings and dashed out the door.

Leaving Mila alone in a building that was too quiet, too still, save the ticking of the wall clock with the second hand perpetually stuck on the number three.

Not much happened in Upton, population 1,498, even at seven at night, and especially not with a winter weather advisory in effect for a spring snowstorm. Who in their right mind would be out in that type of weather?

Besides, this wasn't the first time Mila had been the last one to leave.

Why then were her hands shaking as she completed her time card?

The furnace kicked on with a rumble. The noise startled her, and Mila took a few deep breaths to calm her already anxious mind.

Lights from a passerby illuminated the now nearly dark office, lingering longer than necessary toward where Mila stood.

She just wanted to get home.

Moments later, her clump of keys firmly in one hand and her purse on her arm, Mila stepped out of the clinic, locked the door, and grabbed the black railing as she made her way down the stairs and to the parking lot.

Streetlights overhead cast an eerie glow through the thickly falling snowflakes. A cup of tea and a bubble bath beckoned her before getting some much-needed sleep and repeating the process all over again tomorrow.

When Mila parked her car eight hours ago, it hadn't seemed so far away. But now, doing her best not to slip on the unshoveled parking lot, it could have been five miles to her vehicle.

The wind whipped around her, and she quickened her pace. Her car was just steps ahead.

It was then that she saw two figures to her left near a light-colored car. One person had his back to the car while the other stood facing him. She couldn't hear words being spoken, but she could see spasmodic movements.

Impending doom jolted her, but she shoved the fear aside. This wasn't the time for an overactive imagination.

Mila took a few steps back, debating whether to continue to her car, which was much closer than heading back to the clinic. Perhaps it was just two people in a spirited conversation.

But this late at night and in this weather?

She eyed her car, now only a few paces away, and squinted through the swirling wet snow that hampered her vision. She shuffled toward her car, attempting to hurry, but not slip.

And then Mila noticed something she could never erase

from her memory.

She saw contact made from one person to the other. One withdrew his arm, knife in hand, the street light glinting off a dark substance coating the blade. The attacker braced the victim against the car, then launched into a series of rapid stabs. The victim slumped and crumpled to the ground.

Mila's legs locked and her body went numb. The attacker pivoted toward her.

Move, feet, move!

She willed her feet to obey.

He rushed toward her, knife in hand.

Mila's brain kicked into motion, and she fumbled with the key fob, furiously pushing the button to unlock the door. She reached for the door handle.

The fob had failed.

Again.

If you want to be among the first to hear about Penny's next release, sign up for her newsletter at www.pennyzeller.com. You will receive book and writing updates, encouragement, notification of current giveaways, occasional freebies, and special offers.

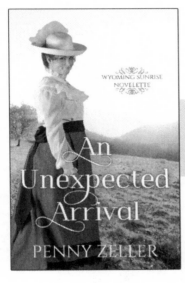

A
WYOMING
SUNRISE
NOVELETTE

If you enjoyed this glimpse into the lives of Mariah and Grant, please consider leaving a review on your social media, Amazon, Goodreads, Barnes and Noble, or BookBub. Reviews are critical to authors, and those stars you give us are such an encouragement.

Authors Note

Dear Reader,

Thank you for joining me for this wild ride in *Forgotten Identity*. I've long loved reading Christian suspense novels, and after Christian historical romance, they are my favorite genre to read (and write!) For me, the thrill is not attempting to find out who the perp is (most of the books by my favorite suspense authors are fairly clear and easy for me to discern who the bad guy is as they *aren't* mysteries) but to find out if the main characters will make it out of their dilemma alive. You may have guessed "George" was a cop early on, but the question remained: *how* and *why* did he find himself near death in the peaceful Mountain Springs? Would he, Mariah, Mom, and the kids make it out alive?

As always, creative license is taken in books. There was some liberty taken with Grant's traumatic brain injury and amnesia, although those do have highly variable presentations. Any deviation from police procedures was me taking intentional fictional liberties.

In addition, I conducted several interviews and partook in numerous conversations regarding so many aspects of *Forgotten Identity*. One of those aspects was the ability for my characters to be completely closed off from the outside world. (Yes, there are still places that fit this description!) These days, we have technology at our fingertips. I hunted down a small mountain bedroom community with a population similar to Mountain Springs as well as a more remote mountain area with cabins. Both receive their share of snowstorms. These locations became the inspiration for my book. With a little help from residents, I discovered that in one of the remote locations, they do not have cell service except for at the top of a hill or in one or two areas. Neither do they have internet. The mountain town has spotty internet affected greatly by the snow. According to my source, "Snowflakes mess with the signal," even though they do have satellite and "line of site wireless". Because it's a higher elevation, it snows earlier in the season and snow and colder temperatures remain longer into the year. In the latter town, my source informed me they have had avalanches that have closed the roads and their cell towers have been down. My source confirmed that in his town, it could take weeks to repair a tower in the winter.

Of course, just discussing these two locations caused the creative juices to start flowing. What if a man, on the brink of death, was found during a blizzard? What if there was no way to contact emergency medical services? What if he suffered a traumatic brain injury and didn't even know who he was? What if bad guys, set on revenge, were out to get him?

In a world where squatting has unfortunately become more common, why not allow the bad guys a place to stay in the nearby home of snowbirds?

Add in some romance (because honestly, that's my favorite genre), two kids, and a dog, and a story was born. As a former homeschool mom myself (our daughters attended and previously graduated from the Zeller Academy), it was fun to revisit homeschooling for Jordan and Presley's education.

Thank you for spending some time in Mountain Springs.

Until next time, happy reading!
Blessings,
Penny

Acknowledgments

Thank you to my family. This crazy lifestyle I call writing would not be possible without you!

To my Penny's Peeps Street Team and my launch team members. Thank you for spreading the word about my books. I appreciate your encouragement and support.

To my beta readers. You are the ones who see my project at its beginning stages. Thank you for all of your wonderful suggestions.

To Gary Ellis, retired law enforcement, for reading my manuscript and ensuring my police procedures were accurate. Your help and suggestions were invaluable, and I couldn't have written this without your insight. Any deviation from police procedures was me taking intentional fictional liberties.

To former law enforcement officer, Scott Brastrup, for answering my question about Grant's ability to go undercover. Your wealth of knowledge is always so helpful!

To other local and national law enforcement officers who assisted me and answered my plethora of questions.

To my cousin, Josh Wageman, PhD, DPT, MPAS, who helped me with Grant's traumatic brain injury, his other injuries, and his recovery. You are absolutely amazing with your bountiful knowledge about all things medical.

To Rowdy Branson, for answering my questions about cell

towers, avalanches, mountain town living, and closed roads.

To my developmental editor at Mountain Peak Edits & Design who helped me make this book the best it could be.

To my proofreader, Amy Petrowich, for catching those pesky errors.

To my readers. May God bless and guide you as you grow in your walk with Him.

And, most importantly, thank you to my Lord and Savior, Jesus Christ. It is my deepest desire to glorify You with my writing and help bring others to a knowledge of Your saving grace.

About the Author

Penny Zeller is known for her stories of faith-filled happily-ever-afters with tender romance, humor, and memorable characters. While she has had a love for writing since childhood, she began her adult writing career penning articles for national and regional publications. Today, Penny is a multi-published author of over two dozen books. She is also a fitness instructor, loves the outdoors, and is a flower gardening addict. In her spare time, she enjoys camping, hiking, kayaking, biking, birdwatching, reading, running, and playing volleyball. She resides with her husband and two daughters in small-town America and loves to connect with her readers at www.pennyzeller.com.

MOUNTAIN JUSTICE

WYOMING SUNRISE

HORIZON SERIES

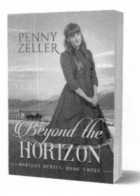

HOLLOW CREEK

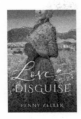   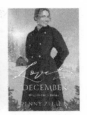

LOVE LETTERS FROM ELLIS CREEK

STANDALONES

SMALL TOWN SHENANIGANS

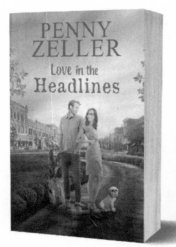

Chokecherry Heights

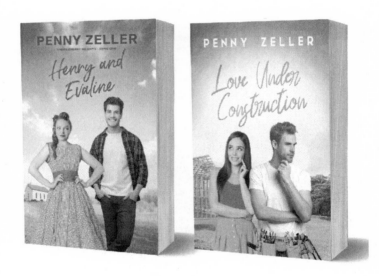

Made in the USA
Columbia, SC
09 February 2025

53268363R00209